MONKEY BUSINESS

A KRISTY FARRELL MYSTERY

MONKEY BUSINESS

LOIS SCHMITT

FIVE STAR
A part of Gale, Cengage Learning

GALE
CENGAGE Learning·

Farmington Hills, Mich • San Francisco • New York • Waterville, Maine
Meriden, Conn • Mason, Ohio • Chicago

GALE
CENGAGE Learning®

LIBRARY OF CONGRESS CATALOGING-IN-PUBLICATION DATA

Names: Schmitt, Lois, author.
Title: Monkey business / Lois Schmitt.
Description: First edition. | Waterville : Five Star Publishing, [2017] | Series: A Kristy Farrell mystery
Identifiers: LCCN 2016041610 (print) | LCCN 2016050591 (ebook) | ISBN 9781432832582 (hardcover) | ISBN 1432832581 (hardcover) | ISBN 9781432834838 (ebook) | ISBN 1432834835 (ebook) | ISBN 9781432832490 (ebook) | ISBN 1432832492 (ebook)
Subjects: LCSH: Women journalists—Fiction. | Murder—Investigation—Fiction. | Zoos—Fiction. | BISAC: FICTION / Mystery & Detective / General. | FICTION / Mystery & Detective / Women Sleuths. | GSAFD: Mystery fiction.
Classification: LCC PS3619.C44643 M66 2017 (print) | LCC PS3619.C44643 (ebook) | DDC 813/.6—dc23
LC record available at https://lccn.loc.gov/2016041610

First Edition. First Printing: March 2017
Find us on Facebook— https://www.facebook.com/FiveStarCengage
Visit our website— http://www.gale.cengage.com/fivestar/
Contact Five Star™ Publishing at FiveStar@cengage.com

Printed in the United States of America
1 2 3 4 5 6 7 21 20 19 18 17

Dedicated to
Peter, always my muse

CHAPTER ONE

Nearly two hours before Long Island's Rocky Cove Zoo opened to the public, the place was empty save for a handful of employees. I passed a gardener replacing dying border plants with red impatiens, and an ice cream vendor fiddling with his frozen yogurt machine.

As I journeyed down a shady gravel path, dark clouds rolling in from the Long Island Sound warned of a summer storm. Wind whistled through trees, whirling leaves and carrying combined scents of elephants and evergreens. In a nearby exhibit, a troop of baboons scurried through tall grasses, hooting loudly.

I quickened my pace, hoping to avoid the storm. Most importantly, I didn't want to be late meeting my brother Tim in the rain forest exhibit. Tim was the zoo's curator of herpetology or, in layman's terms, "the guy in charge of reptiles." He was a source for an article I was writing for *Animal Advocate* magazine on breeding endangered species in captivity. After more than two decades teaching high school English, I'd finally landed my dream job in journalism. This was my first assignment.

As drops of water fell from the sky, I spotted the rain forest up ahead. Thankful I wasn't wearing heels, I dashed toward the building. The door was ajar. I went inside, my eyes adjusting to the darkness.

"Tim, are you here?"

No answer.

He must be here, I reasoned. Otherwise the building would be locked. "Tim?"

Still no reply, only silence broken by the sudden cawing of a bird.

Maybe he'd run out for a few minutes. I decided to explore the exhibit before my brother arrived. The Rocky Cove Zoo had done a good job of replicating the four distinct layers in a tropical rain forest—emergent trees, upper canopy, understory, and forest floor. Since the zoo had constructed viewing platforms at all levels, I started climbing toward the top.

"This would be easier if I were ten years younger and ten pounds lighter," I mumbled, huffing and puffing up the stairs.

Rather than go into cardiac arrest, I stopped at the third tier where I stared out at the lush green garden in the air, watching parrots swoop and monkeys swing. By this time my layered hair had morphed into a mop of curls from the heat and humidity.

Hoping for a bird's-eye view of what was below, I glanced down at the forest floor.

And saw the body.

I felt woozy at the sight of what appeared to be small rat-like creatures gnawing at its face. As I grasped the railing for support, bile rose in my throat.

One thought flooded my mind. *My brother.*
Tim.

I wanted to vomit, but didn't. Suddenly, I heard footsteps. Someone was in the building.

"Kristy, are you here? Sorry I'm late, but I had to drop off dry cleaning."

My legs quivered as I let out a deep breath. *Tim!*

"There's a body," I called, choking on the last word. "In the rain forest."

While scrambling down the stairs, I spotted my brother scurrying toward the exhibit.

"Oh, my God, Kristy," he called out. "It's Arlen McKenzie."
"The zoo director?"

CHAPTER TWO

The rain forest was no longer a scene of peace and tranquility.

Within minutes of calling 911, two police officers arrived. After that came crime scene investigators and the medical examiner.

A uniformed officer, who looked young enough for a milk and cookie break, took our statements, then instructed us to wait until a detective could question us. For the next twenty minutes, Tim and I hugged the corner of the lower platform, watching and waiting. I was holding up pretty well, but my brother looked like he was about to pass out, his normally pallid complexion now the color of a gecko.

"Did the zoo director have a history of heart problems?" I asked Tim.

"I don't know." He pushed his thick-rimmed glasses up the bridge of his nose.

"Could he have fallen and hit—"

"Listen, Kristy. I don't want to speculate. The autopsy will give cause of death."

My brother, a scientist to the end. I hoped when he calmed down, he might venture an educated guess.

I wondered how much longer we would have to wait when two men with badges hanging from their belts strutted toward us. The first, a slender African-American who appeared to be in his early thirties, was impeccably dressed in gray slacks, light blue shirt, striped silk tie, and navy blazer. The other, probably in his late forties, wore a brown suit with pants hanging below his stomach and sweat pouring down his forehead. My guess: homicide detectives.

"Oh, no," Tim said.

As the men approached and I saw them more clearly, I realized the reason for my brother's reaction. The man in the brown suit was Steve Wolfe, a bully who had gone to school with Tim, constantly picking on my younger brother. Granted, Tim was the classic nerd who might as well have worn the sign "KICK ME" on his back.

Since I'd last seen Steve, his muscles had turned to fat. He now sported a receding hairline, pot belly, and blond mustache. But his glacier blue eyes were as cold as when he was a kid, and he wore the same annoying grin that made me want to slap his face.

I could tell by the way he glared at Tim that he recognized my brother, but he introduced himself anyway. "Detective Wolfe. Homicide." He pointed a thumb at his partner. "This is Detective Fox."

Wolfe? Fox? At the zoo? Really?

He whisked me aside. Tim remained with Fox.

I recalled Wolfe came from a cop family with relatives high up in administration, so it didn't surprise me to see him as a homicide detective. I guessed he had a lot of department brass pushing him up the ladder.

Wolfe towered over me, but so did most people. "Kristy Vanikos. Yeah, I remember you."

"It's Kristy Farrell now," I said.

"Yeah, whatever. You always fought your brother's battles. Still doing it?"

"No need. His current acquaintances are mature, intelligent, and civilized."

Wolfe's smirk vanished. His face reddened.

11

I glanced back at my brother who was with Detective Fox in the far corner of the platform. Tim was scratching his cheek.

"How did the zoo director die?" I asked, turning back, now facing Wolfe.

"I'm a homicide detective. You think they sent me here to get your lunch order? How do you think he died?"

"Well, it could be an accident or heart attack or—"

"Yeah, sure." He flipped open his notepad. "I'm asking the questions. Why were you here before the zoo opened?"

"I'm a feature writer for *Animal Advocate* magazine. I'm writing a story on—"

"Wait a minute. Aren't you a teacher? Yeah, sure. You're a teacher. You taught my nephew Jared. He does real good at school."

Obviously, Jared didn't take after his uncle. I refrained from voicing my thoughts.

"I left my teaching position two years ago for a job at *Animal Advocate.*" I didn't tell him that for most of that time, I'd been employed as an editorial assistant. When one of the magazine's writers quit last week, I was given his current assignment, but my editor made it clear the promotion was temporary. I'd be competing for the permanent job along with dozens of other applicants. If I didn't come out on top, I'd be checking other people's work for misplaced commas again.

"I'm writing a story on breeding endangered species in captivity," I continued. "My brother is in charge of reptiles so he arranged to show me the reptile nursery today. Since he was coming in early to conduct research in the rain forest, he suggested we meet here. He left an early admittance pass for me with the guard at the front gate."

"Okay. Walk me through, step by step, from the moment you got here."

I told him exactly what happened.

"So, your brother was in the building earlier, eh?"

"I didn't say that. The door was unlocked. Someone had been here, but it could have been anyone."

"Yeah, sure. But he has a key."

My stomach knotted. I didn't like where this was going.

Wolfe shut his notepad. "You can go. If we need more, we'll call."

I bee-lined toward my brother. He was alone. Detective Fox was now talking to a uniformed officer near the entrance.

"Let's get out of here, Kristy."

"Sure. I could use some coffee."

"There's always a pot in my office. Let's go."

We headed outside where more than two dozen people milled behind the yellow crime scene tape cordoning off the building. Since the zoo normally wouldn't open to the public for another twenty minutes, I assumed they were employees.

"Can we postpone our tour of the reptile nursery?" Tim asked. "I don't feel up to it."

"Of course. We can do it some other time." Then thoughts of deadlines loomed. "But not too long a wait."

I glanced at my watch. Tim had also arranged for me to interview Saul Mandel, the curator of mammals, later today on breeding endangered gorillas. But before I could ask if this appointment would be postponed, I froze at the sound of a scream.

A woman in a champagne-colored dress that clung to her body broke through the crime scene tape and raced toward the building. I couldn't imagine how she ran so fast in her stiletto heels.

A police officer blocked her from reaching the exhibit entrance.

"That's Ginger Hart, the zoo's public relations coordinator," Tim whispered. "She's upset."

Upset? That's my brother. Master of understatement.

13

"Public relations?" I repeated. "She seems concerned with more than damage control."

"Well, she's . . ." Tim blushed. "She's . . . you know."

"I don't know. What is she?"

"She was Arlen McKenzie's lover."

Although I was curious, my taciturn brother said no more, and the zoo director's love life wasn't my concern. The rain had stopped, leaving behind air filled with the fragrance of wet grass and pine needles, and I used the silent walk back to his office to clear my mind.

Making our way down the wide gravel path, I was wondering how the director's death would affect this place when the sudden odor of animal dung interrupted my thoughts. Glancing right, I spied the source, a zoo employee in the camel exhibit toting a shovel full of manure. To my left, a man in a zoo uniform with a basket of fruit paraded into a gated area adjacent to the gorillas. Two gorillas inside the preserve lumbered toward him on all fours over a mound of rocks, making their way with surprising speed.

Business as usual.

Minutes later, we arrived at the herpetology building where we stepped into the main room, which boasted three metal desks, only one currently occupied. A woman with curly white hair sat behind this desk, surrounded by two men wearing brown zookeeper uniforms. Their backs faced Tim and me.

"I don't know if there are suspects yet," the woman was saying to the zookeepers. "But Tim found the body, so I'm afraid he will be—"

"Good morning," Tim interrupted.

The three spun around. One of the zookeepers mumbled something like, "we better get back to work," and the two men scurried down the hall.

"Are you okay, Tim?" asked the white-haired woman, who

bore a remarkable resemblance to Mrs. Santa Claus.

"I'm fine." Tim didn't introduce me. He poured coffee from a nearby machine, handed me a mug, and ushered me into his office. "Good thing you're not a tea drinker. We only have coffee."

Inside the windowless room with its hideous green walls, Tim shut the door. I sank into a worn-out armchair while he sat behind his desk, facing me. My hand was shaking slightly as I lifted the mug to my mouth. "The police think this was murder."

Tim shrugged. "Probably is."

"Well, couldn't it be natural causes, like a heart attack?" Since it was only the two of us, I hoped he would venture an opinion.

Tim shook his head. "We won't know for sure until the autopsy. But since his body was in the rain forest, I doubt it's natural causes."

"Why?"

Tim sat back, appearing more relaxed than he had been. But then he scratched behind his ear. As a kid, whenever Tim was upset, his body itched.

"In zoos, predator and prey are never together," he explained. "The rain forest is barricaded into sections with walls hidden from the public by tropical foliage. In the area where McKenzie's body was discovered, there are no animals that could threaten his life, but there are creatures that do some nasty biting. McKenzie knew enough to never go in there without protective clothing. The only logical conclusion is he was murdered and his body dragged inside."

"How do you think he was killed?" I held up my hand. "I know. We have to wait for the autopsy. But you saw the body. What do you really think?"

Tim hesitated. "My guess is poison. McKenzie wore a short-sleeve shirt so it was visible."

"What was visible?"

"There's a puncture wound on McKenzie's left arm with swelling around it. That means a toxic substance was probably injected."

"Poisoning? Isn't poisoning an unusual method to use on Arlen McKenzie? Injecting poison is more in keeping with frail old ladies. Someone without the strength to fight back."

"Not in this case. McKenzie's left arm was paralyzed from an injury he received while serving in Iraq during the Gulf War. If you stood behind him and plunged a needle into his arm, he wouldn't feel a thing."

I shivered. "I wonder—"

Someone rapped on the door. I jumped, my nerves still on edge.

"Come in," Tim called, then lowered his voice. "We'll talk about this later, Kristy."

A woman dressed in jeans and a lab coat stepped into the room. She was neither attractive nor homely, just plain, wearing no jewelry or makeup. I judged her age to be early thirties.

Tim introduced her as Linda Sancho, the zoo's wildlife nutritionist.

Linda gave a perfunctory nod in my direction before placing a folder on the desk. Her fingernails were bitten to the quick. "This is the data you wanted on the iguana's diet, Tim. By the way, there's a staff meeting at eleven-thirty. Saul sent out e-mails. He wants everyone on time."

"Saul Mandel? The curator of mammals?" I swallowed the last of my coffee.

Linda nodded.

"Well, I guess my interview with him is postponed since it's the same time as your meeting."

"Good luck rescheduling." The wildlife nutritionist shook her head. "Saul has lots of other matters on his plate now."

16

"What do you mean?" I asked Linda.

"He's not only curator of mammals. Saul is Rocky Cove's assistant director. With McKenzie gone, he's in charge for the time being."

"When our former director died a few years ago, most of us expected Saul to be appointed," Tim added. "We were shocked when the trustees brought in Arlen McKenzie."

Linda bit her cuticle. "Hopefully, the trustees will now appoint Saul permanently."

"That certainly gives him motive for wanting McKenzie dead," I said, thinking aloud then wishing I hadn't.

"He hated McKenzie. That's for sure." Linda snorted. "But he's not the only one, right Tim?"

Tim didn't reply. But as Linda exited, he began scratching his neck with a vengeance.

Chapter Three

My editor, Olivia Johnson, was one tough lady who'd worked her way up from the streets of the South Bronx.

Exiting the zoo, I'd phoned her about the murder of Arlen McKenzie.

"I heard," she'd said, cutting me off. "It's on the news."

"I discovered the body."

Did I expect sympathy? Even a cliché like "how terrible for you." Not from Olivia. She responded with, "What about your interviews?"

"They've been postponed."

"Not for long, I hope. We've got deadlines. Did you reschedule?"

"Everyone is really shaken up. I thought I'd wait—"

"Don't wait. Make new appointments." She paused. "Journalism isn't for the sensitive. You've got to be aggressive, especially if you want your temporary promotion to become permanent."

I winced. But that was Olivia. Right to the point. Taking a deep breath, I said, "When I get back to the office—"

"About the office," Olivia interrupted. "Our air conditioning is malfunctioning."

Malfunctioning? The temperature had hit ninety.

"Work from home the rest of the day," she suggested.

Since I was at the stage of life where I was always hot to begin with, I jumped at my editor's offer.

"Don't forget to reschedule those interviews." Before I could get a word in, she hung up.

I sighed. Ever since watching *Superman* as a kid, I wanted to be Lois Lane. Instead, I wound up teaching high school English. Two years ago, when I heard about an opening for a feature writer at *Animal Advocate* magazine, I decided to go for it. Someone else got the position, but I was offered an editorial assistant spot with a future promotion held as the dangling carrot.

Now that I had the carrot, I intended to keep it—even if that meant dealing with Olivia.

When I arrived at my home, Brandy, an eight-year-old collie, and Archie, a mixed breed who looks like a small black bear, greeted me at the door, tails wagging. To my surprise, I found the third animal member of the family curled up on the living room sofa.

"Owl, how nice to see you." My veterinarian husband had found the badly matted cat, all skin and bones, in a box dumped behind his animal hospital. The calico, who had been part of the household for nearly a month and had fattened up considerably, usually stayed far away from the dogs.

Archie, noting the cat's presence in the room, bounded toward the sofa, tail still wagging. Owl hissed, then jumped to the floor and raced out of the room. Archie cocked his head.

"When will you learn, Archie?" I leaned over and stroked the dog's spongy black fur. "Owl is afraid."

After brewing a pot of coffee, I rescheduled today's cancelled activities. Despite the director's death, Tim managed to arrange an interview for me tomorrow with Saul Mandel, the mammal curator who now served as acting director. After my interview, I'd tour the reptile nursery with Tim.

With my laptop set on the kitchen table, I spent the next two hours researching endangered species, but I couldn't concentrate. My mind kept wandering to the murder and Linda Sancho's comment. Who hated McKenzie and why? I tried recalling if Tim had ever mentioned the new director, but my memory came up blank.

Curious and determined to find out, I began searching the Internet for information on Arlen McKenzie and the Rocky Cove Zoo. Totally immersed in what I soon discovered, I was jolted out of my thoughts when I heard a car pull up.

"Hi, Mom. Thought I'd join you on my dinner break." My twenty-six-year-old daughter Abby paraded through the doorway. With her dark hair, olive skin, almond-colored eyes, and aquiline nose, she looked like a younger and much thinner version of me.

A recent veterinary school graduate, she had joined her father's practice on Long Island. She rented a beach house with two friends but frequently stopped here for meals.

"Hey, did you hear about the murder at Uncle Tim's zoo?" she asked, kneeling down to greet Archie and Brandy who had bounded into the room and now provided her with a face washing.

"Your Uncle Tim and I discovered the body."

As Abby stood with her mouth wide open I gave a detailed narration of what happened.

"Well, your new job's not boring," Abby said when I finished my story.

"It beats teaching teenagers the difference between an infinitive and a gerund." I grinned.

Abby glanced at her watch. I knew she had to get back to work.

"If you want dinner, you'll need to cook something," I said, pouring more coffee against my better judgment. After a day like today, the last thing I needed was more caffeine. "With your father away at the veterinary conference, I'm eating at the Woodland Inn with your Uncle Tim and Aunt Barbara, although I really don't feel like food right now, which is surprising since I usually eat more when I'm upset."

"I'm surprised Uncle Tim didn't cancel, considering what happened."

I shrugged. "You know your aunt. Barbara planned on eating out, and Barbara doesn't like changing plans."

Abby chuckled. She swung open the refrigerator door and stuck her head inside. So did Archie and Brandy. "I'm starved. Good, there's feta cheese. Think I'll make an omelet."

Yawning, Abby pulled out butter, eggs, and cheese, then stretched up her five-foot body, reaching for a mixing bowl from the top cabinet. She also inherited her height genes from me.

"Didn't you work a late shift last night too?" I asked.

"With Dad away, we're all pulling double duty. These late nights are getting to me. I don't know how Dad does it. He's not as young as he once was."

I wouldn't call fifty-one old age but maybe that's because I was only two years away.

As Abby lined up the ingredients on the counter, the dogs remained glued to her side. They adored my daughter. Besides, if they were lucky, a little food might drop to the floor. Dogs are so hopeful.

"So, do the police have any suspects?" Abby asked while grabbing a cheese chunk that was dangerously close to Archie's nose.

"Don't know. But lots of people have reason to hate him." I spun my laptop screen toward her. "Look at this news article. It was published the weekend your father and I visited your grandma in Florida. That's why I never saw it."

Abby sat down at the table, facing the computer. "Uh, oh. The dreaded budget cuts." She skimmed the article. "Reorganization of staff. Twenty-five jobs slashed." She paused. "It's a reason to hold a grudge, but is it enough to kill someone?"

"This may just be the tip of the iceberg. A week after your father and I returned from Florida, we went to dinner with Tim and Barbara. I remember Tim alluding to problems at work. He never mentioned McKenzie or this article, just that working at the zoo wasn't like it once was. But I didn't realize until today the problems were that severe."

Thoughts of my brother flashed through my mind. Shy and bookish, I think he liked reptiles because they were so quiet. And he'd always been secretive. Even as a child, he rarely confided in me. Yet, I could usually tell he was troubled when he avoided my eyes or scratched his body.

Had I been so absorbed in my new job that I'd missed the signs?

Tiffany-style lamps illuminated the eight booths and seven tables that made up the Woodland Inn's dining room, creating a cozy atmosphere. I spotted my brother and sister-in-law immediately, seated in the back by the knotty pine wall. Tim stirred a scotch and soda while Barbara sipped white wine.

Unlike me, with our Greek father's complexion, my brother inherited our Irish mother's fair skin, looking as if he never came in contact with sunlight. By comparison, Barbara sported a deep summer tan, providing a striking contrast to her short blond hair. I often wondered when Barbara found time to sunbathe or visit a tanning salon. A pharmaceutical executive, she always complained about the long hours she worked.

Wearing a mint green sundress, Barbara looked perfectly groomed as usual. The woman, always color coordinated, never had bags under her eyes or dog hair on her clothes.

Barbara's mouth formed a mulish pout and Tim was frowning. As I approached, Tim's frown disappeared, but Barbara's expression remained the same. Surely, Tim had the murder on his mind.

"Good. We can order now." Barbara glanced at her watch, her way of letting me know I was ten minutes late.

After thanking Tim for arranging tomorrow's interview with Saul Mandel, I parked myself down. A red-headed, freckle-faced waitress in a black mini-skirted uniform approached. I ordered a pomegranate martini. Pomegranate was loaded with antioxidants, so if I was imbibing, I might as well get nutrients out of it. That was my theory even if no one else agreed.

"How are you holding up?" I asked my brother.

"He's fine," Barbara said. "It's not as if he liked McKenzie. He hated the man."

"From what I hear, so did everyone else." I grabbed a roll from the bread basket and slathered it with butter. My appetite had returned. I hadn't eaten since breakfast.

"Not everyone hated him." Barbara smirked.

"What do you mean?" I kept slathering.

"Ginger Hart. The public relations coordinator. She liked McKenzie—a lot."

"Ah, yes." I bit into my buttered roll, recalling the scene outside the rain forest. "Tim told me she was Arlen McKenzie's lover."

Tim blushed as he downed more of his drink.

A Cheshire cat grin appeared on Barbara's face. "Did he also tell you McKenzie was married to Amanda Devereux, the curator of ornithology? She's his widow. Nice little love triangle—McKenzie, Amanda, and Ginger. Must have made for tense staff meetings, don't you think?"

"It didn't matter to McKenzie." Tim swallowed what remained of his scotch in two big gulps, then motioned for the waitress to bring another. I'd never seen my brother down more than one drink before dinner.

"He probably stashed a woman in the next room on his wedding night," Tim continued. "He never cared who he hurt."

Barbara shot Tim a look, but he avoided his wife's eyes.

I caught the look. "What's going on?"

Tim chewed on his lower lip.

"Tim?" I stared my brother down.

He crumbled his napkin into a ball and squeezed it with his fist. "McKenzie wasn't renewing my employment contract. He was hiring the son of a wealthy donor as the new curator of herpetology."

I dropped what remained of my buttered roll. I never expected this. "You've been there more than twenty years. Could he do that?"

"Unfortunately, yes. The director has sole power to hire and fire. My last contract was for five years, and it's up in two months. It had always been renewed but not this time."

"Tim saw his replacement's resumé," Barbara said. "The Sunday comics are more impressive. This kid wouldn't be considered for the job if it weren't for his father's money."

I stared at Tim, gauging his reaction to Barbara's statement. His eyes had hardened and every muscle was tense, but he was working hard not to show it.

"What about the zoo's board of trustees?" I asked. "Wouldn't they question this?"

"The trustees aren't involved in day-to-day operations." Barbara pushed back a strand of hair that dared to fall out of place. "I told Tim to spend less time with his snakes and crocodiles and more attending social functions. But he wouldn't listen. Maybe if he had cultivated the board members, they would have gone to bat for him."

Nothing like being supportive. I bit my tongue. Barbara had the warmth of a hyena circling a carcass.

"Now what?" I asked. "With McKenzie gone, what happens to your contract?"

Tim scratched his neck. "With Saul Mandel as acting direc-

24

tor, I'm sure it will be renewed."

My eyes met Tim's. I realized how much he benefitted from the murder of Arlen McKenzie.

But was it a motive for murder?

Driving home from the restaurant, I reflected on my brother's career. Tim was a scholar, renowned in the field of herpetology. But he wasn't media savvy. He didn't have the ability to charm wealthy donors. Still, shouldn't two decades count for something?

The phone rang as I stepped into my house. Glancing at the caller ID, I recognized my husband's cell number.

"Sorry, honey. I just got your message," he said. "I've been tied up at the conference and had the phone off. You sounded worried. Is everything okay at home?"

"Not really." I hesitated while deciding the best way to give him the news. I wanted a way that wouldn't upset him. Realizing there was none, I simply said, "I discovered a dead body this morning."

"My God, Kristy! Who? What happened?"

I visualized the worry in Matt's large doe-like eyes and his nervous habit of running his hand through his thinning sandy hair. As I slid into a chair, the two dogs at my feet, I told him about Arlen McKenzie, ending with, "It gets worse. Tim has a motive."

After recapping Arlen McKenzie's plan to replace Tim as curator of herpetology, I added, "It's not even the money. I'm sure they could live comfortably on Barbara's salary. But Tim loves the zoo. It's his life."

Matt hesitated. "It's also the money. I didn't say anything to you at the time, but do you remember the diamond necklace Tim gave Barbara for her birthday?"

"Of course. It's gorgeous."

"Tim wanted to borrow the money from me to buy it."

"What! How much?"

"Seven grand."

"That's ridiculous." My muscles tightened. "What did you say?"

"That I'd need to discuss it with you first."

"And he said?"

"He said never mind. He didn't want you to know."

"How could I not know? Did he think I wouldn't notice a withdrawal for that amount? Why didn't he use a credit card?"

"I don't know any details," Matt said in his soft-spoken voice. "Tim only said that he was experiencing a small cash-flow problem."

Archie's huge bear-head now rested on my right foot. Brandy's chin was on my lap, so I scratched behind his furry collie ears. "Then buy a cheaper gift." All I could think of was our mortgage and Abby's college and veterinary school tuition, which we were still paying off. Barbara and Tim's house was twice as large as ours, and they had college expenses with their two sons. How could they afford seven thousand dollars for a necklace?

"Why didn't you tell me this, Matt?"

"Because I didn't give him any money. He must have gotten it somewhere else."

"It's not about the money." I jumped up, nearly toppling the dogs. "It's about my brother."

I slumped back down. Archie, the canine tank, laid his head back on my foot. Brandy's chin was once again on my lap.

Silence. Matt finally spoke. "You're right. I should have told you. I'm sorry, honey."

After hanging up, I rose and shook my foot, numb from

Archie's head cutting off my circulation. Although still annoyed at Matt, my thoughts focused on my brother and his out-of-control spending.

CHAPTER FOUR

The next morning I entered the zoo's administration building and headed toward the information desk, which in true bureaucratic fashion was at the far end of the lobby, away from the entrance.

"I'm paying for the liquor, but her bridesmaids are chipping in for the food," a squatty middle-aged receptionist with tortoise-shell glasses was saying into the phone. Deep and throaty, her voice sounded like a bullfrog.

I waited.

"They can't decide between butter cream or whipped cream cake," she continued, apparently oblivious to my presence.

I inched in closer.

"Chocolate's my favorite," she said.

I cleared my throat.

"We'll have fruit too. Possibly, strawberries dipped in—"

"Excuse me," I interrupted. By now, I was practically leaning on the counter. I needed to be on time for my appointment. "I'm Kristy Farrell from *Animal Advocate* magazine. I have an appointment with Saul Mandel, but I received a message to stop here first."

"Just a minute." She punched the hold button. "You're to see Ginger Hart before your interview."

"Ginger Hart? The public relations coordinator?"

"Yes." The receptionist rolled her eyes as if I had asked who was President of the United States. "Sign the visitor's registry

28

here, then take the elevator to the third floor. She's the last door on the left."

"Are you sure she wants to see me now? Before my appointment with Mandel?" I asked, scribbling my name in the visitor's log.

The receptionist held up a yellow post-it. "This note says to see her as soon as you arrive. And before you ask, I've no idea why."

The elevator doors opened on the third floor, and I stepped out onto the carpeted hallway. With cherry-wood walls, recessed lighting, and potted plants, there was no question this was the executive wing. Walking down the corridor, I noted most office doors were closed with not a soul in sight.

I entered the public relations suite where a young man who resembled a stick insect sat behind the front desk, pecking at his computer keyboard. His long, fast-moving fingers reminded me of spider legs. The name plate identified him as Lyle Llewelyn.

"Good morning. I'm Kristy Farrell from *Animal Advocate* magazine." I had the feeling I'd be repeating that phrase a lot today. "I'm interviewing Saul Mandel but was told to see Ginger Hart first."

He stopped pecking and lifted his head, glancing first at me, then the door. "Ms. Hart's expecting you but she just stepped out of the office."

"Do you know why she needs to see me?"

He hesitated, glancing again at the door. "She didn't say. She'll be back in a sec."

"But I don't want to be late for my appointment."

"We don't want that either." He shuddered. "Saul Mandel can be a bit intimidating."

A bit intimidating? His reputation was worse than that. According to my brother, Mandel's fierce temper had earned him the nickname Taz—a reference to the bad-tempered Tasmanian devil.

"I'll let you know as soon as Ms. Hart returns. Why don't you have a seat?" Lyle gestured toward a sitting area at the far corner of the suite.

"Thanks." Since I still had time, I decided to give Ginger Hart a few more minutes. I made my way across the room, gazing at Aborigine paintings, African carvings, and Native American pottery. Whoever had decorated had spared no expense. Quite different than my brother's small office with its ugly green paint and tile floors.

As I sank into a black leather couch, I wondered about Ginger Hart. Her boss, who also happened to be her lover, was murdered yesterday. Her personal and professional life should be in turmoil. Why would she want to see me?

"Here's Ms. Hart now," Lyle called out from the front desk, jolting me out of my thoughts.

The scent of jasmine perfume filled the air as the public relations coordinator strutted into the room.

"You must be the reporter from *Animal Advocate*. Kristy, is it? Call me Ginger." The woman smiled and extended her arm.

At yesterday's crime scene, I'd guessed her age in the mid-twenties, but now after a closer look, I raised that estimate about ten years. With her short skirt, strappy high heel sandals, and stylishly layered auburn hair, she oozed sex appeal. But there was an intelligence and hardness radiating from her jade-colored eyes, warning me she was not someone to take lightly.

"Let's go into my office." She motioned toward a nearby room.

"Here are your messages," Lyle said as Ginger neared his desk. There was a quake in his voice that hadn't been there before. "I'll have the material you requested ready by lunch time, Ms. Hart."

"Of course, you will. That's why we pay you." She snatched the pink message slips from his hand. "And bring me a cup of tea."

Lyle blushed. I stared at my feet.

"Would you like a cup, too, Ms. Farrell?" he asked.

"She doesn't have time." Ginger swung open the door to her office and went inside.

"I'm a coffee drinker, anyway," I said with a wink at Lyle.

I entered, quickly surveying the room—a corner office with a view. The panoramic window looked out on the African Plains exhibit, where a trio of hippos wallowed in a muddy brown watering hole. In front of the exhibit, more than a dozen visitors lined up by a red and white soda wagon for cold drinks, reminding me today promised to be a scorcher with temperatures again reaching ninety. You couldn't tell that in here where the air conditioning made me feel like I was in the midst of a polar ice cap.

Ginger handed me a business card, then slid into her leather swivel chair, and motioned me to a seat in front of her desk.

"I'm sorry to hear about the zoo director's death," I said, curious to see her reaction.

"Thank you. It's a great tragedy for the Rocky Cove Zoo."

If Ginger ever played poker, today was the day. Her face and movements showed no emotion. She leaned forward and tapped a crimson fingernail on her desk.

"Saul Mandel told me about your meeting today," she said without missing a beat. "I know our curator of herpetology is your brother Tim, and he set up your interview directly with Saul. And I understand Tim also scheduled a tour for you at the reptile nursery. In the future, call my office. It's my staff's job to coordinate all press contacts."

I sank back in my chair thinking how typical of Tim. He hadn't cleared the interview.

"Gee, I violated your protocol on my first assignment," I joked, attempting to lighten the situation, but Ginger did not appear amused.

I had little patience for bureaucracies, and the zoo appeared to be a big one. But if I landed the permanent feature writer position at *Animal Advocate* magazine, I'd be covering lots of stories here, so it wouldn't be smart to make an enemy of the public relations coordinator. I changed my tone.

"Seriously, I apologize for the misunderstanding. I still need to interview—"

"Just call my office and set it up with Lyle." The corners of Ginger's mouth curved into a slight smile. "You can leave now for your interview with Mandel. But your tour of the reptile nursery has been cancelled for today."

"What?" I felt the heat creep up my neck and onto my face as I realized the reason for this meeting. It was to teach me a lesson. A power play.

Ginger must have read the expression on my face. She held up her hands. "I had nothing to do with this. I was told Tim isn't coming in this morning. Since he can be a little absent-minded, even though he's your brother, I didn't know if he had called you to cancel, so I'm informing you as a courtesy."

She was right. Tim hadn't contacted me, and I wasn't surprised he'd forgotten our appointment. This from a man who remembered the scientific name of every reptile that crawled the earth.

"Tim never takes time off," I said as Lyle entered with Ginger's tea. "Did he say why he'd be late today?"

"He had an unexpected visitor at his home." Ginger grabbed the teacup, then sat back, crossing her legs. "Detective Steve Wolfe."

CHAPTER FIVE

Saul Mandel loomed behind a metal desk, facing me. The man must have weighed more than three hundred pounds. With his heavy jowls, big lips, and bushy eyebrows, he looked like a fairy tale ogre. Stifling a nervous giggle, I resisted the urge to mumble, "Fee, fie, fo, fum."

Mandel gestured toward a folding chair across from him. "Just put that pile on the floor."

Slightly flustered, I removed a stack of papers from the chair. I sat down, wondering why he hadn't moved into the director's office now that he was temporarily in charge.

Mandel glanced at his watch. "I only have thirty minutes so we better get started."

I hoped that was enough time. A bad interview could end my career before it began. Although filled with thoughts of Detective Wolfe interrogating my brother, I willed myself to concentrate on the task at hand.

"I'm writing an article on breeding endangered species—"

"I know why you're here. What information do you need?" He pulled out a handkerchief and wiped the perspiration off his forehead, even though the air conditioning emanating from a wall unit behind him blew full blast.

"Why don't you tell me the reason for the breeding program?" I said.

"You came to this interview without knowing the reasons?" His ice blue eyes met my brown ones.

Not about to let him intimidate me, I smiled. "Of course, I know. But I want to hear it in your words so I can quote you in the story."

Silence. It was my turn to sweat as I wondered if he intended to answer. Saul Mandel's reputation seemed right on the mark. He was as gruff as my brother Tim was meek.

Finally, he spoke. "This program may be the only chance certain species have for survival." As he talked, the fleshy waddle of skin beneath his chin quivered. "Habitat loss from the development of land is a major threat to their existence."

The intercom rang.

"And, of course, the hunting and poaching of animals for their body parts. Take the gorilla."

The intercom buzzed again.

Ignoring the ring, his voice grew louder. "Gorillas are highly prized. Their meat goes to restaurants that specialize in exotic game, the heads are sold as trophies, and the hands are made into ashtrays for people who consider them conversation pieces. The animals don't breed quickly enough—"

The intercom sounded a third time.

Mandel frowned, furrowing his forehead. His eyebrows melded together, now looking like one giant caterpillar. "Let me get rid of this call." He grabbed the phone, buried under the clutter on his desk. Papers cascaded to the floor. "Can I get back to you?" he said into the receiver. "I have someone—" He stopped abruptly to listen to the person on the other end.

"What? When did this happen? Wildlife nutrition isn't incidental. Don't worry, Linda. That was last week. You're dealing with me now, not McKenzie." Mandel, whose face was now the color of a holiday ham, slammed down the receiver, then stared at the water-stained ceiling tile, his hands trembling.

"Problems?" I asked, but wished I hadn't when he turned his cold eyes on me.

I was here to learn about the zoo's breeding program, nothing else. But once again, thinking of Detective Wolfe's visit to my brother's house, I concluded there was no question that Tim was a person of interest in McKenzie's death. It wouldn't hurt to collect information about other zoo employees who had reasons to despise, and perhaps kill, the zoo director. I jotted down *Linda* and *wildlife nutrition* for future reference.

Mandel continued, "Now, what was I saying? Oh, yes. We need to . . ."

We talked for another half hour about the procedures and problems of breeding endangered gorillas in zoos. Upon completion of the interview, Mandel said, "I'll walk out with you." He pushed his bulky frame out of his chair. "I'm on my way to the elephants."

Despite his weight, Mandel marched briskly down the hall. As we exited the building and crunched down a wide path lined with tall oaks, the aroma of fresh popcorn from a nearby vendor reminded me I had skipped breakfast.

During the interview, I hadn't been able to make out the design on Saul Mandel's green suspenders, but now that he stood next to me, I saw it was a pattern of purple monkeys. I couldn't quite reconcile this with his stern image.

"Have you known my brother long?" I asked, curious as to how the friendship between this bear-like man and my mild-mannered brother had developed.

"Tim and I both started here twenty years ago."

He wiped his brow. I'd never seen anyone perspire like this man. Raising his voice to be heard above the noise of a passing brood of children, all wearing red T-shirts emblazoned in white lettering with the name of a local summer camp, Mandel added, "We need more people like Tim. There's no substance to this new breed McKenzie wanted to hire."

Before I could ask what he meant, Mandel greeted a couple

walking up the path. "Good morning, Amanda, Frank."

I couldn't help but stare at this unusual pair. The woman, several inches taller than her companion, with raven hair styled in a French twist, wore white summer slacks, a peach silk blouse, and pearl earrings. I instinctively stood straighter and pulled in my stomach.

The man was someone you wouldn't want to meet in a dark alley. Dressed in a brown zoo uniform, rings pierced his ears, nose and eyebrows. Tattoos of angry-looking black widow spiders covered his muscular arms, and a snake with enlarged fangs marked his lower right cheek.

"Good morning," the woman said, glancing at Saul Mandel. She immediately turned back to her companion.

The man scowled and did not return Mandel's greeting. As he passed by, I caught the odor of stale cigarettes. He and the woman continued on their way, each one apparently absorbed in what the other was saying.

"That's Amanda Devereux, curator of ornithology, and Frank Taggart, bird keeper in charge of the incubators," Mandel said. "They must be in a rush to get to the bird nursery."

Had I heard correctly?

"Amanda Devereux? McKenzie's widow? Her husband died yesterday and she's here today?"

Mandel nodded. "Yes. The memorial service isn't until next week. Meanwhile, she might as well immerse herself in her work."

"I guess everyone mourns in their own way." I didn't know what else to say.

The sharp sound of a trumpeting elephant filled the air. Before turning toward the pachyderm's call, Mandel grinned for the first time since I had met him. "Mourns? Knowing Amanda, she's celebrating."

CHAPTER SIX

The next morning I left two voice messages for my brother, asking him about yesterday's police visit. Backing out of the garage, I clipped the mirror off Matt's car. Then my laptop crashed, my washing machine broke, one of the dogs threw up on the bedroom comforter, and the cat discovered the fun of fringe with my favorite Pashmina scarf.

And then Detective Steve Wolfe called.

"The day McKenzie's body was discovered, you planned to meet your brother in the rain forest at eight, right?"

"Right."

"But you *claim* he didn't get there until later."

I didn't like his emphasis on "claim."

"Yes. I told you that before," I said. "He was about ten minutes late."

"That's unusual, eh?"

"I don't think so."

"You claimed you entered the building because you thought your brother was there. When you realized you were alone, you thought he'd been there and left."

"I admitted I was mistaken. When Tim finally came, he apologized for being late because he had dropped off his dry cleaning."

"You believe that, eh?"

"What's not to believe? You never dropped off dry cleaning?"

"Just wanted to make sure my notes are clear. That's all. We'll be talking again soon."

I slammed down the phone, muttering words that would make my priest blush. I would have loved a pomegranate martini, but since I couldn't justify vodka before noon, I settled for coffee. I had taken my first sip when I heard someone approaching the kitchen door.

"Oh, good, it's you," I said.

"Of course, it's me." Dressed in khakis and a sleeveless yellow cotton top, Abby strolled into the house. "I came by to pick up some papers from Dad's study. Who were you expecting?"

"The way things have been going, a process server." I told Abby about my call from Detective Wolfe.

"He's just trying to push your buttons, Mom."

Abby swung open the refrigerator door, poured iced tea into a glass, then pulled out a chair by the table and slid down. The two dogs were now chasing each other in the backyard. Owl wandered into the kitchen and rubbed against my daughter's leg. Abby bent down and scooped Owl up, cradling the cat in her arms.

"So," she said, removing her sunglasses. "How are Uncle Tim and Aunt Barbara?"

I sipped my coffee before recapping last night's conversation, ending with, "I'd no idea Tim was so heavily in debt. And I can't believe your father never told me. That's not like him."

"Maybe Dad had other thoughts on his mind."

"You may be right," I admitted to my daughter, recalling Matt's behavior the week before the veterinary conference. "Last week, he never came to bed before midnight, and he even missed two televised Yankee games."

Abby said nothing. She held her iced tea with one hand and stroked Owl with the other.

"He's been preoccupied lately," I said. "So much so, I plan to ask him about it when he returns from the conference this weekend."

Abby didn't respond. She just stared at her iced tea.

"There's a problem at work, isn't there?" I asked, guessing my daughter knew something.

She hesitated. "A new veterinary service is opening in town this fall. I think Dad's worried it will affect business."

"Surely, there's room for another veterinarian in the community."

"This is more than another veterinarian, Mom. It's a health and wellness center for companion animals. The facility will be state of the art and provide a host of services including chiropractic adjustments, acupuncture, massages, water therapy, and herbal remedies."

"A new-age spa for dogs and cats." I shook my head. "I don't know. Sounds like it belongs in Beverly Hills or Manhattan, not Long Island's south shore. Besides, everyone loves your father. Do you really believe this new facility threatens his practice?"

"This center is part of a national chain. It's hard for small independent businesses to compete." After sipping the last of her iced tea, Abby set down her glass, jostling the cat on her lap. Owl meowed in protest. "Uncle Tim isn't the only one with financial trouble. I think Dad's veterinary business is in for hard times."

I exhaled as Abby's statement sank into my brain. Matt had built the veterinary hospital from scratch. Next to family, it was the most important thing in his life.

"Mom, are you okay?"

"Oh, I'm just great. My husband's veterinary hospital is at risk, and a lunatic detective wants to pin a murder on my brother."

★　★　★　★　★

Abby fixed the glitch in my laptop, but I wasn't so lucky with my washing machine. Deciding not to put more money into repairing the eleven-year-old appliance, I spent the afternoon shopping for a new one. I also took Matt's car in for an estimate, amazed at how much it would cost to fix a side-view mirror. And I still hadn't heard from my brother.

My cell phone trilled as I pulled into my driveway. Barbara's name popped up.

"Good," I mumbled. If Tim wasn't about to return my calls, I'd find out what happened from my sister-in-law.

"A Detective Wolfe was here yesterday," she said. "He asked if Tim was home the night McKenzie died."

"Was he?" I stepped into the house, pulled out a chair, and slid down.

"Well, yes, as far as I know. I attended a retirement dinner for a colleague in Manhattan, so I didn't get home until midnight. Tim was here then but—"

"But he has no alibi before that time. Do the police have a handle on time of death?"

"No later than ten Monday night, and since McKenzie met with three trustees until eight, it had to occur between those hours," Barbara replied.

"Did Tim say he was home between eight and ten?"

"Tim swears he arrived home by seven and didn't leave the house. I believe him but I don't know if the police do. Wolfe asked if Tim received any phone calls or had visitors. He said no. I hoped you spoke with him on our home phone and he forgot. You know how absentminded he is. Even though the phone company will have records, I wanted to check."

"I didn't call, but don't worry. They need a lot more evidence before they can arrest Tim."

"I know you're right. Only I can't afford to have him mixed

up in a murder investigation. I'm up for a promotion and my company is ultra conservative."

Her concern wasn't about Tim. As usual, it was all about Barbara.

"I don't think the police have enough evidence to arrest him," Barbara continued, "but I'm afraid of how the press could damage both our reputations. Whoever committed the murder would need access to the rain forest."

"Who besides Tim can get in there?"

"The building is locked after hours. The police found the master key in McKenzie's desk, and I understand only five other employees have keys. Tim is one, and so are the other curators, Saul Mandel and Amanda Devereux."

"Okay. That's three accounted for. What about the other two?"

"I've no idea."

"Do the police know the cause of death yet?" I asked.

"Wolfe said the autopsy results would be released soon."

After Barbara said good-bye, I poured wine in a glass and carried it to the patio where I sank into one of my cushioned lounge chairs.

Would Detective Steve Wolfe make Tim a scapegoat?

I remembered back to Tim's high school senior year. After his harassing my brother and two other students in gym class, school authorities banned Steve from the senior prom. "You'll regret this," Steve had threatened at the time. "I don't know when, but I'll get even."

My brother went away to college and never saw Steve again until this week.

Had Steve changed or remained a bully? He needed evidence, of course, but would he frame Tim?

I sighed, realizing I had always protected my little brother, and I guessed I'd be doing it again.

To prove Tim's innocence, I needed to find the real killer.

CHAPTER SEVEN

The next morning, with my fingers crossed, I phoned the police department and asked for Detective Fox. Finger-crossing didn't work. Detective Wolfe answered.

"My editor is considering doing a small piece on McKenzie's murder," I lied, praying this wouldn't get back to Olivia.

"I thought you worked for some animal magazine, not *Crime Gazette.*"

"McKenzie was a prominent member of the zoological community so its fitting we write a little blurb—"

"Don't stick your nose where it doesn't belong."

"I only want to know who has access to the rain forest."

"Your brother." He snickered.

"Who else?" I gritted my teeth.

"It's not my job to answer your questions. Call the press office. But remember, this is an open investigation. They probably won't tell you anything either."

"They can't decide what to put behind the chair." The zoo's receptionist was talking on the phone as I approached her desk. "The pink umbrella with the red hearts or the life-size cut-outs of the bride and groom."

"I like the pink umbrella," I said, signing the visitor's log and putting down the pen.

The receptionist glanced up at me. "That was my first choice too."

Sarcasm doesn't work with everyone.

I scooted into the elevator, pressing the button for the third floor. When the door opened, I spotted Ginger Hart in conversation with a young woman who looked familiar.

"Mei?" I said, stepping into the hallway.

She spun around. "Mrs. Farrell, what are you doing here?"

We hugged.

"I almost didn't recognize you," I said.

"It's been more than six years since I graduated." Mei grinned. "I've contact lenses now. I let my hair grow, I've lost about thirty pounds, and—"

"I take it you two know each other," Ginger interrupted.

"Mrs. Farrell was my first teacher when I arrived in America, and she was always my favorite."

I smiled, remembering the awkward teenager who came from Hong Kong to live with her aunt on Long Island after her parents died.

"Mrs. Farrell," Mei said, "this is Ms. Hart, the zoo's—"

"We've met," said Ginger. "Although I didn't realize you were a teacher, Kristy."

"I heard you left Jefferson High, Mrs. Farrell. What are you doing now?" Mei asked.

"I'm working as a writer for *Animal Advocate* magazine. How about you?"

"Graduate work in zoology. I'm interning at the zoo. I've been—"

"Don't forget those reports, Mei," Ginger interrupted again. "I need them by ten tomorrow." She turned toward me and asked, "What brings you here today?"

"Research in the zoo's library. But right now, I thought I'd stop in your office. I need to schedule an interview with the ornithology curator."

"Our curator of ornithology is McKenzie's widow. I can't

imagine she'd be up to an interview."

Being every bit the diplomat, I refrained from mentioning that I saw Amanda Devereux at the zoo the day after the discovery of her husband's body. Instead, I countered with, "There must be someone else in ornithology I can talk to."

"I suppose I could arrange something. I'll have my staff work on it and contact you."

Ginger took off down the hall, vanishing into her office.

"I'd love to catch up on what you've been doing," I said to Mei.

"I'm free now. How about we go to the cafeteria? If I remember, you love your coffee."

It was such a hot and humid day, animal smells lingered in the air. As Mei and I strolled down the main path, my nose told me the elephants were near.

Mei pointed to the approaching exhibit—an African savannah with grassy plains, scattered trees, and a watering hole. One elephant calf, submerged in the pool, squirted water at two adult elephants.

"I wish he would spray me," I joked, wiping the perspiration off my forehead. My blouse clung to my body.

"Isn't this exhibit super? Saul Mandel worked with the architects to ensure it duplicated the elephant habitat. And he did a fantastic job on the new rain forest, too."

"Mandel designed the rain forest? The newspapers credited McKenzie with that."

Mei frowned. "That's wrong. McKenzie only cared about attracting media attention and worming donations out of rich people. He hadn't a clue about designing habitats."

Climbing up the cafeteria steps, she added, "Trust me. If it weren't for Mandel, the Rocky Cove Zoo rain forest wouldn't exist."

The air-conditioned cafeteria buzzed with conversation. As Mei and I maneuvered our way through the crowded building, I spied Linda Sancho alone at a table. The wildlife nutritionist held a cup in one hand while pecking at a laptop keyboard with the other. She nodded as we went by.

"Do you know Linda?" Mei asked.

"We were introduced this week."

"Linda works harder than anyone I know." Mei handed me a tray. "McKenzie planned to eliminate her position. He spent a fortune renovating the administration building, but he said the zoo couldn't afford the luxury of a wildlife nutritionist."

After grabbing a chocolate doughnut, I scooted my tray along to the coffee urn. "I hope Linda's job remains in the budget," I said, filling my cup to the brim.

"With McKenzie gone, I think it will. It's always hard to lose a job, but it's especially rough in this case." Mei grabbed a bottle of diet iced tea from the refrigerated compartment. "There aren't many jobs for a wildlife nutritionist. Linda said there were no openings in the New York or New Jersey area. If she lost her job here, she would need to move off Long Island."

"And she didn't want to do that?"

"Her husband is a lawyer with a big firm, Webster, Mayer, and Hammond. He's up for a partnership and refuses to relocate. Linda loves her job. She's not about to abandon her career."

"So, what would she have done?"

"A commuter marriage to start with. That's if she could get a job in another state. But she received tremendous pressure from her husband, who thought the idea was absurd, although he couldn't come up with a better plan."

Mei rooted around in her wallet as we reached the cash register.

"I got it," I said and paid the cashier.

"Thanks." Mei grabbed a straw before we headed toward the dining area. "It gets worse. Linda's mom lives nearby and has cancer. She goes for chemotherapy. If Linda moved, her mom would be alone during the week. How's that for a guilt trip?"

I nodded, realizing that with McKenzie dead, Linda might no longer have to make this tough choice.

"By any chance, do you know if Linda has access to the rain forest?" I asked.

"She sure does. She's in there all the time, researching edible rain forest plants."

"Do you know who else has a key?"

"The three curators, of course." Mei furrowed her brow and didn't speak for a few seconds. "I'm sorry, but I can't think of anyone else right now."

We located a vacant table in the back of the cafeteria. "I loved your journalism class," Mei said as we sat down opposite each other. "Remember how you made us keep daily diaries?"

I laughed. "Yes. And I remember how most of the class didn't want any part of it."

"No one wanted to bother, including me." Mei raised her voice to be heard above the chatter and giggling of three teenage girls sitting at an adjacent table. "But it turned out to be one of the most useful things I did. I keep a daily diary now, and I write all my thoughts in it. Seems strange to write long hand in this computer age, but I find it helps me focus."

"Good." I beamed, always pleased when something I did made a lasting impression on a student. "But enough about the past. What are your responsibilities here?"

"I rotate a few weeks in each department, assisting curators with research projects. I began with Saul Mandel and mammals, followed by Amanda Devereux and birds. I started this week with Tim Vanikos and reptiles."

"Tim's my brother."

"Really? I didn't know that." Mei frowned.

"What's wrong?"

"Nothing." Mei smiled but it quickly faded. She looked down and opened her iced tea.

I wondered why her expression had changed so quickly. Thinking back to my teaching days, I knew I wouldn't get more of an explanation, at least not now. Mei would talk when she was ready.

"How's McKenzie's widow holding up?" I asked, changing the subject. Since Mei knew all three curators, I figured she'd be a good source of information.

"Amanda Devereux? I guess okay. She never shows emotion so she's hard to figure out."

"Don't the police view the spouse as a murder suspect?" I sipped my coffee.

"Not in this case. Her alibi is airtight. She was too drunk that night."

"Drunk?" I put down my cup.

"That's what I heard. McKenzie must have really upset her." Mei glanced over her shoulders, then leaned forward, lowering her voice. "On the day of the murder, Amanda called a staff meeting after work. By the time everyone arrived, she reeked of alcohol, couldn't control her balance, and was slurring her words."

Mei paused to sip her iced tea through a straw. "Luckily, her two bird keepers, Jill and Jeremy, carpool to work. They convinced Amanda to postpone the meeting. Jill took Amanda's Mercedes and drove her home while Jeremy followed in his car. The housekeeper was off that night, so Jill settled Amanda into bed."

"Does Amanda live far from here?"

"The Village of Stone Mount. That's about an hour west. Jill and Jeremy left Amanda's house around eight-thirty. The murder occurred no later than ten so it's unlikely Amanda sobered up in time to drive back to the zoo and murder her husband."

"What if she wasn't drunk? What if she faked it?"

"I guess it's possible. But she'd need to fool her entire staff. That's difficult."

"You're sure of this?"

"First, I heard the story from Frank Taggart. He's in charge of the bird nursery and incubators. He takes great pleasure in telling everyone."

I remembered Frank from my last visit to the zoo. He'd been deep in conversation with Amanda Devereux. "He's the zookeeper with the body piercings and snake and spider tattoos, right?"

Mei nodded. "If Frank was the only source, I might not believe it. But Jill told me the same story when I ate lunch with her the other day. She's worried about her boss."

Suddenly, Mei's eyes widened. She stopped talking and stared straight ahead. I couldn't see what she saw, but it was obvious that she didn't want our conversation overheard.

I turned around but didn't recognize anyone.

"Jill is afraid Amanda has a drinking problem," Mei continued. "There've been other signs. I wonder what McKenzie did?"

"That's the second time you blamed McKenzie. Why?"

"When I first started at the zoo, Amanda was the perfect model of poise and good manners, but lately . . . you wouldn't believe what happened only a week before McKenzie's murder."

I sipped more coffee. "Why don't you tell me?"

"Amanda stayed home from work, claiming she had a stomach virus. Rumor was she had a hangover. Anyway, later that day, she felt better and asked me to stop by her house that evening to review reports. Amanda and I had just finished analyzing the health reports on the hawks when her husband came home. He apologized for being late, claimed he had an emergency meeting with the Chairman of the Board of Trustees."

"Didn't Amanda believe him?"

"No. Because the chairman called the house an hour before, looking for him."

"Caught." I grinned.

"Amanda confronted McKenzie. He tried changing the subject, but Amanda hung on like a pitbull. She accused him of being with Ginger Hart. They argued right in front of me."

"That put you in an awkward spot."

"Tell me about it. The fight got real ugly. McKenzie finally admitted to meeting with Ginger but claimed it was only to tell her she wasn't getting the promotion he'd promised."

"What promotion?" I bit into my doughnut.

"Vice President for Public Relations and Development, a new position the zoo director created just for Ginger. But Amanda had found out about it. Since this wasn't a simple hiring or firing but involved creation of a new job, it needed the approval of the Board of Trustees. Amanda lobbied her friends on the board to turn it down, and they rejected it at their monthly meeting that morning. So, McKenzie met with Ginger later that day to deliver the bad news."

"Did Amanda believe her husband's version of the story?"

"I don't know. A delivery from a local pharmacy interrupted their argument. When Amanda answered the door, McKenzie scooted upstairs. Since I'd finished my work with Amanda, I left . . ." Mei paused. "McKenzie was telling the truth this time. Lyle, who works in the public relations department, overheard the zoo director telling Ginger about the board's decision. Lyle told me that when Ginger heard she wasn't getting the promotion, she exploded, creating quite a scene in the office."

I sat back, processing all that Mei had told me.

Mei glanced at her watch while sucking the last of her iced tea through a straw. "Time to get back to work."

"Me, too." I wiped doughnut crumbs off my chin and rose from my chair. "I'll be spending the rest of the morning at the zoo library, immersed in research."

"You're still easy to talk to," Mei said as we threw our trash in the receptacle and maneuvered our way to the exit. "You'll be here again, right?"

"At the zoo? Many more times. I need lots more material for my article."

"Good. I may need your advice."

"Something wrong?"

Mei shrugged. "Something doesn't make sense. But too many pieces are missing, and I can't explain it without more information. I'll let you know once I find out more."

We strolled out the cafeteria doorway in time to spot Ginger Hart hurrying down the path.

"Wonder where she's headed in such a rush," I said.

"Probably to the rain forest. The crime scene tape has been removed."

"Why would Ginger go to the rain forest?"

"She's planning a big fundraiser there next month. Cocktails on the viewing platforms. One thousand dollars a ticket." Mei frowned.

"What is it?"

"You asked me before about access to the rain forest. I just remembered. Ginger has a key, too."

CHAPTER EIGHT

An idea flashed through my mind.

I'd finished my research in the zoo library. On my way to the parking lot, I grabbed my phone and punched in my brother's work number. "Tim, do you have the McKenzies' home address?" I didn't tell him I was at the zoo, only a few yards from his office.

"Sure. Everyone is listed in the staff directory. Why?"

"It's complicated. I'll tell you later. Can you give it to me?"

"I'll look it up, but something tells me I don't want to know why you need this."

Now that I knew the five zoo employees with rain forest access, I needed to check out where they were the night of the murder. I'd start with Amanda Devereux. My idea was to verify the driving time from the zoo to the McKenzie house. Amanda's alibi rested upon her level of intoxication. If the curator wasn't as drunk as everyone claimed, could she have driven back in time to murder her husband?

Leaving the zoo, I drove west on the Long Island Expressway, then turned north, heading to Stone Mount Village, part of Long Island's infamous Gold Coast. Soon the scenery became horse farms where sleek thoroughbreds gazed in grassy paddocks, abutting estates whose upkeep could support entire third-world nations. I snaked around the narrow, winding roads until I reached the McKenzie home.

Stopping my car, I gazed at the iron gated entrance anchored by two stone pillars connected to a stone wall. McKenzie hadn't bought this place on a zoo director's salary.

I checked my watch. Fifty-seven minutes since leaving the zoo. There were no street lamps in this tony area, and the lights from the homes would be far off the road, making the drive more difficult once night fell.

Roads that twist and turn. Total darkness. If Amanda drove here while even slightly drunk, she'd be apt to hit a tree. No way could she have driven back to the zoo to murder her husband.

I managed a U-turn and headed back down the road. About a half mile later, a black Escalade appeared in my rear window, barreling at a speed well above the posted limit. It was less than a car length behind me.

"Great," I mumbled. "A tailgater and no place to pull over."

The Escalade soon came so close I feared it would bump me. I accelerated. The Escalade accelerated. I couldn't go faster—that would be foolhardy on these winding lanes.

At the crossroads, I swerved left. The black SUV followed. Gripping the steering wheel, bile rose in my throat. This wasn't a tailgater. Someone was after me.

I flashed around another bend with the Escalade in pursuit. As I maneuvered a sharp right turn, I came within inches of ramming into a tree.

I careened around the next corner, the Escalade on my tail. The end of this road spilled out onto a more heavily trafficked main thoroughfare. If I made it there, I'd be safe. *If I made it.*

Seconds later, the intersection came into view. Breathing a sigh of relief, I veered off onto the main road. The Escalade followed but now maintained a respectable distance.

Up ahead was a gas station with cars lined up at the pumps. I pulled in, screeched to a halt by the mini mart, and held my breath. The Escalade drove out of sight.

Still shaking, I tried to convince myself that this was just some jerk getting kicks harassing others. A spoiled rich kid seeking thrills. After all, no one knew I was here except my brother.

Determined not to let the incident with the Escalade ruin my day, I decided to visit The Scarlet Noose, a bookstore specializing in mysteries and crime stories. I parked in front of the store, then I wandered through the narrow aisles for nearly twenty minutes, finally selecting an anthology of short stories. While a clerk processed my credit card, I spotted a poem taped to the cash register. The author was anonymous.

> *Arsenic and Cyanide*
> *Curare, Foxglove, Aconite*
> *From pills come sleep and ecstasy*
> *Or a death that's crowned in agony*
> *Guns and knives scream of violence*
> *Deadly poisons kill in silence*

I couldn't recall where, but I remembered reading death by poison often indicated a female killer, and I wondered if this theory held true for the murder of Arlen McKenzie.

But those thoughts were swept out of my mind as I exited the store. Pulling out of the parking space behind my car was a black Escalade.

CHAPTER NINE

Saturday.

"How was your conference, Matt?" I asked, stretching up to kiss my six-foot-four spouse. "Learn anything?"

Matt sighed and dropped his suitcase by the door. "Unfortunately, yes. I learned new medical equipment will cost a fortune."

I debated telling him that I knew about his new competition, the animal health and wellness center. One look at his face told me the time wasn't right. Worry lines creased his forehead, and his eyes reflected more worry than usual. I'd let him bring up the topic when he was ready.

"I'm bushed." Matt stretched out his arms and yawned. "I need to shower and change. Then we can go out back and have a drink."

"Abby's coming later with patient updates so I'll make a pitcher of iced tea. What about you?"

"I want a cold beer."

An hour later, Matt and I were relaxing on our patio, enjoying the late-afternoon breeze and fragrance of lavender from the garden. Matt, with his beer, sat by the patio table and rummaged through his conference reports. I settled down on a chaise lounge with my new anthology, hoping to forget about my husband's business problems, McKenzie's murder, and the Escalade incident, at least for a little while.

"Hey, did you hear the news?" Abby barged into the yard. "The medical examiner released the autopsy findings. McKenzie was poisoned by venom from a Russell's viper."

I dropped my book. "A snake? Does this mean his death was accidental?"

"No. The venom didn't come from a bite. It was injected."

"That means there's no doubt it's murder." My shoulders slumped.

"I'll bet Uncle Tim knew viper venom killed McKenzie."

"Why would he know?"

"Because viper poisoning leaves physical evidence. The skin around the wound turns purple. The victim vomits blood and bleeds from the nose and eyes. Since Uncle Tim saw the body, he had to notice this."

I guessed my face showed my thoughts because Matt said, "Just because your brother is herpetology curator doesn't mean he's the only one with access to venom."

"He's the only suspect who works directly with snakes. How else would someone get hold of it? You can't just go into a store and say 'I'd like three ounces of snake venom, please,' can you?"

"In a way, you can. There are companies that extract venom to sell. It's used to make snake bite antidotes and in the treatment of neuralgia and rheumatism. Some medications that coagulate blood actually contain Russell's viper venom."

"So it would be easy to obtain?"

"Anything is easy if you have money and know where to go," Abby said. "Especially online."

"I would still feel better if Tim had an alibi."

"I take it he doesn't," Abby said.

"Not one he can prove. Tim was home alone most of the evening."

"An ironclad alibi would be great, but not having one doesn't prove a thing."

I realized there was nothing I could do now, so I picked up my book and continued reading.

Abby placed a manila folder on the patio table. "I'm going to grab an iced tea, Dad. You can start looking at this."

Abby scooted into the house. A few minutes passed.

"How long does it take to pour iced tea?" Matt sounded testy. I was sure the future of his veterinary practice weighed heavily on his mind.

Abby came back. "It's a good thing I went inside. I cleaned up the accident."

I dropped my book again. Something told me I wasn't going to get much reading done today. "What accident?"

"One of the dogs. By the sofa."

"Are you sure. Neither has had an accident since puppy-hood."

"Of course, I'm sure. A cat never lived here before. They're acting out against Owl."

"This situation is getting worse, not better." I picked up my book and attempted to read.

Abby pulled up a chair next to Matt. "Before I forget, you may be called to testify in court. The Polichaks are divorcing and a custody battle is shaping up for Jake."

"They're both crazy for that little terrier," Matt said. "I can't believe they're divorcing."

Abby turned toward me. "Speaking of marital break-ups, do you think Uncle Tim and Aunt Barbara will hold off on the divorce?"

My book fell to the ground for the third time. "What divorce?"

"Nicholas told me how his parents fight all the time," she said, referring to Tim and Barbara's oldest son. "Usually about money."

Abby was close to both my brother's children, but especially Nicholas who now attended graduate school in Boston. "Lots of people fight but don't divorce." I waved my hand to fend off a nearby bee. "Did Nicholas say they were divorcing?"

"He told me his mom brought the topic up twice, but he's not sure if she's serious."

"When I joined Tim and Barbara for dinner the other night, they had been arguing. But that's nothing new. They've been fighting since the first day they met. Otherwise, they seem fine."

"Aunt Barbara always seems fine in public. But I think Nicholas is wrong. They won't divorce. A divorce will only make their money matters worse. It would require supporting two households. Aunt Barbara wants more money to spend, not less."

Despite the severity of the situation, I chuckled. Abby always zoomed right to the practical issues in any situation. But I agreed.

Tim adored Barbara. A divorce would devastate him. And Barbara was motivated by money and prestige, which would be gone if Tim lost his job.

As Abby continued updating Matt on veterinary business, I no longer listened. Instead, I thought about my upcoming visit to the zoo this Monday, when I planned to somehow check out the alibis of zoo employees who had access to the rain forest. It was unlikely but not impossible that Amanda drove back to the Rocky Cove Zoo. What about Saul Mandel, Linda Sancho, and Ginger Hart? Where were they the night of McKenzie's murder?

In the meantime, a knot tightened in my stomach as I envisioned Detective Wolfe examining motives, means, and opportunity.

Since no one could verify Tim's alibi, a case could be made for opportunity.

As a herpetologist, he had means.

And his motive kept growing.

CHAPTER TEN

Matt got called into the veterinary hospital Sunday afternoon to perform emergency surgery on a three-year-old Golden Retriever hit by a car. I decided to spend this time finding out what I could about Rocky Cove's late zoo director.

After whipping around the house and picking up my husband's extraneous laundry, I settled down at the kitchen table with my laptop and searched for Arlen McKenzie's obituary.

Basically a puff piece, the obituary extolled McKenzie's financial acumen. It told how, as former CEO for three major Long Island corporations, he reorganized the businesses and increased profits.

One company struck a familiar chord. I remembered a former neighbor who'd worked there for more than fifteen years. After some quick math, I realized that three months after McKenzie took control, my neighbor lost his job, the victim of corporate streamlining.

To Arlen McKenzie, reorganizing meant downsizing. When he came into a company, lots of people wound up unemployed. It appeared he followed the same pattern at the Rocky Cove Zoo.

"No wonder everyone at the zoo hated him," I muttered.

"Talking to yourself?" Matt trudged into the kitchen carrying a large bag emblazoned with the logo of our favorite Chinese restaurant. Partners in crime, Brandy, the collie, and Archie, the mixed breed, rushed toward him.

"Scat. You'll get your dinner later." He shooed them away.

"How's the Golden?"

"Fine. Operation successful."

My husband began removing carton after carton from the brown bag.

"How much did you buy?"

"I'm hungry. Abby watches me at work like a hawk. My days of jelly doughnuts are numbered."

I grinned as we parked ourselves down at opposite ends of the table with the two dogs at my feet. I palmed off two pieces of dumpling to the dogs as the cat stuck her head around the doorway. "Poor Owl. She won't come anywhere near Archie or Brandy." I walked across the room and fed the cat a shrimp.

Returning to the table, I said, "I just finished reading Arlen McKenzie's biography, but something doesn't make sense. Why would McKenzie take a job at the zoo? He probably earned three times as much when he headed private corporations."

"Political ambition."

I looked up from my white carton.

"I read about McKenzie in a financial magazine," Matt said. "He made a killing in the stock market. Now he wants to run for congress, but he needs to make a name for himself on Long Island first. How? Become associated with a high-profile organization. The Rocky Cove Zoo fit the bill."

"But Matt, he was downsizing the zoo. Is that a smart political move?"

"The Rocky Cove Zoo isn't located in McKenzie's congressional district."

"But being responsible for massive lay-offs couldn't be good for his political career," I argued.

"Most people don't care, unless they're the ones laid off. Arlen McKenzie would have portrayed himself as a successful businessperson who brought the zoo out of financial chaos and would do the same in government."

"I see what you mean. McKenzie knew the value of public relations, too. He'd make sure the public saw him as a hero who saved the zoo from financial ruin."

The phone rang. I dropped my chopsticks and grabbed the receiver as I recognized my brother's home number on the caller ID.

"Kristy, I need your help," Barbara pleaded before I could say hello. "What's the phone number of the criminal lawyer Matt knows? The police are here again."

"Why?"

"Tim lied about his alibi. An eyewitness spotted him in front of the rain forest the night of the murder. Tim was arguing with Arlen McKenzie."

CHAPTER ELEVEN

I didn't make a conscience decision to sit, but I felt my knees folding.

"Barbara, what did the police say?" I couldn't believe my brother lied.

"Otto Kravitz, part of the zoo's cleaning crew, overheard McKenzie and Tim arguing a little after eight. McKenzie wanted Tim gone by the end of next month. Tim told McKenzie to drop dead." Barbara sighed loudly.

"Where was Otto when this occurred?"

"Sweeping by the side of the exhibit. That's why he heard the conversation without anyone noticing him."

"I don't understand. Why was Tim there?"

"He had an appointment with McKenzie. Tim had ideas for the rain forest that he hoped would impress McKenzie."

"And McKenzie would change his mind about firing Tim."

"But that didn't happen. Now Tim's motive is stronger than before. Detective Wolfe is salivating over this. He told Tim not to leave town. I need a good lawyer."

"I'll put Matt on the phone. He'll give you the information." I handed my husband the phone while briefly filling him in on the situation.

Matt's patients included an Old English bulldog owned by one of the top criminal lawyers on Long Island. He was smart and ruthless—the lawyer, not the bulldog. Nicknamed the "courtroom carnivore," no one would arrest this attorney's client without a solid case.

As Matt hung up the phone and returned to the table, he shook his head. "I can't believe your brother's stupidity."

After the phone call, we both lost our appetites.

"There's a Yankee game starting in ten minutes," Matt said while stuffing leftovers in the refrigerator. "Want to watch it?"

"No thanks. I know you're trying to take my mind off my brother, but I've work to finish. I think I'll go up to the bedroom where it's quiet."

I propped myself up in bed, opened my laptop, and began reorganizing my notes. But I couldn't concentrate. I kept conjuring up images of Tim arguing with the zoo director. Deciding to postpone working on my magazine assignment, I hit another button on the keyboard and brought up a blank screen. I listed the five zoo employees with keys to the rain forest, leaving space between each name to jot down my thoughts.

TIM VANIKOS: McKenzie refused to renew my brother's employment contract. How quickly could Tim secure another job? How long could Barbara and Tim cope financially with Tim unemployed?

With McKenzie out of the way, this problem no longer existed.

AMANDA DEVEREUX: She knew about her husband and Ginger. She blew up at him a few days before the murder.

Was she angry enough to kill him? Was she sober enough to return to the zoo?

LINDA SANCHO: Elimination of the wildlife nutritionist job meant an upheaval in her family life, possibly forcing her to choose between marriage and career. And what about moving away during her mother's chemotherapy?

Now Linda didn't need to make these decisions.

GINGER HART: McKenzie's lover. They'd fought bitterly when she received the news that she'd been denied the promotion he promised. The fight was overheard by her staff. For an employee to confront her boss in public, she had to be stupid or filled with fury.

Ginger is not stupid.

SAUL MANDEL: He had lost out to McKenzie for the top position at the Rocky Cove Zoo.

Would he now become director permanently?

I felt a glimmer of hope. All suspects had motives that were as strong as my brother's.

Chapter Twelve

Abby had always been a great sounding board, so when she stopped by the house for bagels the next morning, I told her about Tim's false statement to the police and my incident with the Escalade. She appeared more interested in the vehicle that chased me than in her uncle's dilemma.

"But who knew you were there?" she asked, pouring her second glass of orange juice. She had just come from running two miles on the boardwalk near her home.

"I don't know. Maybe someone heard me ask Tim for the address. Or perhaps someone was near the McKenzie estate and saw me stop." I shrugged. "Someone knows I'm looking into the zoo director's death."

Abby bit into a bagel smeared with cream cheese. "What did Dad say?"

I sipped my coffee. "He doesn't know."

"You didn't tell him?"

"Why upset him? He's got enough on his mind. He's worried about that new veterinary facility, isn't he?"

"The health and wellness center for companion animals. He certainly is. The corporation that owns the center is renovating a huge facility only two blocks from Dad's veterinary hospital. By the way, where is Dad?"

"At work. He left early. Ann Carroll called here this morning and asked if she could bring Ivan the Terrible in before regular office hours."

Ann Carroll was a long-time friend. Lord Ivanhoe of Britain, her hyperactive cocker spaniel, had been nicknamed Ivan the Terrible by Matt's veterinary staff.

Abby devoured the last of her bagel. "I still think you should tell Dad about the Escalade."

"No. Dad's a worrier, and there's nothing anyone can do." Glancing at the clock, I sprang from my chair.

"Where are you off to, Mom?"

"The zoo. I'm touring the reptile nursery with Tim. And I intend to find out why my brother lied about his alibi."

I swung open the French doors and clapped. The two dogs bounded in from the yard and raced to Abby. "I'm out of here," I said. "Lock the door when you leave."

"I'll be gone momentarily. Jason's great aunt is bringing in her Manx cat. She thinks the cat has ear mites."

"Jason's great aunt?" I stood by the counter, facing my daughter. "He's introducing you to the extended family? Sounds serious."

Abby rolled her eyes. "His aunt moved into senior housing only a few blocks from the veterinary hospital. She didn't want the long drive to her old vet, so Jason suggested me. That's all it is."

Abby had been dating Jason for five months, but she hadn't seen much of him lately because he was busy studying for the bar exam. I really liked the recent law school graduate.

After breaking a bagel in half, I palmed the pieces to Archie and Brandy. Expecting a lecture from Abby on weight and canine nutrition, I was surprised when she ignored my actions.

"Be careful," she instead said. "You and I both know the Escalade that chased you is tied to McKenzie's murder. You were right with what you said before. Someone knows what you're doing and that someone doesn't want you snooping."

★ ★ ★ ★ ★

Tim fiddled with his pen.

"Why did you lie?" I sat across from my brother's desk with his office door shut.

"I didn't think anyone saw us. I could only imagine how bad my presence at the rain forest would look to the police."

"It looks worse now."

Tim glanced down, avoiding my eyes. "I know Saul believes me. But not everyone else does. I can tell by the way my colleagues stared at me this morning."

"How did they find out so quickly?"

"I'm sure someone here has a pipeline into the police. All you need is one person to hear the news and it spreads. I've never seen Barbara so mad. I humiliated her."

"She'll get over it."

"She might leave me." He squeezed an eraser between his two fingers. "With McKenzie refusing to renew my contract, I had motive. Now, I have no alibi."

"You're not the only one with motive. As for alibis, what about the others, like the wildlife nutritionist?"

"Linda Sancho? She attended an animal behavior conference at Ridge River University. The police verified it. Linda asked a question and the speaker remembered her."

I crossed my legs. "Maybe she slipped out before or after her question."

"I don't know. I guess it's possible."

"Tim, what exactly does a wildlife nutritionist do?"

"She's responsible for the diet of every animal here." Tim stretched back in his chair, his arms behind his head. "Saul almost lost a baby zebra this spring. It couldn't eat because it couldn't use its tongue. Do you know why?"

"I haven't a clue."

"Lack of vitamin E. Zoo nutritionists not only need to know

what animals eat in the wild, but they have to determine the nutrients in the food. Sometimes—"

"Okay, I see."

"Wait. There's more. Take the anteater—"

"I get the idea." My brother either gave one word answers or he sounded like an entry in an encyclopedia. But I needed to find out about Linda's job, not the anteater's diet. "As a nutritionist, Linda must be pretty good at chemistry."

"Her undergraduate major."

"I guess she works with all types of animals, including snakes."

"Sure. I've consulted with her on more than a dozen occasions."

Filing that information in my mind, I moved on to the next zoo employee with access to the rain forest. "How about Saul Mandel? What's his alibi?"

"He arrived home at seven and stayed all night. His wife backs him."

I didn't say a word.

"I know what you're thinking, but I can't imagine Saul killing anyone."

"What about Ginger Hart? I heard she exploded when told she wasn't getting the promotion McKenzie promised."

"What are you doing? Playing Nancy Drew?"

"Call it a writer's curiosity. What about physical evidence? Hair? Fiber?"

"McKenzie met with more than a dozen staffers in the rain forest the afternoon of the murder. He was finalizing plans with Ginger for a fundraiser featuring the new exhibit. So, finding DNA evidence in the area wouldn't mean a thing. It could have been there hours before. Enough talk of murder. Let's go to the herpetology nursery. That's why you're here, isn't it?"

Tim rose from his chair. As we entered the outer office, talking among the staff suddenly ceased. Tim pretended not to notice, but his face reddened. He walked with his head down as if fascinated with his shoes.

We headed down a narrow corridor until we reached a door with a sign identifying it as the herpetology nursery. As we stepped inside the facility, the stillness reminded me of the silent nature of reptiles. I heard the sound of my footfalls on the concrete floor as I wandered through the room and gazed at tanks housing newborn snakes and lizards.

"Unlike baby birds and mammals, reptile hatchlings emerge ready to catch prey," Tim explained. "The hatchlings emerge from eggs," he added.

I shuddered. Aside from a warning hiss, snakes didn't make a sound. Noiseless, odorless, and well camouflaged. You might not know one was near until it was within striking distance. No wonder they were such formidable enemies.

After the tour, we returned to Tim's office where he explained egg fertilization procedures and discussed the successes and failures of the breeding program. He began talking about his current project, breeding the Morlett crocodile.

"On Thursday my intern will remove crocodile eggs from their nest for incubation."

"Intern?" I said. "Is that Mei Lau?"

Tim nodded.

"Mei was my high school student."

"I didn't know that. Would you like to watch the egg collection?"

"I'd love it," I said, rising from my chair. Besides providing insight for my article, I knew something was bothering Mei, and I hoped she was ready to talk.

"Then be here by eleven-thirty." He glanced at the stack of papers on the side of his desk. "Now I need to get back to these reports."

Before exiting, I turned to say good-bye. But my brother wasn't reading his reports. His chin rested on his hands, and he was staring into space.

CHAPTER THIRTEEN

"You're as bad as he was," said a voice from behind the cafeteria. "You only care about appearances. You don't give a damn about the animals."

"Without publicity, there wouldn't be any animals. Is that what you want? Do you want the zoo to close, you stupid idiot?"

Recognizing the second voice, I crept along the side of the building and peeked around the corner.

"That money is from a federal wildlife nutrition grant. It's meant for research, not promotional videos." Linda Sancho pointed a finger in Ginger Hart's face. "I'm reporting this to Saul Mandel."

Ginger pushed down Linda's hand. "Go right ahead. But remember, the Chairman of the Board of Trustees is enthusiastic about the project. And Saul is only the acting director. Do you want Saul to squash a project the board chairman likes?"

"You are despicable." Linda whirled around and stomped off.

I scooted back to the front of the building and waited. A few seconds later, a scowling Ginger came forward.

"Ginger. I'm glad I ran into you."

The anger on Ginger's face dissipated, a smile quickly appearing. "I'm glad you did too. I've good news. Amanda Devereux is willing to be interviewed, so my assistant set you up with an appointment at ten-fifteen this Thursday. He was planning to call you later."

"Perfect."

"Contact my office if you need anything else." Ginger started to walk away.

"Do you have a few minutes for me now? I need more background information on the zoo."

Ginger paused as if considering her response. "I usually assign someone from my staff to work with writers from minor publications like yours. But I could use a cup of tea. Why don't we go inside the cafeteria and talk?"

"Great. I'd like some coffee." But more than coffee, I wanted the opportunity to question Ginger about the murder.

"We have a special here today," Ginger said as we navigated through the crowd inside the building. "Sugar cookies shaped like elephants. Part of our Pachyderm Power Program. It was my idea. Each week, the cookies are in the form of a different animal. Next week is Monkey Madness."

Upon reaching the food line, Ginger grabbed a tea bag, poured hot water, and selected an elephant cookie with white icing. "They still have quite a few left. I'll have to talk to the food service manager about displaying them more prominently."

Deciding it might be smart to support Ginger's public relations stunt, I chose a pink iced elephant along with my coffee, then joined her at a small corner table, away from the noise. Ginger described upcoming projects, sounding like a public service announcement.

"Besides the emotional impact of Arlen McKenzie's death, it must affect the zoo's daily operations," I said, weaving the murder into our conversation.

"You better believe it. I'm so busy handling the media I don't have time to perform my normal functions. Of course, the rain forest was closed for several days, too. That's one of our biggest attractions." Ginger sipped her tea. "Your magazine should do a feature story on the rain forest."

"I'll mention it to my editor. The police must be a disruptive influence. I understand they're questioning all staff with keys to the exhibit."

Ginger nodded.

Deciding a smooth segue was impossible, I came right to the point. "Did they ask you for an alibi?"

"Yes. I had dinner that night at my favorite Greek restaurant, Treasures of Zeus. Not that it's any of your business." She rose from her chair. "I know what you're doing. You're trying to take the heat off Tim. It's not happening. At least not with me. My alibi is airtight."

Chapter Fourteen

After leaving the zoo, I drove to the *Animal Advocate* magazine office, located in a two-story building in the downtown business district. The first story housed a law firm and insurance agency. *Animal Advocate* occupied the second floor. The publication operated on a tight budget with barely more than a dozen full-time employees.

I trudged up the stairs and pushed open the office door, first to be confronted by a blast of air from the recently repaired air-conditioning system, then by Clara Schultheis, resident gossip and conspiracy theorist. She was also administrative assistant to the editor.

"Kristy, I've been waiting for you," she called out from her desk, located only a few feet from the door. "What's the inside scoop on McKenzie's murder?"

"All I know is what I read in the papers." I tried scooting around her.

"Want to hear my theory?" she whispered loudly, stopping me in my tracks. "I think Arlen McKenzie was involved with blackmail."

"What are you talking about?"

"Remember the stories about the former director, the one before Arlen McKenzie? The one who died of cancer? There were rumors about funny stuff involving the zoo's money during his tenure."

"My brother told me all about that at the time. He says it

wasn't true, just media sensationalism. There's no evidence of embezzlement, only bad business decisions made by a dying director who wasn't really paying attention to business."

Clara scratched her head, oblivious to the mess it made of her short gray hair. "I don't believe that's the whole story. My personal theory is that when McKenzie was hired, he uncovered a money scandal, swept it under the rug, and blackmailed the embezzler. That's who killed him."

"Come on, Clara. How can you say that? You have no proof."

Clara winked over the top of her half-moon glasses. "I'm usually right about these things."

"And Elvis has been sighted in Afghanistan," I mumbled under my breath.

"Did you say something?"

"Is Olivia in?" I asked, quickly changing the subject.

The office of the magazine's editor, Olivia Johnson, was less than fifteen feet away from Clara's desk. Her door was shut.

"She's interviewing someone for feature writer," Clara said. "He majored in journalism at some Ivy League college. Just graduated this May."

"Damn!"

"Don't worry. I still think you'll get the job. I'm rooting for you."

"Thanks, Clara." I felt like a deflated balloon.

"He's arrogant. You know the type. He comes from money and expects things to fall his way as a natural right. Olivia hates that attitude."

"If he's good, Olivia won't care if he has the personality of Attila the Hun."

"You got the temporary position," Clara said. "That gives you a heads-up on everyone."

Fretting about my competition wouldn't help but writing a good story could. I wandered back to my cubicle and spent the rest of the day researching the mating habits of endangered gorillas.

Late afternoon, with my mind chockful of facts about gorilla sex, I shut down my computer and sat back. As my thoughts wandered to my earlier conversation with Ginger Hart, an idea popped into my head. I located the phone directory and thumbed through the pages.

The same town. My hunch was right. I grabbed the phone and punched in Abby's number.

"Have you plans for dinner?" I asked my daughter. "Are you going out with friends? Or Jason?"

"Jason's living on take-out pizza until the bar exam. Actually, I have no plans, but I wanted to make it an early night. I thought I'd eat something from the four basic food groups. You know, restaurant, take-out, microwave, or sandwiches."

I laughed. "Let's make it restaurant. My treat. Tonight is your father's monthly poker game, so it will be just the two of us."

"A Mexican restaurant just opened up on the boardwalk near my place."

"We'll try that some other time. I feel like Greek food tonight."

"We never go to Greek restaurants. What's up, Mom?"

"There's a place called Treasures of Zeus that I've heard is excellent. It's right off exit 60 on the expressway."

"That's the exit you take for the Rocky Cove Zoo. This has to do with McKenzie's murder, doesn't it?"

"It's the restaurant where Ginger Hart supposedly ate that night."

"Supposedly? You want to find a hole in her alibi? Don't you think the police checked?"

"Maybe they missed something."

When Abby didn't respond, I added, "The police may be satisfied with the answers they received, but did they ask the right questions?"

"I suppose you know what to ask."

"I certainly do. I'll pick you up at the veterinary hospital after work."

After battling the Long Island Expressway traffic, I pulled into the parking lot behind my husband's veterinary hospital, where I noticed a dent in the green Ford Mustang belonging to Matt's office assistant.

Katie had only bought the car two months ago.

My husband's car was not in his reserved parking space. I remembered he'd scheduled a meeting to inquire about financing for new veterinary equipment.

A sinking feeling arose in the pit of my stomach as I wondered what would happen if he couldn't get the money he needed. I pushed that thought out of my mind as I crossed the parking lot and pulled open the building door.

A large woman held a cat carrier on her lap. Across from her, a man restrained a barking German shepherd on a short leash, while at the opposite end of the room, a woman cradled a yapping Pomeranian, lovingly referred to by the veterinary staff as a canine dust bunny.

Business appeared to be good. But I couldn't help but wonder about the new health and wellness center. Would these clients abandon my husband for the services of an impersonal national chain?

At the reception counter, Katie Kelly, the twenty-two-year-old office assistant, handed a brown and white packet of pills to a small wizened man.

"Hi, Katie," I said. "What happened to your car?"

"Parking lot accident. And what's going on at Rocky Cove? Abby said you found the body."

"I certainly did."

"It was on the news again at lunch. The police commissioner issued a statement about how the department would be working swiftly and diligently to solve the case, blah, blah, blah."

I couldn't remember the last time the commissioner called a press conference on an individual crime. Such remarks came from the detective in charge of the case or the department's press office. But Arlen McKenzie had powerful connections. That meant they'd be looking for a quick solution and that didn't bode well for Tim.

"Is Abby still with a patient?" I asked.

"She just finished with Cyrus," Katie said to me, gesturing toward an old-looking Doberman being led to the door by a teenager.

I spun around and saw my daughter, stethoscope swinging from her neck.

"Mom, I texted you earlier. When you didn't respond I phoned and left a message."

"What's up?"

"We've had a few minor emergencies. I still have patients to see so I'll be working at least another hour."

"We can still go to the restaurant. I'll run some errands and come back for you, okay?"

Abby agreed and made her way toward an examining room. I wanted to ask Katie more about her car accident, but she was on the phone describing the pros and cons of a gerbil as a house pet, so I waved good-bye and decided I'd get the scoop on the accident when I returned.

When I arrived back at the veterinary hospital, Katie was gone for the day. Abby sat behind the desk and stared at the computer screen.

"I finished earlier than expected," she said, "so I decided to check out that new animal health and wellness center." She shut down the computer.

"So, what did you find?" I asked as she flipped off the light switch and we exited the building into the parking lot.

"Their website is incredible. I understand why Dad's so worried. The first center started up six years ago in California. Now there are more than forty facilities in eighteen states, most on the east and west coasts. And the corporation plans to double that amount in the next five years."

"I still wonder if it will make it here."

"Mom, when I was eight, you claimed computers were a passing fad."

Economics is not my strong point.

But I hoped finding a killer was.

CHAPTER FIFTEEN

I had no idea if my plan would work. We exited the expressway and continued down the main road until reaching the village of Rocky Cove. Famous in past centuries as a fishing and whaling center, Rocky Cove had undergone a revitalization of its downtown area. Main Street—now lined with newly planted trees, Victorian-style street lamps, wrought iron benches, and hanging flower pots—featured ethnic restaurants, outdoor cafés, and trendy boutiques.

Treasures of Zeus sat between a bookstore and an art gallery. I parked in a large municipal lot in back of the buildings. Abby and I entered the restaurant through the rear door and wandered down a short hallway until we reached the dining room with its white stucco walls, wooden beams, and pictures of the Greek Islands.

This was a summer tourist area so the dining area was crowded, and I regretted that I hadn't made reservations.

"I hope we can get a table," I said.

Ten minutes later we were shown the only empty booth in the restaurant.

"Now that we're here, what's your plan?" Abby asked.

"To find out when Ginger Hart left here the night of the murder. Supposedly, the police verified the time, but I can't believe the staff in a busy restaurant constantly checks their watches. Fifteen to twenty minutes could make a difference."

"And how will you find this out?"

"By casual conversation with the wait staff. Some people love to talk, others clam up. Here comes a waiter now. Let's hope he's a talker."

"Welcome to Treasures of Zeus," said the waiter, a short man built like a fireplug. He handed out menus. "I'm Demetrius. I'll be your server tonight."

After we ordered two glasses of the house wine, I said, "One of your regulars recommended this restaurant. Do you know Ginger Hart?"

He hesitated. "Yes. I'll be right back with your wine." He headed for the bar.

"Sorry, Mom. You got the clam, not the talker." Abby glanced at her menu. "How do you know Ginger's a regular customer?"

"She claims this is one of her favorite restaurants."

Demetrius returned with our wine. "Are you ready to order?"

"My father was born on Santorini," I said, hoping some ethnic bonding might loosen our waiter's tongue. "I grew up with Greek food and I love it all. It's hard to choose. I wish I'd asked Ginger for a recommendation. She was here last Monday. Do you remember what she ate?"

"I don't know. But I recommend the spanakopita. It's the house specialty. Comes with Greek salads."

Abby and I decided that sounded like a good choice. He scribbled down our order and turned toward the kitchen.

"Give it up. You're not getting information from him." Abby sipped her wine.

"You're probably right." I rose from my seat. "I need a trip to the ladies' room."

I maneuvered around the tightly packed dining area to the hall where I spotted a poster I hadn't noticed before. I returned just as Demetrius delivered pita bread to our table.

"Demetrius, I saw a sign for *Taverna Night*. It features a Greek buffet and music." I made a sweeping gesture with my arm. "Where is there space?"

"We move out the tables and chairs from the middle and set up a long buffet. The band is at the far end. We still have booths so guests can sit and eat, but most of the time, everyone congregates near the bar and in the center of the room."

Once he moved out of earshot, I leaned toward Abby. "According to the poster, the last *Taverna Night* was the evening of McKenzie's murder. Ginger wasn't here for a sit-down dinner. *Taverna Night* is a typical singles cocktail party. Wall-to-wall people, drink in one hand, plate in the other."

"I'm sure the police are aware of that. It doesn't make a difference."

"Yes, it does. Ginger had the opportunity to sneak out. The zoo is on the outskirts of town, less than four miles away."

"It's risky. What if someone spied her skulking away?"

"The ladies' room is near the end of the hall by the exit. Ginger could have gone there, then easily slipped out and exited through the back door when no one was watching."

"And what about coming back? What if someone saw her?"

"She could say she went to retrieve something from her car."

"I still think it's risky."

"Murder is risky."

I waited until he put our Greek salads in front of us. "Demetrius, I was in this area last Monday, and I swear I spotted Ginger Hart entering the book shop next door at about eight-thirty." This was a lie, of course, but it was worth trying. "Do you remember if she stepped out for a few minutes?"

Demetrius stiffened. "You're asking lots of questions. Does this have to do with the murder where Ms. Hart works?"

Abby narrowed her eyes. I could read her mind. She was wondering how I planned to get out of this.

"Not at all," I said to Demetrius. "I'm just curious because I'm sure I saw her, but my daughter says it wasn't Ginger. We have a small bet riding on this. The loser does the winner's laundry for a week."

"I didn't see her leave, but I was busy. Can I get you anything else? More wine?"

We nixed the wine and Demetrius left.

"A laundry bet?" Abby laughed. "That's so strange it's hard to believe it's not true." She glanced at the curved archway leading to the back hall. "It's highly improbable that Ginger slipped out of here and returned to the zoo."

"To quote Sherlock Holmes, 'Once you eliminate the impossible, whatever remains, no matter how improbable, must be the truth.' " I sipped the last of my wine. "Or, to put it another way, Ginger Hart is not in the clear."

CHAPTER SIXTEEN

A talking chipmunk? I shook my head. This would be a long day.

Although temporarily assigned as feature writer, I still performed a few of my old editorial assistant tasks. Since freelance articles accounted for twenty percent of *Animal Advocate,* I spent the following day at the office, where I read unsolicited stories from the slush pile, forwarding those appropriate to the editor for consideration.

"How's it going?" Clara asked when I emerged from my cubicle for my fifth coffee.

"The last article featured a talking chipmunk who tells the reader about the importance of trees. Before that was a story about a worm who wants to be an eagle. What do they think *Animal Advocate* is? *Aesop's Fables?*"

"Aren't there any decent articles in the pile?"

"A few." I glanced at the editor's closed door. "Is Olivia in?"

"No. She had a luncheon engagement. Why?"

I hesitated. "Have you heard anything about the feature writer's job?"

Clara winced. "Olivia called a few professors of that kid who came in for the interview. She's checking his references."

"We need to stop referring to him as a kid. Does he have a name?"

"Schuyler Adams."

"Why is that familiar?"

"His father, also named Schuyler Adams, owns a company

operating eco-tours and wilderness camping vacations."

"The one advertised in our magazine? The full-page ad in each issue?"

"Yes."

I was ready to call it quits for the day when Clara barged into my office.

"I've great news." She waved a paper in her hand. "Do you remember the proposed story on wildlife smuggling?"

"The one Olivia assigned to a freelancer?"

"The freelancer is out of town on assignment for another magazine. Olivia wants you to write the article."

Great news would be the permanent promotion to feature writer. But this was good news. The more I had to write, the better my chances of proving to Olivia I could do the job.

"Here's the phone number of Roy Maxwell, New York Director of the United States Fish and Wildlife Service." Clara placed the paper she was waving on my desk. "Olivia said to start with him."

"Thanks." I picked up the phone to call when I noticed Clara still hovering in front of me.

"Anything else?" I asked.

"I was listening to Horatio, the radio talk-show host."

"The obnoxious one who's always being sued?"

She ignored my comment. "He was discussing Arlen McKenzie's murder. One of his call-in listeners thinks, just as I do, that the murder involves financial embezzlement."

"You may be right." Sometimes it didn't pay to argue with Clara. I pointed to the stack of papers on my desk. "I need to get back to work."

Once Clara left, I phoned Roy Maxwell at Fish and Wildlife and was lucky enough to arrange an interview. After hanging up, I leaned back in my chair, pondering Clara's last statement.

The argument I'd witnessed between Linda Sancho and Ginger Hart the other day had dealt with federal grant money. Of course, Clara had a vivid imagination, as probably did the call-in radio listener, but maybe the theory concerning misappropriation of funds had merit.

I grabbed the phone and punched in my brother's number.

"Ridiculous," Tim said after I explained my theory. "When McKenzie took over as zoo director, he hired an accounting firm to check the books. The audit showed no illegal transactions, just sloppy practices."

"Sloppy practices? Maybe someone didn't want their sloppy practices stopped."

"Enough to kill for?"

"What if someone has something to hide? Think about it. Do you pay attention to the finances of departments other than yours? How can I get a look at the zoo's financial records for the years before McKenzie became director?"

"Easy. That information is in the annual reports, and I have copies in my desk. I'll drop them off at your house on my way home."

"By the way, do you know anyone at the zoo who drives a black Escalade?"

"I don't think so, but I don't pay attention to what people drive."

"What about the suspects in McKenzie's murder? The ones with the keys to the rain forest."

"What about them?"

I sighed in exasperation. "Do you know what they drive?"

"Not the make and model, but I'm pretty sure none has a black car. Why this obsession with what everyone drives?"

"It's not important. I'll see you tonight." I said good-bye, hanging up before he could question me further.

I punched in the number for the animal hospital. Katie, the

office assistant, picked up.

"I'll get Abby for you. Let me put you on hold for a minute."

After listening to a recorded message on fleas and ticks, Abby came on the line.

"Can you stop by the house on the way home from work?" I asked.

"Provided I don't stay too long. Jason and I are having dinner out."

"I thought he was living on pizza until after the bar exam. He's taking a break?"

"A short one. That's why I want to be on time. What's this about?"

"Uncle Tim is dropping off some papers that I want you to examine. I need your animal expertise since I may not be familiar with some of the items the zoo purchased, and I don't know what your uncle knows outside of reptiles. I'd ask your father, but he's working late. I'll tell you more tonight."

After hanging up, I sat back in my chair, pondering possible financial scenarios. I was anxious to read the Rocky Cove Zoo reports. Follow the money.

Embezzlement of funds would certainly be a motive for murder.

Before meeting my brother and daughter, there was something I needed to do.

I left my office early. Instead of driving directly home, I headed for Ridge River University. I wanted information on the animal behavior conference attended by the zoo's wildlife nutritionist, Linda Sancho, the night Arlen McKenzie was killed.

An accident on the Long Island Expressway delayed traffic. I arrived at the Student Union scheduling office at the same moment a young woman, whose hair resembled a lion after a bad perm, exited the room and locked the door.

"Excuse me," I said. "Can you tell me where I can get information on last week's animal behavior conference?"

"Sorry, I was on vacation last week."

"Is there someone else I can talk to?"

"Professor Patel from biology coordinated the conference. He might be in his office in the Life Sciences building."

"Do you know where the conference was held?"

"Sure. It was in the auditorium at the end of this hall."

After grabbing a campus map from a nearby information rack, I wandered over to the auditorium and peeked inside. In addition to the main entrance, two exits were located on either side of the room.

I left the Student Union and headed to the Life Sciences building. Once there, I found Professor Patel's office locked, but an idea came to mind. Campus announcements usually stayed posted for weeks after an event occurred, so I searched the department bulletin board and discovered a schedule. It included a video presentation on territorial behavior at eight p.m.

The lights would be off during the video presentation, making it easy for someone to slip out unnoticed. Without a traffic jam, the drive from Ridge River University back to the zoo would be no longer than fifteen minutes.

Linda's alibi was flawed.

CHAPTER SEVENTEEN

"Not again," I muttered.

Upon my arrival home, I saw that one of the dogs had peed in the living room. Luckily, it was on the hardwood floor and not the blue and green area rug.

I sighed. Another protest against Owl?

I didn't have time to think about my animal problem. I'd no sooner cleaned the mess when the doorbell chimed. As I swung open the door, the two dogs barked and rushed into the living room. I stepped aside so Tim could enter.

"I didn't expect you so early. Abby's coming, but she's not here yet."

"Since McKenzie's murder, no one wants to work late." He handed me a manila folder. "These are the annual reports. They're for the last five years of the old administration. I also included the report issued after McKenzie's first year in case you want a comparison."

"Why don't you make yourself a drink while I read these? And a snack if you're hungry. I think there's cheese in the refrigerator."

I settled on the sofa and scanned the reports. I would study them carefully later, but for now I wanted an overview.

According to the reports, zoo spending had skyrocketed during the previous director's last two years during the time he had been ill. Comparing those budgets to his three prior years, I noted dramatic increases for computers, software programs, lab equipment, office furniture, and exhibit renovations.

"All legitimate expenses," I mumbled, "unless . . ." An idea shot through my mind.

Tim returned carrying a scotch and soda and a small plate of food. While he sipped and nibbled, I read, every so often glancing at my brother, who looked more disheveled than usual. Dark, heavy bags appeared under his thick glasses.

The dogs sat on either side of Tim's chair, staring up at him with their big brown eyes. This tag team mooching technique usually earned a tasty tidbit from Tim, who was a soft touch, but tonight my brother appeared so absorbed in his thoughts, I was sure he didn't notice.

"Tim, how does your budget process work?"

"The head of each department submits a budget for the upcoming year to the director." He paused, cutting a slab of brie and shoving it on a cracker. "In addition to normal yearly expenses, like salary and supplies, we include a wish list."

"Seems like wishes came true at Rocky Cove."

Tim smiled. "Here's where it's a game. We always ask for more than we expect because we know the director is going to eliminate a percentage of the request."

"But that didn't happen the last two years of Jay Allen's administration, did it?"

"Jay's cancer was killing him. He was in lots of pain and couldn't focus on the zoo. He approved the budget with most requests intact."

"So after he died, McKenzie was hired to balance the budget?"

"Yes. We're not totally out of the woods, but we're back on track. But McKenzie didn't need to propose the drastic cuts and slashing of wildlife conservation projects the way he did, Kristy, especially since he always found money for his pet projects, like refurbishing the administration building."

"Let's get back to the old budgets. Didn't they need approval of the Board of Trustees?"

"Our board pretty much relies on the judgment of the director."

"I can see that during normal circumstances. But with the director ill—"

"It fell through the cracks. Remember, our board trusteeships are honorary, volunteer positions. The zoo's board members don't get paid, so their businesses come first. The board chairman was involved in a corporate merger of his company during this time. He missed more than half the board meetings. The vice-chairman is a state senator who spends most of her time in Albany. No one minded the store."

Suddenly, the door sprung open, and Abby paraded into the living room. The dogs rushed to greet her.

As she plopped down on the sofa, I explained what Tim and I had discussed, ending with, "These purchases involve major money. What if a vendor charged the zoo inflated prices and kicked back to a department head?"

"All my purchases are one hundred percent legitimate." Tim's voice was huffy, and a deep flush crept up his neck to his cheeks.

"Whoa. Take it easy. I'm not accusing you. But what about the other departments?"

Tim shook his head. "Couldn't happen. The individual departments don't select vendors. All purchases are funneled through the zoo's purchasing division."

"Supposing a purchasing agent collaborated with a department head. That's possible, isn't it?" I glanced down at the reports. "We need to find out if the zoo overpaid for any products or services."

"I know a purchasing agent at a zoo in New Jersey," Abby said. "Give me the reports. I'll send him a copy of Rocky Cove's expenditures. He'll be able to tell me if the costs are legitimate."

Tim rose from his chair. "I better go. I didn't realize the time. I'm in enough trouble with Barbara without coming home late."

Tim opened the door as Matt pulled up in front of the house.

"Oops. I better go too," Abby grabbed the annual reports from my hand. "I'm blocking the driveway."

After dinner, I poured a beer for Matt and mixed a pomegranate martini for me.

"Let's take these out on the patio," I said, handing Matt his glass.

We settled in lounge chairs under the saucer-like moon, the silence of the evening broken only by the rhythmic chirping of crickets and the occasional hoot of an owl.

After a few minutes of silent stargazing, I said, "I've been assigned a second story. It's on wildlife smuggling."

"Sounds good. How's your first feature, the one on breeding endangered species, coming along?"

"Not as quickly as I'd like. I still have more research. But that gives me reason to keep visiting the zoo. That's good because I can delve deeper into McKenzie's murder."

"I think you should stay away from the murder. It could be dangerous. In fact, what exactly are you doing?"

"For now, I'm checking alibis." I sipped my martini, then told him about my visit to Ridge River University.

"Maybe Linda Sancho left the animal behavior conference," I said.

"I think you're stretching it."

"Not at all. The auditorium holds up to four hundred. It's possible she slipped out, and the same holds true for Ginger Hart at Treasures of Zeus."

"But that's normal. Most people don't have eyewitnesses verifying where they spend every minute of the day."

"My point exactly. Tim lacks an ironclad alibi, but so do Linda and Ginger. There's no difference."

"Lacks an ironclad alibi?" Matt shook his head. "There's proof he was at the zoo. That's a big difference."

CHAPTER EIGHTEEN

"Smugglers take risks because of the huge profits," Roy Maxwell said. "Without a market for tortoise shell jewelry or alligator shoes, these items wouldn't be brought into the country."

I scrambled through my bag and searched for my pen, having arrived ten minutes late for my interview with the New York Director of the United States Fish and Wildlife Service. Although the agency was less then ten miles from my home, today's morning rush-hour drive took fifty-five minutes, with enough traffic congestion to give Mother Teresa road rage.

Maxwell, an African American with a face just beginning to show age lines, cut to the chase. He pointed to a side credenza displaying a tiger head, leopard skin, stuffed turtle, crocodile bag, and ivory carvings.

"That's just a sample of what our inspectors confiscated at Kennedy airport. Tourists think it doesn't matter because the animal is already dead. They don't realize the more they buy, the more animals are killed." He paused. "That's why I'm glad you're writing this story. We need the public on our side."

He opened the top drawer of his desk and removed a picture. "I hope this isn't too graphic."

I winced as Maxwell handed me the photograph of a dead rhino in a pool of blood. Its horn had been hacked off. A baby rhino stood beside the lifeless form.

"In the Middle East, rhino horns are used as dagger handles. An intricately carved horn can sell for twelve thousand dollars,"

Maxwell said. "The powder from the horn is considered an aphrodisiac in Asia, selling for $450 an ounce. One weighing six pounds brings in more than $40,000. In this instance, a poacher wounded the animal and chopped off its horn. He left it to bleed to death with her baby watching."

"What happened to the baby?"

"Rescue workers transported him to a nearby center for orphaned animals. Eventually he'll be released in the wild. Most aren't that lucky." Maxwell leaned forward, arms folded on his desk. "Now, I'm sure you have some questions about our agency?"

"I do. Let's start with how successful you are in catching the bad guys."

"Just like the police don't catch every thief, we certainly don't catch every smuggler." He picked up a paperclip, straightened it out, and bent it back and forth until it snapped. "You wouldn't believe how wildlife comes into this country. Yesterday, an inspector discovered a tourist who had shoved a parrot up his jacket lining. He'd taped the parrot's mouth shut."

"A live parrot?"

"Yup. Smuggling involves more than products made from endangered species. It's live animals too. Just last week, we uncovered a shipment of six baby lemurs smuggled in a crate filled with books. They were stuffed in a hidden compartment. Five suffocated to death."

"But if the animals died—"

"The dealer would have made enough on the one survivor to more than cover the losses."

The phone buzzed. Maxwell ignored it and began telling me how smuggled animals are often transported in plain sight. "The animals, usually endangered species, are often accompanied by forged documents saying they were bred in captivity through a legally sanctioned program. It's difficult to

94

prove the papers are false, and it's a time-consuming process."

The receptionist stuck her head in the room. "Johnson from Washington is on the phone. Do you want to call back?"

"No. He's impossible to reach. I'll talk with him now." Maxwell handed me a folder. "This contains two press releases involving major agency cases, both less than two years old. Look them over while I take this call."

One press release said: "The owners of a Manhattan pet store pleaded guilty in federal court this week to violations of the Lacey Act, which prohibits the sale of protected wildlife. Tom Booker and Nancy Booker, owners of Booker's Amazing Pet Emporium in New York City, netted more than $500,000 for the illegal sale of two hundred rare and endangered snakes and lizards. The Bookers were part of an international wildlife trafficking operation that smuggled reptiles from Africa, Australia, and Indonesia.

"The Bookers created false documents identifying the reptiles as being captive bred and legal to sell. Included in this collection of smuggled reptiles was a Komodo Dragon. This was the third series of violations for the couple."

The second release said: "A federal judge sentenced Clayton Malur, owner and operator of Malur's Animal Auction in Razorville, Ohio, to six months in jail and a $5,000 fine for his role in the transport and sale of six endangered Bengal tigers to hunting ranches, taxidermists, and exotic meat dealers.

" 'It is estimated there are fewer than seven hundred Bengal tigers in the wild,' said a spokesperson for the agency. 'Tiger parts sell for substantial money. The hide goes for several grand, and the internal organs find their way to the traditional Asian medicine market.' Malur has a prior conviction for selling endangered macaws."

When Maxwell finished his call, I asked, "What exactly is an animal auction?"

"Auctions serve as middlemen for buyers and sellers of livestock and exotic animals. Most auction houses deal only with animals that are lawful to sell. But Malur's reputation is that you can get pretty much any creature you want if you're willing to pay."

"What led you to Malur in the first place?"

"Rumors persisted about him, including some interesting Internet chatter. We'd been watching for a while so we placed an undercover agent at his auction facility as barn help. While this agent hauled feed bags and shoveled manure, he listened in on Malur's conversation and heard about the tiger shipment."

I absentmindedly twirled my pencil between my fingers. "This press release is several months old. Think Malur's still dealing in illegal wildlife sales?"

"I can't say. Agency policy is to comment only after making an arrest. Even if we know something is happening, we can't say anything publically." He smiled. "That's the lawyers talking, not me."

"When are the auctions held?"

"The last week of every month."

"The auction could provide a great angle for my wildlife smuggling story. I could use the information from your press release, but it would help if I could get a feel for what goes on. I'd like to attend if my editor will spring for the airfare."

"I'd rethink that idea if I were you," Maxwell said. "A few months ago, one of Malur's goons roughed up a humane society investigator, who wound up in the hospital."

"I wouldn't identify myself. I'd go undercover."

"An animal rights attorney visited the auction undercover last year. No one has heard from her since."

CHAPTER NINETEEN

The press release was informative, but I wanted a sense of the place, so I decided to visit Booker's Amazing Pet Emporium. My goal was to describe the store, then point to its past violations, illustrating the underground trade in exotic animals. Despite Director Maxwell's warning, I hoped to visit Malur's animal auction too.

During the train ride into Manhattan, my mind flashed back to last night's conversation with Matt. I needed to delve further into the alibis of Linda Sancho and Ginger Hart. Since I'd be at the zoo tomorrow, I grabbed my pen and pad and began jotting down questions that would lead me to the truth.

After locating Booker's Amazing Pet Emporium, squeezed between a vintage clothing store and an antique shop, I pulled opened the door and strolled inside.

Although grateful for the air conditioning, nothing else looked inviting. The place was dark, dirty, and smelled like rotting turtles. Aquariums with fish ranging from three-dollar tetras to three-hundred-dollar clown fish covered the right wall. Dead fish floated on top of the water. The middle aisle overflowed with pet supplies, kibble spilling out from a torn food bag. Hamsters, mice, and other small creatures occupied the left side, their cages containing waste excretions, accounting for the stench. Further up the aisle were reptiles.

A shrill yelp echoed from the back right section of the shop. Tripping over boxes, I hurried to that section, where I found more dirty cages filled with sickly looking puppies. The smell of urine permeated the area. Two Yorkshire terriers, probably the source of the yelp, nipped each other's ears. A beagle puppy sat listlessly in the corner of another cage. Pus oozed from its left eye.

My face flushed from the heat of anger.

"May I help you?" A man, appearing to be in his early forties and wearing horn-rimmed glasses, approached.

I spun around, ready to complain about the dirty conditions but quickly changed my mind. I doubted he'd clean up the place because of anything I said. If I antagonized him, I might not be able to come and go as freely as I wanted. I'd call the appropriate authorities later.

"No. Just looking," I said.

"We can give you a good price if you buy today. These pups are for sale."

"I'll think about it."

"They may not be here when you return. Where else could you get a purebred dog for two hundred dollars?"

"Why are they so cheap?"

"I'm cutting my profit. I want them placed in good homes."

I doubted that. According to the signs under the cages, the dogs were about nine months old. The store needed to make room for a shipment of younger puppies, and I wondered what would happen to those that didn't sell.

"I'm sorry. I can't make a commitment now," I told him.

His facial expression said he knew I was a browser, not a buyer. Still, he handed me a business card and suggested I contact him when ready. Then he wandered away, approaching two teenage boys hunched over a cage of white rats.

Exiting the store, I glanced at the business card. The name on the card was Tom Booker, one of the owners.

I rummaged through my bag for my cell phone, and punched

in 3-1-1, the number used to report animal abuse in New York City. Next, I brought out my notepad and jotted down facts for my magazine article. With what I'd seen, my description of the shop would be vivid.

I wondered about the animals. Where did they come from? Where would they go?

While deep in thought, a familiar figure turned the corner and strolled down the block. I stared as the figure pulled open the door to Booker's Amazing Pet Emporium, glanced furtively over her shoulder, and stepped inside the shop.

The familiar figure was Rocky Cove's wildlife nutritionist, Linda Sancho.

CHAPTER TWENTY

What business did Linda have with Booker's Amazing Pet Emporium?

During the train ride back to Long Island, I tried convincing myself that Linda Sancho didn't know about the shop's history of violations. Still, why would anyone with concern for animals deal with such a sleazy place?

As I pushed open the door to the *Animal Advocate* office, I was greeted by Clara, motioning with short, staccato waves of her hands while mouthing the words, "He's here."

"He's here," Clara whispered loudly as I approached her desk.

"And good afternoon to you, too. Who's here?"

"The kid. You know who I mean. The one who wants your job. Schuyler Adams."

"It's not my job yet, but thanks." I strolled over to the table outside the editor's office and poured coffee into a mug. "What's Schuyler doing here? Another interview?"

"No. He dropped by fifteen minutes ago and asked if Olivia was in. He had something to show her. I told him to leave it with me, but Olivia wandered out and invited him into her office."

"I wonder what he's showing her. Probably a stellar piece of journalism from his time at college." I tried downplaying my concern but knew my voice held an edge. "Do you have a travel authorization form?" I asked, changing the subject.

"Sure." She reached into a desk drawer and handed me a form. "What's this for?"

While I filled out the paper at her desk, I told Clara about Malur's Animal Auction in Ohio. As the door to Olivia's office swung open, Clara whispered, "Here he comes now."

Schuyler Adams, dressed in khaki pants and a pale blue open-neck shirt, was tall and skinny with dirty-blond hair.

"Hi, I'm Kristy Farrell." I extended my hand.

He limply shook it. "Schuyler Adams."

"Kristy's writing two articles for our next issue," Clara said.

"Really?" Schuyler scanned the room as if searching for someone more important. "Olivia's a superb editor. I'm sure your articles will be fine with her supervision."

"Kristy taught a journalism course in high school."

"Ah, a teacher." He smiled.

Clara opened her mouth, about to say something, but I shot her a look. As Olivia's administrative assistant, Clara would have to work with the new feature writer, whether it be Schuyler or me.

Schuyler glanced at his watch. "I better go. Nice to meet you, Christine."

"It's Kristy."

He was out the door.

"He's got an attitude, don't you think?" Clara said.

I nodded absentmindedly. As concerned as I was about my job, my thoughts had suddenly drifted back to Linda Sancho and Booker's Amazing Pet Emporium. As dozens of thoughts whirled through my mind, I formulated a theory.

"Matt, could Linda be selling zoo animals?" I asked my husband while we sipped coffee in our den that evening. "What if she was involved in illegal sales and McKenzie found out about it? My theory is that Linda killed the zoo director to keep him from talking."

Matt shook his head emphatically. "Impossible. The Rocky Cove Zoo is a major institution. Every animal is accounted for. Do you think no one would notice a missing lion?"

"Somehow, I don't think Linda's selling lions." But Matt had a point. Even if a small monkey or lizard was taken, the zookeepers would instantly notice.

"I still believe there's some type of connection between Linda, Booker's Amazing Pet Emporium, and Arlen McKenzie's murder." I held up my hand, ticking off the points one by one as I listed them. "One, she has motive. Two, her alibi is weak, so she had opportunity. Lastly, as a wildlife nutritionist, she works with all species, including snakes, giving her access to venom. Therefore, she had means. I like her as a suspect."

"You'd like anyone as a suspect if it cleared your brother. But whether or not she killed McKenzie, I still don't see how it relates to the pet store."

My gut told me they were connected.

Next, I told Matt about meeting Schuyler Adams and how his father's company advertised in *Animal Advocate*.

"I hope Olivia makes her hiring decision for feature writer based on the merits of the candidates, not on financial pressure from an applicant's father," I said.

"She may not have the option. *Animal Advocate* needs advertising revenue. She may be forced to hire him."

I didn't respond. Although Matt tended toward pessimism, I expected a little encouragement. "You're the best one for the job" or "Olivia thinks highly of you" would have been nice.

"What will you do if Olivia hires him, Kristy? Stay on as editorial assistant?"

"I don't know. I haven't gotten that far."

"Can you get your teaching job back?"

"I don't want it even if I could."

"At one time, you liked teaching."

"But I love writing. I've dreamed of doing this." I stared at my husband. As a former teacher, I had long since learned to read people's faces.

"Matt, what's wrong?"

"There's something I haven't told you." Matt put down his cup. "A health and wellness center for animals is opening a few blocks from my veterinary hospital."

"I know. Abby told me."

"In addition to traditional and alternative veterinary medicine, it offers spa treatments and will be open twenty-four hours, seven days a week."

"You've always had someone on call for emergencies."

"It's not the same. I've spoken to other veterinarians where these facilities have sprung up. It impacts on existing businesses. More than a dozen veterinarians have sold out to the new company."

"But your clients love you. You can't think they'll leave?"

"Dogs are loyal. Humans are fickle."

"So, I need to stay employed," I said. "My job and salary take on a new importance."

He sighed. "I need to modernize. If I don't get a loan, I'll have to sink most of what I make back into the business to buy new equipment. If I can't do that, I may need to close the veterinary hospital."

I firmly believe that no matter how bad your problems, there's someone whose situation is worse.

The phone rang and my brother said, "I just finished talking to my lawyer."

"What did he say, Tim?"

"He told me Steve Wolfe has an appointment next week with the district attorney."

"Why?" I held my breath.

"Wolfe wants the district attorney to convene a grand jury to indict me for murder."

CHAPTER TWENTY-ONE

I'd never expected a curator's office to look like it came straight from the pages of a decorating magazine, with white walls, white rug, and black furniture. All room accessories adhered to the color scheme too, down to the white mints in Amanda Devereux's black candy dish.

Providing a striking contrast to the black and white room, Amanda held court in a sea foam–colored silk dress with a Hermes scarf. Unlike Tim, a hands-on administrator, I imagined Amanda let staff handle day-to-day operations while she avoided any direct involvement with the birds.

She gestured toward a black leather armchair. I slipped into the seat, inhaling deeply and thinking that she had to know I was Tim's sister. Did she believe Tim killed her husband?

"Before we start, I want to offer my condolences."

"Thank you. Arlen was a wonderful man. But the best thing to do is keep busy and not dwell on his death."

I thought briefly about what my brother had said concerning Arlen McKenzie's recent memorial service. It was a private service with no one from the zoo invited. I found that strange. Then I remembered Saul Mandel's comment.

"Mourn?" he had said. "She was probably celebrating."

Amanda Devereux appeared to be a woman who masked her feelings.

She folded her perfectly manicured hands in front of her. "How can I help you?"

"Why don't you start by telling me what species of birds are bred at the zoo?"

"We're known for our parrots and macaws. We have several species at Rocky Cove, including the Puerto Rican parrot and the blue-throated macaw, which are near extinction in the wild. We have state-of-the-art equipment, including new incubators in our nursery."

There was a loud thud. I jumped.

"Crap! There's no place to put the boxes," yelled a voice in the next room.

Amanda smiled. "That was a carton hitting the floor. The custodians are rearranging the supplies next door. With these thin walls, you hear everything." She rose from her chair. "I have an idea. I wanted to show you the ornithology nursery anyway. Why don't we continue the interview there? It's hard to believe, but the birds aren't as noisy as our custodial staff."

After a short walk to the far end of the building, I began hearing peeps and chirps.

"This is it." Amanda swung open the door and stepped inside the nursery.

"Ah, the smell of birds in a closed environment," I joked. "Where are my stuffed sinuses when I need them?"

Amanda didn't smile or comment. Some people never see humor in their work.

"Those are the incubators along the back wall," Amanda said. "The aviaries lined against the side walls are home to our newborn birds."

In front of the incubators, a man wearing a zoo uniform slouched in a chair behind a metal desk. I couldn't help but stare at the large black widow spider tattooed on his muscular upper arm.

Frank Taggart, the bird keeper in charge of the incubators and nursery.

"You startled me." He jumped up from his chair. "I'm not used to visitors."

"Frank, this is Kristy Farrell, a writer from *Animal Advocate* magazine. Why don't you show her our nestlings?"

"You're the boss." His clenched jaw indicated he didn't agree with this decision.

"Come on," he called, glaring at me. "I don't have a lot of time." As I approached, even the strong smell of the birds couldn't mask the odor of stale tobacco on his clothing.

The nursery currently housed more than a dozen baby birds. Frank grudgingly identified each species. The last aviary he showed contained only one nestling.

"What bird is that?" I asked. "Its talons are huge."

"A bald eagle."

"There's just one?"

"Do you see more?"

"An only child." I ignored his sarcasm. "Is that unusual?"

Before he could respond, Amanda answered, "Not at all. A bald eagle lays one to two eggs, on rare occasion three. In this case, there was only one eaglet."

"I have paperwork in the main office," Frank said. Without a good-bye, he strutted out of the room.

"I don't think your bird keeper thought much of my visit," I said.

Amanda smiled. "He can be a little gruff."

A little gruff? Something about Frank Taggart sent a shiver down my spine.

Chapter Twenty-Two

As I emerged from the ornithology building, I blinked in the strong sunlight. Two figures caught my eye.

Ginger Hart trotted down the path accompanied by a pear-shaped man with owl-like eyes and a receding hairline. When they reached me, Ginger introduced her companion, Norm Dembrowski, Chairman of the Board of Trustees.

"*Animal Advocate* is a small magazine, but it targets a readership interested in wildlife," Ginger said to the chairman. She turned to me. "How was your interview with Amanda?"

"Fine. She provided plenty of information."

"I never asked you about your interview with Saul Mandel the other week. I hope that went okay too. I know how abrupt he can be. He's had trouble in the past with reporters."

Mandel wasn't the easiest person to interview, but I didn't like Ginger's comment in front of the board chairman. It reminded me of kids who snitched on each other. "The interview was great. Saul Mandel is dedicated and knowledgeable."

"I'm glad to hear that." For an instant, Ginger's mouth formed into a mulish pout. "We'll be going now. Norm and I are meeting with a few trustees to do damage control on the zoo director's murder, and we don't want to be late."

"Nice meeting you," the chairman said as she whisked him away.

I realized it was almost eleven-thirty and quickened my pace until I reached the herpetology building.

"I'm here to see Tim Vanikos," I said to the woman sitting behind the front desk. I remembered this woman from my other visits since she looked like Mrs. Santa Claus. "I'm Kristy Farrell. I'm his—"

"Sister. I saw you with him the other day." She smiled. "I'm Mary. Tim's expecting you, so go right in."

"Morning, Tim," I said, entering his office and shutting the door behind me. "Any more news on the District Attorney's meeting with Wolfe?"

"I told you last night the meeting is next week," he said, turning away from his computer to face me. "How could there be any news?"

"You're right." I quickly changed subjects. "I just met your board chairman, Norm Dembrowski. He was with Ginger Hart."

"It didn't take her long. With McKenzie gone, Dembrowski's her new target."

"Romance?"

"No. Power. Ginger had influence on McKenzie's decisions, not only because of their relationship, although that helped, but also because of the important role public relations played in his agenda. Now, with Saul temporarily in charge, she doesn't get her way. Ginger and Saul are like a snake and a mongoose."

"What do they fight about?"

"I'll give you some history." Tim leaned back. "Their most recent blow-up occurred two months ago. One of the zoo's donors had wanted to borrow a capuchin monkey for her daughter's jungle-themed sweet sixteen party. Ginger, who will do almost anything to please a donor, agreed, but Saul refused. He went straight to Arlen McKenzie, and for once the zoo director backed him. Of course McKenzie's reasons weren't the same as Saul's. McKenzie was concerned about liability if the monkey bit someone."

"Do you think Ginger is now using the board chairman to go around Saul?"

"More than that. She wants Saul to look bad in the eyes of Dembrowski and the other trustees. This way, maybe they won't appoint Saul permanently."

"But don't you think the zoo director needs social skills?"

"It has to be balanced, Kristy. I also think Saul would schmooze more if the position called for it."

I wasn't sure I agreed. My brother thought highly of Saul Mandel, but I wondered if he was blinded to Saul's faults. More importantly, was he blinded to the possibility that Saul could be the murderer?

Tim shut down his computer and sprang from his chair while grabbing a paper off his desk. "It's time to go. The crocodiles are waiting."

Despite my brother's fondness for snakes, I regard them as the most sinister of predators.

"That's an Asian cobra," Tim said as we passed the snake exhibit on the way to the crocodiles. A long, limbless body glided along the rocks in its terrarium. With its mud-brown coloring, it blended in with the large stones. As it stopped and lifted its head about twelve inches, I stared at its cream-colored underbelly. A chill ran through my spine. I remembered what I'd once read about this snake. It was responsible for the majority of deaths by snake bites in Asia.

"Isn't she beautiful?" Tim said.

"If you say so."

Tim smiled as if reading my mind. "The Asian cobra is a killer but so are lions, bears, and hippos. People may be afraid of large mammals, but no one views them with disgust."

"I admit it's irrational." Determined to ignore my fear and loathing of anything serpentine, I pointed to a gunmetal-gray snake uncoiling in a corner tank. The snake appeared to be nearly five feet in length and as wide as a man's upper arm.

"I can't read the print on the sign from here. What type of snake is that?"

"Black mamba. Fastest snake on earth. It reaches speeds of fifteen miles per hour."

I shuddered. I had read about the black mamba, too. Deadly venom and a bad attitude. Some herpetologists described the snake's temperament as warlike.

Tim glanced at his watch. "We better go. I'll bring you back here later and show you more. Just remember, ninety percent of all snakes are harmless."

"Turn that statement around and ten percent are venomous. And that venom is deadly as hell. I still prefer lions and hippos, thank you."

We continued down the hall.

"Just a second." Tim stopped in front of a door with a sign reading STORAGE ROOM. "I need to leave a form in here. Mei is coming in at seven tomorrow morning to work on inventory."

Tim placed an inventory form on a table in the middle of the room. Five large boxes were piled nearby on the floor.

"Mei has to inventory everything in these cartons?" I asked.

"No. Just the loose supplies in the closet over there." He pointed to a door at the far end of the room.

We headed back down the corridor until reaching another room with a sign that read STAFF ONLY. Tim unlocked the door. "This is our access to the crocodiles."

Inside, Mei Lau was talking to a man in a zoo uniform. He had straw-like hair and skin pale as mashed potatoes. Mei appeared agitated. She kept shaking her head and making wide, swooping gestures with her hands.

My mind floated back to my time as Mei's teacher. I

remembered the anxiety bottled up inside the young teenager. Mei suffered from stomach aches before exams and developed migraines during the college admission process. Had she changed or were those same characteristics still part of her personality?

Tim introduced the man talking with Mei as Gary Larsen, a reptile keeper.

"Let's get started," my brother said. He led the way through the back to the glass-enclosed crocodile exhibit. As I gazed at the fierce-looking reptiles, lounging in their swampy habitat, it reminded me of Marco Polo's description of those creatures as "great serpents with feet."

"The crocodile in the exhibit to our right is resting in front of her nest," Tim said. "After we remove those eggs, we incubate them at a specific temperature."

"Why?" I pulled out my pen and pad.

"The sex of a crocodile is determined by the amount of heat the egg receives. Temperatures below eighty-eight yield a higher percentage of females. By altering temperatures, it's possible to produce the desired sex."

"How do you remove the eggs?"

"Carefully."

I chuckled. My brother usually didn't have a sense of humor.

"With this species, the female guards her eggs ferociously. She won't hesitate to attack if her nest is threatened. Gary will distract the crocodile, then lock her up in the holding area while Mei collects the eggs."

Gary emerged near the side of the exhibit furthest away from the nest. Through a trap door, he extended a dead chicken on a long stick. The crocodile dashed toward the food with a fierce burst of speed.

"Now that we have the crocodile where we want her, Gary will press a button on the wall panel and a gate will descend."

Tim had no sooner finished speaking when the gate slammed down in the middle of the exhibit, entrapping the crocodile away from the nest. Mei stepped into the nesting area through a back door, scooped up the eggs, and placed them in a bucket.

Suddenly, Tim gasped.

I screamed.

The gate separating the crocodile from Mei jerked up. It rose nearly two feet before slamming back on the floor. It repeated this in rapid succession.

Mei's back faced the crocodile. But the sound of the metal hitting the ground caused her to spin around. At the sight of the gate moving up and down, she squealed like a mouse in an eagle's claw.

"The gate's malfunctioning!" Tim yelled. "Get out!"

Instead of running to the exit, Mei froze to the spot. The crocodile hovered at the gate, ready to make its move.

Gary threw meat through the trap door. As the crocodile gobbled it up, Tim shot in through the exhibit's back entrance, grabbed Mei's arm, and pulled her out.

"Are you okay?" Tim asked.

Sweat poured down Mei's brow. She tightly clutched the bucket of eggs. "I guess so."

"It must be an electrical short. I'm calling maintenance and insisting they send a mechanic immediately. No matter how careful you are, a freak accident can always happen in a place like this."

I put my hand on Mei's shoulder. "You're safe. It's over."

"I hope so."

I stared at the intern.

Mei's eyes welled with tears. "What if it was deliberate?"

"What do you mean?"

"Nothing." Mei recovered her composure. "My nerves got the best of me. I guess it was an accident."

I shot my brother a look.

"Of course it was an accident," he said. "If you feel okay, Mei, why don't you take these eggs to the incubator?"

I knew my brother wanted to take Mei's mind off what happened, but he still seemed a little callous. Meanwhile, my brain raced, wondering if someone had sabotaged the gate. I needed to talk with Mei.

"I'd like to see the incubators. I'll go with her, Tim."

My brother shook his head. "Not a good idea. Too much is happening now. You can go another day."

"But I need information—"

"Not today, Kristy. Mei, you better go now."

Mei departed.

I stood between my brother and Gary, annoyed I'd never asked Mei for her phone number.

CHAPTER TWENTY-THREE

I pulled into the zoo parking lot at eight o'clock the next morning. I had wormed an early admittance pass from Tim by telling him I needed more animal photos and that they'd be easier to obtain before the zoo opened to the public. My real reason was to question Mei, who would be conducting inventory.

Despite the early hour, the zoo buzzed with activity. Zookeepers and food vendors were all getting ready for the expected crowds. As I entered the herpetology building, I heard voices coming from the office, but I veered in the other direction, toward the storage room. Making my way down the dark corridor, a chill ran up my spine. Not a soul in sight. I was surrounded by venomous snakes, even if they were behind glass.

The door to the storage room was ajar.

"Mei?" I called, stepping inside.

I heard a sound but saw no one. I spotted the five cartons from yesterday. Only now, they were piled in front of the closet, blocking the door.

I heard a moan coming from inside the closet.

"Mei, is that you? Are you okay?"

No response. I couldn't open the door without moving the boxes.

Moans, now fainter than before, echoed from inside the closet.

Using my entire body, I pushed the cartons aside.

The door was clear. I swung it open and stared at Mei

sprawled on the floor.

Spread across the intern with its head lifted more than two feet, an Asian cobra fanned its dark brown hood, facing me.

It was ready to strike.

CHAPTER TWENTY-FOUR

I slammed the door shut.

A wave of nausea swept through my body. With my hands shaking, I pulled out my phone and punched in 911.

"Don't be a hero," the emergency operator warned. "Don't go into the room."

"But she—"

"You'll make matters worse. We're sending help immediately."

I stashed my phone back in my bag while glancing at the closet. With a cobra bite every second counted. I wanted to pull Mei out, but no way could I handle a cornered venomous snake. I needed to find my brother or someone else from herpetology.

I raced down the corridor to the office. Mary, the clerk, was the only one there.

"Oh, my God, no one's here now who can handle a snake," she said with panic in her voice. "Gary went to the cafeteria to get a muffin. Fred has a later shift, and Jennifer's on vacation. I don't—"

"Where's Tim?"

"I don't know. I saw him earlier, but I've no idea where he is now."

"Let me see if I can find someone."

I ran out of the building in the direction of the cafeteria, hoping to find my brother or Gary, the reptile keeper. I stopped for a second to catch my breath, and from the corner of my eye, I spied a figure headed away from the herpetology facility. It was

Saul Mandel, or at least I thought it was from the brief glimpse I gleaned before he vanished.

Thinking he might know what to do, I was about to run after him when Tim approached from the opposite direction.

"A cobra's loose in the storage room," I yelled. "It bit Mei. I called 911, but I don't know if she's alive."

My brother ran quicker than I'd ever seen. He pulled out his two-way radio.

"Gary, get over here now. The cobra escaped."

Once in the building, Tim darted into the storage room and grabbed a large container, a long hook, and heavy gloves.

He slowly opened the door to the closet. "Damn!"

My heart pounded. Was Mei dead? I edged closer to the closet until I could see inside.

Tim was having difficulty. It wasn't easy picking up a reptile measuring more than four feet. He grabbed the snake with the hook, but the creature slipped off and slithered back onto the floor.

"Get out of here, Kristy!" he ordered.

As I scurried away from the closet to the far side of the room, I heard someone running down the hall.

"What's going on?" It was Gary, huffing and puffing.

"A snake bit Mei. Tim's trying to capture it."

Gary didn't say a word, and he didn't rush to assist Tim. He picked up gloves, but he stayed far away from my brother and the snake.

"Gary, are you okay? Maybe you should help Tim." I was puzzled by his strange reaction. As a reptile keeper, he should have been trained for situations like this.

Tim grabbed the cobra again with the hook. "Got it. Get the cover, Gary." Tim dropped the snake into the large container.

Gary didn't move.

"Gary!" Tim yelled.

I shot by Gary and slammed down the lid.

"What the hell's wrong with you, Gary?" Tim secured the lid, then dashed into another room while yelling, "Kristy, that was plain stupid!"

I wasn't listening. I made my way into the large closet and now knelt next to Mei's body. But before I could do anything, Tim returned carrying a small box marked *Antivenin.*

"She's still alive." Tim inserted a syringe in Mei. "Kristy, go to the entrance and wait for the ambulance."

I raced down the hall as sirens blared in the distance, becoming louder with each second. An ambulance and a police car pulled up on the grass in front of the building.

"The victim's in there." I pointed to the storage room. "The snake's been captured so you can go in." The medical technicians hurried into the room with a gurney. One police officer pulled Tim aside and another began talking to Gary.

After what seemed an eternity, but was probably only a few minutes, the medical technicians rushed Mei out of the building into the ambulance. Tim followed.

"How bad is she?" I asked, running alongside Tim.

"She's alive but barely." Tim's voice cracked as he spoke. "I don't know if the antivenin is too late. I'm driving to the hospital."

The ambulance sped off with sirens blasting. When I spun around, I found myself facing a police officer whose badge identified him as Officer Cooper. I was thankful it wasn't Detective Wolfe, although a sinking feeling told me that he would be contacting me soon.

"Are you the one who found the victim?" he asked.

"That's right."

He scribbled down my name, address, and phone number. "If you don't mind, I'd like you to tell me exactly what you saw."

Even if I did mind, it's not like I had a choice.

"Mei sprawled on the floor with the cobra atop her body," I said. "I thought it was about to strike. I slammed the door shut and called for help. Then I spotted the herpetology curator coming up the path. He captured the snake and administered the antivenin."

"Did you see anyone near the storage area?"

"No, but I did see someone outside the building. I'm pretty sure it was Saul Mandel."

Officer Cooper's big, horsey eyes narrowed into slits. "The reptile keeper told us you're the herp . . . herpa . . . you're the sister of the guy in charge of the snakes. Is that true?"

"Yes."

He paused then shut his notebook with his meaty hands, apparently satisfied for the time being. "Okay. We'll contact you later for a formal statement."

Before I left, the second police officer returned. I overheard his comment to his partner. "The cobra is missing from its tank. I think we can assume it's the same one that bit the victim."

It felt like tiny spiders crawling in my intestines as I considered the most likely possibility. Someone had deliberately released the snake?

CHAPTER TWENTY-FIVE

Would Mei survive?

Dozens of questions shot through my mind, but that was foremost. The day I'd first run into Mei, she had mentioned keeping a diary and writing her thoughts in it. Instinct told me the diary held the answer to a lot of my questions. I wanted to go to the hospital, but I needed to find this book. Since the intern's current assignment was herpetology, my search would begin there.

I hurried back to the office where Mary appeared to be fidgeting with a pencil. I would have to get rid of her before snooping. Luckily no one else was here.

"Is Mei okay?" Mary asked immediately. "I can't stop thinking of her."

After providing a rundown of what happened, I said, "Mei was currently assigned to this department, wasn't she? Do you know her well?"

"Not really." Mary pushed a wisp of white hair away from her eyes. "She hasn't been with herpetology that long. She worked in the small room next to Tim's office. He assigned her to special projects, so she really had little contact with me."

Glancing at the coffee machine on a nearby shelf, an idea formed in my mind. I didn't know if I could pull it off but decided to try. "I better sit down. I feel dizzy." I made my way to a chair.

"It's no wonder, you poor thing. You had a horrible morning.

Sit here and rest a while."

"I'd love a cup of tea to settle my stomach."

"I wish I could offer you some, but everyone here drinks coffee, so we don't have tea."

"Maybe once I feel better, I'll walk to the cafeteria, but I feel too shaky now."

"I tell you what, honey. I'll go to the cafeteria and get it for you. Tim would want me to do this for his sister."

Once Mary disappeared out the door, I scooted into the small room off Tim's office. Mei's desk appeared the same as when she was my student—like the aftermath of a nuclear explosion.

I sorted through the clutter atop the desk and found nothing resembling a diary. The top right drawer contained only stationary supplies and a few candy wrappers.

I yanked opened the drawer to the left and there it was, a spiral notebook with the words *Daily Journal* scrawled across the cover. After stashing the book in my bag, I dashed into the main room and slipped back into the chair as the front door opened.

"Here's your tea, dear," Mary said, handing me a cup. "Have you heard from Tim? Any word on Mei?"

"No. I'm anxious to get to the hospital." After taking a few sips of tea, I rose from my chair. "I should get going."

"But the rest of the staff will be here soon. They'll want to know what happened. Besides, you haven't finished your tea."

"I'll take it with me. I feel much better." I bolted for the door. "Thanks again."

As I hurried down the path, bird keeper Frank Taggart emerged from the ornithology building. He took giant strides until he caught up with me.

"I heard you found the intern. You may have saved her life." With his face now inches away from mine, his breath smelled like a dirty ashtray.

"I hope so," I said, quickening my pace. "I know cobra venom is powerful."

"Was she conscious?"

"I don't think so, but I'm not really sure."

"If they got the antivenin in her in time, she could recover. If not . . ." He shrugged. "Cobra venom acts real fast. Twenty minutes can do it." He vanished in the direction of the cafeteria.

If I wasn't worried before, I sure was now. *Twenty minutes.* How long had Mei been in that room?

CHAPTER TWENTY-SIX

No antiseptic can take away the smell of fear in a hospital waiting room.

I found Tim in a corner of the waiting area, his head in his hands. He looked up at me. "No one here can tell me anything. I don't know if Mei is alive or dead."

"How could a snake have gotten in the closet?" I asked after hugging my brother.

Tim glared at me, his body stiffening. "Why are you asking me? You think I did it, don't you?"

"Of course not, Tim. I only thought that as a curator you could explain how the snake could escape from an exhibit."

"There's no way in hell that cobra could escape. Someone deliberately removed it from the tank and dropped it in the closet."

"But why? Isn't a snake bite an unreliable method of killing? Whoever did it had to realize Mei might be rescued in time."

"The Asian cobra's bite is among the deadliest in the world. But still, this isn't like McKenzie's murder where a specific amount of venom was injected through a needle. No one knows how much venom a snake will release when it bites."

"Do you think someone was trying to scare her?"

"It's a risky way to scare someone." He stared at the ceiling. "The whole thing is crazy."

I gently placed my hand on my brother's arm. "Do you have an alibi?"

"Not really. Saul called a breakfast meeting at seven for Linda to present her latest nutrition findings. The meeting ended in thirty minutes. I didn't feel like returning to the office, so I sat on a bench by the polar bear exhibit and went through my reports. I'm sure no one saw me."

"Besides Saul and Linda, who attended the meeting?"

"Amanda, of course. And Ginger, too. That's it."

"What did everyone do afterward?"

"We all went our separate ways. I think they headed back to their offices, but I don't know for sure."

I flashed back to when I ran out of the herpetology building seeking help.

"Tim, I'm pretty sure I saw Saul—"

"Excuse me," a nurse interrupted. "The doctor will see you now. You can go in there." She pointed to a room on the other side of an open doorway.

"Is Mei okay?" Tim asked.

"Dr. Aghassi will tell you everything."

We stepped into a small, windowless room furnished only with a couch and a table. A pitcher of water and a stack of plastic glasses rested on the table.

A few minutes later, Dr. Aghassi arrived.

CHAPTER TWENTY-SEVEN

"I'm sorry. We couldn't save her," the doctor said.

My eyes filled up. I couldn't believe this was happening.

The next moment, I heard the sound made by high-heeled shoes clicking across a tile floor.

"They told me you were in here." Ginger Hart, in a peacock blue sundress, strutted into the room.

Tim blurted out the news. "Mei's dead."

"Oh, no. This is the second murder at the zoo in less than two weeks. I can just imagine the newspaper stories. This is terrible."

"It's not too good for Mei, either," I said, thinking this woman had the warmth and compassion of a scorpion.

"I'll contact the family." Ginger seemed oblivious to my sarcasm. "I'll check our records to find the name of her closest relative."

"Mei's parents are dead." I wiped a tear from my face. "As far as I know, she only has an aunt in this country."

"I'm sure that will be in our files. Tim, why don't you go home? You look awful."

"I'm heading back to Rocky Cove. I need to find out how that snake got into the storage room closet."

"Maybe you shouldn't." Ginger was texting while talking. She didn't look up as she spoke. "The police need to talk to you. I don't think that should occur at the zoo."

"You have an attorney," I reminded my brother, suppressing my urge to rip the phone out of Ginger's hand. "When you meet with the police, make sure Stan Margolis is present."

Tim looked at me with a deer-in-the-headlights stare.

Work was the furthest thing on my mind, but, unfortunately, I was expected at *Animal Advocate*.

"Did you hear?" Clara called out as I stepped into the office. "There was another murder at the zoo. A student intern."

I blinked, afraid I might tear up.

"We'll talk later," I said, taking off down the hall. I didn't want to discuss this with Clara or anyone else now. "I've a ton of work to complete."

Once I settled in my cubicle, I pulled Mei's journal from my bag and began reading. The book detailed Mei's daily responsibilities. I paid particular attention to Mei's notes on the day immediately preceding Arlen McKenzie's death. Although scheduled to work in herpetology, Mei had been called away from her regular duties and assigned to a special public relations program titled "Keeper for a Day." A handful of sixth graders had been chosen to shadow Rocky Cove's zookeepers. McKenzie had made sure he took a photo with each student. Mei's responsibilities had consisted of assisting the photographer in setting up the pictures near various animal exhibits.

I rubbed my forehead. When I had first run into Mei, she told me there were things at the zoo that didn't make sense. My gut told me she would have written about that in this book. But everything I read appeared straightforward—except one item. By process of elimination, I determined that had to be it. I flipped back to the beginning of the journal.

I scanned a list of four names, each one accompanied by a number.

MAX—720
MYRA—420
SCOTT—570
TORY—105

A note, scrawled on the bottom of the page, read: "SM concerned about Tory. Please keep advised."

SM must stand for Saul Mandel, I thought. But who are Max, Myra, Scott, and Tory?

I was ready to call it a day. I rose from my chair just as my cell phone trilled. Abby's number popped up.

"I just heard about the murder of the student intern, Mom. A *cobra!*"

I closed my eyes and held the phone away from my ear.

"Why didn't you call me?" Abby asked. "I know you were there. You told me you were going to the zoo this morning."

"I planned to phone you later. How did you find out?"

"Jason called me at work. He heard it on the news."

"I thought Jason was studying for the bar exam every waking hour."

"He was taking a break. Don't change the subject. He called and told us what happened."

"Us? Does your father know?"

"He sure does."

"I guess Dad's upset."

"He's ranting about how dangerous the zoo is with a lunatic killer running around. He feels you should concentrate on your articles, not the murders."

This was not the time to mention that I was the one who discovered Mei in the closet with the snake. Instead, I proceeded to tell Abby about the list of names and numbers in Mei's journal.

"Maybe Dad's right," Abby said. "Maybe you should stop

asking questions. In fact, maybe you should stay away from Rocky Cove. At first, I didn't think there was any problem with a little harmless snooping. But that's changed. I'm betting Mei was murdered to keep her from talking. What if the killer thinks Mei passed information to you before she died?"

"I don't think—"

"You could be the next victim, Mom."

Chapter Twenty-Eight

Since I accomplished nothing at the office, I spent the next day working at home. Roy Maxwell from Fish and Wildlife had sent me more material, so I started with a recent press release.

It read: "A joint effort between the United States Drug Enforcement Agency and the Fish and Wildlife Service has resulted in the arrest of Wayne Babcock, owner of B & S Animal Importers, and the seizure of eighty-seven boa constrictors arriving at Kennedy airport in New York from Columbia, South America. The snakes had been implanted with cocaine-filled condoms inserted through their rectums, which were then sewn shut.

"The shipment of boa constrictors entered the country under a legal permit. An inspector for the United States Fish and Wildlife Service, performing a routine verification, noticed more than half the snakes were dead on arrival and several others bleeding from both ends. Suspecting drugs, the inspector contacted the Drug Enforcement Agency for further investigation. X-rays revealed foreign objects inside the snakes.

"Each snake contained a minimum of two drug-filled condoms. The packets were surgically removed, resulting in the seizure of more than one hundred pounds of cocaine.

"A spokesperson for the Fish and Wildlife Service stated, 'This is not the first instance of illegal drugs hidden inside animals. Most people fear snakes, even nonvenomous ones, so drug lords stuff packages inside legal snake shipments because they think inspectors are reluctant to examine snakes too closely.' "

Although this press release didn't involve the smuggling of endangered species, the connection between Fish and Wildlife and the Drug Enforcement Agency fascinated me, and I hoped to tie it together in my article. But that was for another day. After shutting down my computer, I decided to see if I could find out more about the names and numbers in Mei's diary. I phoned my brother.

"How's it going, Tim?"

"Terribly. No one will tell me anything. Not even Saul. Everyone must think I'm the one who killed Mei."

"I'm sure that's not true. But maybe we can find out who is responsible. Do you know anyone at the zoo named Max, Myra, Scott, or Tory?"

"Nope. And I know just about everyone here."

We talked a few more minutes. Tim told me he'd been called into police headquarters and interrogated again by Detective Wolfe. Tim's attorney, Stan Margolis, had been present.

It started off as a typical Sunday evening. Matt sat glued to the television, watching the Seattle Mariners clobber the New York Yankees. Dressed in my pajamas, I was debating whether to tackle a crossword puzzle or settle down with my mystery anthology when Abby barged through the door with Jason close behind her.

Jason stared at my fuzzy bunny slippers. "I told Abby to call first, Mrs. Farrell, but she assured me that popping in was no problem."

"It's fine, Jason," I said weakly. "What's up?"

"Jason needs a break, so we're on our way to a movie," Abby said. "But I wanted to bounce an idea off you first. Actually, it was Jason's idea."

They made a cute couple. A former college basketball player, Jason was tall and athletic-looking with dark brown hair.

"Remember when I sent Rocky Cove's annual reports to my purchasing agent friend at the New Jersey zoo, Mom?"

"Of course. Did he get back to you yet?"

"I heard from him this morning. He couldn't find any financial shenanigans. But that started me thinking. We only checked annual spending for individual departments. We never looked into capital projects like the new rain forest. To build the rain forest, the zoo had to deal with architects, engineering firms, and construction companies. What if that involved kickbacks?"

Abby handed me the stack of annual reports. "I'm returning these to you. The corporations involved in the rain forest development are listed in the back of last year's report. Maybe you can come up with something." After glancing at her watch, she turned to Jason. "We better go if we want to make the movie." She grinned at me. "Nice slippers, Mom."

Once they left, I scanned the last annual report, discovering three corporations, all located on Long Island, who worked on the rain forest project—Pharrel Architects, Wantag Engineering, and Orville Construction. Then I thought about the four names in Mei's journal. Could they be associated with these businesses?

I grabbed the phone and punched in my brother's number.

"Remember the other night when I mentioned Max, Myra, Scott, and Tory?" I said.

"And hello to you too. Yes, I remember."

"Could they be connected to Pharrel Architects, Wantag Engineering, or Orville Construction?"

"Those are the corporations that designed and built the rain forest."

"That's right."

"Sorry, Kristy. I've no idea if there's a connection."

"Who would?"

"Saul handled most of the details. He might know."

Saul Mandel was a suspect, so I couldn't question him without putting him on alert. "Anyone else?"

"McKenzie, of course. He would have attended meetings with corporate reps. But since he's dead, that won't help."

Somehow, I needed to find out if the list of names in Mei's journal had anything to do with the corporations involved in developing the rain forest.

Yawning, I realized I was too tired to hatch a scheme tonight. I wandered into the den as the Yankee game ended with the Mariners winning twelve-to-three. Matt grumbled about bad calls from the umpires and began channel surfing.

The next moment, an image on a commercial flashed across the screen. Matt flipped to another station, but I'd seen enough to jog my memory.

The commercial featured a Long Island wedding caterer. It reminded me of the receptionist at the Rocky Cove Zoo. She was the one who had kept me waiting while she chatted on the phone about a bridal shower.

Anyone from Pharrel Architects, Wantag Engineering, or Orville Construction, anyone who had an appointment with Arlen McKenzie, would have signed the visitor's log at the front desk. The receptionist would be aware if one of the signatures was a Max, Myra, Scott, or Tory, especially if that person met frequently with McKenzie.

I needed to find out what the receptionist knew.

Chapter Twenty-Nine

"Larger crowds than at a Manhattan sample sale," I grumbled as I circled the zoo's parking lot and looked for a spot. I wondered how many people visited here out of morbid curiosity. Two murders, both front-page news, proving bad publicity is still publicity.

On my way, I had stopped at a local craft shop and purchased a magazine, hoping it would do the trick. Entering the administration building, I proceeded to the receptionist's desk.

"We need to call those who haven't responded to the shower and find out if they're coming," the receptionist said into the phone.

She hadn't held the shower yet. That's what I'd hoped. With a smile, I stood by her desk.

The receptionist looked up, scrunching her nose as if she'd entered a room where Brussels sprouts were cooking. "Hold on, Agnes." She slapped her hand over the phone. "May I help you?"

"The few times I've been here, I've overheard you talking about a bridal shower." I pulled out the arts and crafts publication I'd purchased earlier. "Here's a magazine that should interest you. It has a section on making party favors."

She snatched the magazine from my hand, her eyes narrowing. "Are you selling magazine subscriptions?"

"Absolutely not. I thought you might find some ideas you could use."

She thumbed through the pages. "Are you selling arts and crafts supplies?"

"No. I'm a writer for *Animal Advocate* magazine, and I've been here before. My name is Kristy Farrell. I'm not selling anything." I sighed in frustration. If she didn't recognize me from my previous visits, I wondered if she would remember a Max, Myra, Scott, or Tory.

She eyed me suspiciously but continued leafing through the pages.

"I'm into crafts," I lied. "If you have time, I could tell you about them."

"My lunch break is in thirty minutes. We could meet at the cafeteria. I usually sit near the entrance. By the way, my name is Phyllis."

We agreed to meet. As I stepped away, Phyllis called out, "But this better not be a sales scheme. I'm not buying anything."

With forty-five minutes to kill, I headed to the herpetology building. I was hoping to find Gary, the reptile keeper. Since he'd worked with Mei the day before her death, I wondered if she had confided in him.

Gary had called in sick. I still had time left, so I revisited the rain forest, hoping that returning to the scene of the first murder would jar something deep in the crevices of my memory, but that didn't happen.

I had just settled down in the cafeteria with a cup of coffee when Phyllis waddled through the door.

"I started looking through your magazine," she said as she plopped down across from me. "But I kept getting interrupted with phone calls." She pulled the publication out of her bag. "I need party favors for the shower."

"Working at the zoo must be interesting," I said, wanting to guide the conversation to the real purpose of my visit, the names in Mei's journal. Otherwise, I was afraid she'd lead me down the path of potpourri and scented candles. "You must meet lots of people."

Phyllis opened the magazine to the table of contents. "You can't believe how many people I deal with during a day. I'm overworked."

I bit my lip. "Have you ever met a Max or Myra here? I believe they work for Pharrel Architects."

"They don't sound familiar." She began thumbing through the magazine.

"Maybe it's not an architect's firm. They might work for an engineering or construction company. Maybe Wantag Engineering? Or Orville Construction?"

"I've never heard of anyone named Max or Myra." She continued flipping pages.

"How about Scott or Tory? They're friends of my husband, and they had once mentioned doing business with the zoo." I was afraid my nose would grow if I told more lies.

"Sorry, but I don't remember half the people who come through the door." She pulled her sandwich out of her bag and bit into it as she flipped the magazine toward me. "Now, tell me," she said with her mouth full. "How difficult is it to make these swan candy cups?"

CHAPTER THIRTY

My plan to get the zoo receptionist to identify Max, Myra, Scott, or Tory was a total bust.

I left the cafeteria and meandered through the North American mammal section. While lingering at the grizzly bear exhibit, I heard someone approaching.

"You spend more time here than most of our employees."

I gritted my teeth as I turned and faced Frank Taggart.

"Lots to do." I stepped back on the path.

"You're Tim Vanikos's sister, right? I hear he's meeting with the public relations gal right now. Ginger's not pleased with having a murderer on staff." He lit his cigarette.

I glowered at him. He had the charm of a short-order cook during the morning rush. "Tim's not guilty."

He puffed on his cigarette. "Tim's the only one who has keys to both the rain forest and the snake room."

"I don't believe in a place as large as Rocky Cove no one else has access."

"You are stubborn, aren't you? Dream on." He puffed on his cigarette as he swaggered down the path.

Still steaming from Frank's comments, I headed to the parking lot and, on the way, passed the gorilla preserve. Animals always relaxed me, so I stopped. While watching the keepers feed the three adult gorillas and one baby, I spied Saul Mandel by the side of the exhibit.

I maneuvered my way toward him. "Hello, Dr. Mandel. I'm

glad I ran into you. I wanted to let you know that I'm almost finished with my article on breeding endangered species in captivity."

He spun his head toward me and stared, first with a puzzled expression, followed by a sudden look of recognition. "Good. Our breeding program is an important topic."

He turned back to his gorillas.

Undaunted, I said, "I interviewed Amanda Devereux too. I must say, she's holding up well, considering everything."

"Considering what?"

"Considering her husband's death?"

"Oh, yes, well, Amanda is a professional. Her work is important to her. I'm sure she wouldn't let her personal life interfere."

I suppressed a smile. Saul Mandel sounded like we were discussing Amanda's bridge schedule, not the murder of her husband.

"I know what you mean," I said. "My brother is involved with his work too. He's here all hours."

Saul Mandel turned his head to follow the movements of the gorillas.

"You must work late too and miss lots of dinners at home with your wife."

"No. I usually leave here shortly after six."

"Good for you. Everyone needs time for themselves."

"My evenings, young lady, are when I work on my research in the peace and quiet of my home, without senseless interruptions and mindless chatter."

"Your wife doesn't mind?"

He glared at me. "My wife is an amateur wildlife photographer who shares my fascination with animals. By profession, she's a systems expert, and she assists me in my computer research. I've been involved with an elephant tracking project in

Botswana." He coughed, his body shaking like an erupting earthquake. "Been doing it every night for more than a month."

"Every night? No breaks for family or social events? Dinner out? A movie?"

Saul Mandel waved a sausage-like finger in my face. "The world of nature is far more interesting than some film about a serial killer or space alien with an infectious disease." He focused his attention back on the gorillas.

I couldn't find a hole in Mandel's alibi, but that didn't mean he had told the truth. Since a male gorilla decided it was time to relieve himself, and the strong odor was none too pleasant, I turned to leave. But before I stepped away, one of the zookeepers exited the exhibit, locking the gate behind him. He approached the curator.

"I just weighed Tory," the young man said, scratching the skin under his mustache. "She gained five pounds."

"That's good to hear." Mandel nodded. "Be sure to write this up in her record. Now, excuse me. I must get back to my office."

Mandel departed. The zookeeper headed in the other direction, but I quickly said, "Tory? Who's Tory?"

The keeper turned around, grinning sheepishly. "I shouldn't have said anything in front of you. People don't realize it, but Dr. Mandel has a great sense of humor. He named the gorillas after his wife's family, but only his staff knows this. Tory is his niece."

Although sure of the answer, I asked anyway, "What are the names of the three other gorillas?"

"Max, Myra, and Scott."

After questioning the zookeeper, it became clear that the names in Mei's journal were gorillas, and the numbers next to each name referred to the animal's weight. The cryptic line, "SM concerned about Tory," dealt with the curator's concern about the baby gorilla's size, which now had improved. The list had nothing to do with trouble at the zoo. Maybe the diary didn't hold any answers. But I didn't believe that. Mei had told me she wrote all her thoughts in her diary.

My thoughts were interrupted when I spotted my brother exiting the administration building.

I rushed toward him. "I heard you met with Ginger Hart. How did that go?"

"Not well. She wants me to keep a low profile. Says I'm ruining the zoo's reputation. Can you believe that? She's the one who's publicity crazy. I never wanted to do anything but my research and care for my reptiles."

"This will all pass. Before you know, she'll be hounding you to pose for photos with the lizards."

"Well, I really don't have time for this, especially with one of my reptile keepers out sick."

"Is that Gary?"

Tim nodded. "He's been out since Mei died. Says he has the flu, but I think her death really affected him. What brings you here again, Kristy?"

"Oh, tying up loose ends. I ran into Saul Mandel."

"So he did come in today. I knew it. Saul never takes a day off."

"He wasn't supposed to come in?"

"Saul's wife, Sylvia, is exhibiting her photographs at a show this week, and I think she wanted his help with set-up. Tomorrow is the grand opening."

"Saul isn't helping her?"

"I'm sure he is. He probably rose before dawn to provide assistance. But its unlikely he'd devote a full day to the project. Saul doesn't take time off unless it relates to mammals other than the two-legged kind."

"Where is the photo show?"

"It's at the Community Art Center in the Village of Sea Breeze. Nothing elaborate, but his wife is real excited. It's her first exhibition. I understand she took a week off from work so she can be there the entire time."

"Really." An idea flickered in my mind. "I'd like to see her photographs. I assume the exhibit is open to the public."

Tim nodded. "I saw the flyer. Ten dollars admission, which includes punch and cookies."

I was about to say good-bye when I spied Frank Taggart leaning against a nearby building, cigarette dangling from his mouth.

My brother must have seen him too. Frank smirked and my brother frowned.

"What's the matter?" I asked.

"Frank Taggart." Tim shook his head. "I can't believe Amanda thinks so highly of him."

"He doesn't appeal to me either, but maybe she likes him because he's good at his job. Do you know if he's a decent worker?"

Tim shrugged. "He's not bad. Frank originally worked in a small zoo in Arizona where he cared for mammals, birds, and reptiles—a jack of all trades. So when he came here, he started with me in herpetology. I have to admit he did a good job with the reptiles, but he had an attitude. I was glad when he left last year for a position in ornithology."

I felt my eyes widen. "I didn't know he worked for you. He had access to the snakes?"

"At one time, but he doesn't have access anymore."

"But what if he made a copy of the key before he left?"

"All keys say 'Do Not Duplicate.' But it doesn't matter. He never had a key to the rain forest."

Frank Taggart's earlier comment about my brother being the only one with access to the two murder sites came to mind. I didn't want to badger Tim, but I needed to be sure of my facts.

"Only herpetology staff can unlock the snake room door, right?"

"Pretty much."

"Pretty much?" I sighed. "The other day you told me only herpetology. What does 'pretty much' mean?"

"Well, there's a master set of keys for all exhibits, of course."

"Where are they kept?"

"The director has them. In this case, the acting director."

Saul Mandel.

CHAPTER THIRTY-ONE

The next morning, I headed out to the photography exhibition where I planned to talk to Saul Mandel's wife.

The Sea Breeze Community Art Center was located in a French Mansard Victorian house. I paid my ten-dollar entrance fee to a patrician-looking woman with an expression as frosted as her hair.

The photographs were arranged by subject: gardens, wildlife, people, and seascapes. I guessed Mrs. Mandel's specialty would be wildlife, so I wandered toward that section, where a woman with a shape reminiscent of Reuben's cherubs stood in front of a photo of a coyote pup. My guess was right. The nametag on the lapel of her olive green pants suit read *Sylvia Mandel*.

"Your photos are terrific," I said. "I particularly like the one of the coyote pup. Where was it taken?"

"Yellowstone Park. My husband and I vacationed there last year."

"Really? I met your husband at the Rocky Cove Zoo. He doesn't seem the type who would ever take vacations. I guess that shows how wrong first impressions can be."

"You're partly right. It was a working vacation for him. He conducted wolf research. I have a photo of a wolf here." She pointed to an eight by ten photo titled *Wilderness King*.

"He certainly is dedicated. He told me about his current research on elephants and that he works on it every night."

"He certainly does. Never takes a break. Here's my picture of a squirrel holding a nut."

"It's charming. Saul said you help him?"

"Saul is very gracious. He credits me with a lot more than I actually do."

"He makes it sound like you're there for him twenty-four/seven."

"I assist him with his computer, but for the last few weeks, I've been too busy preparing for this exhibit to spend much time with him."

"Are you saying you didn't work with him recently because of the photo show?"

Sylvia scratched her head. "I can't remember exactly. If he developed a computer glitch, I'd try to help him resolve it, but for the most part I burrowed myself in my basement studio after dinner. I concentrated on my project while he worked in his office upstairs. By the way, my photos are for sale. If you buy today, ten percent goes to the art league. Perhaps you're interested in the coyote?"

With coyote photo in hand, I left the exhibit. Saul Mandel never said his wife worked with him every minute. He had only said she helped him with the computer. He hadn't lied, but still . . .

Sylvia Mandel's commitment to her photography equaled Saul's passion for his elephant research. Absorbed in her work in her basement studio, Sylvia would assume Saul was upstairs the whole evening.

Bottom line was, she wouldn't have noticed if he'd left the house.

CHAPTER THIRTY-TWO

The next day, I sat hunched over my desk, staring at Mei's journal. The intercom buzzed, jolting me out of my thoughts. I grabbed the phone.

"Kristy," Clara said. "There's a Detective Steve Wolfe here to see you."

Damn! "Send him in." I stashed Mei's book in a drawer seconds before he marched into my cubicle. Obviously, he'd started down the hall before Clara had called.

"Have a seat." I pointed to a folding chair in the corner.

"I won't be here that long." He pulled out a notebook and pen. "I have a question about the murder of that girl at the zoo."

I gritted my teeth. "What do you want to know?"

"The report says you discovered the body. Is this becoming a hobby?"

"I don't think the death of a young woman is a joking matter."

"Yeah, sure. What is it with you always being at the zoo before it opens to the public? Normal working hours not good enough?"

"There are often times when my research requires—"

"Let me be more direct. Why were you in the herpetology building so early?"

"I hoped Mei would be available then to be interviewed about her internship program," I lied. I wasn't about to tell him that

Mei suspected someone of deliberately sabotaging the crocodile gate, at least not until I investigated.

"You saw no one else in the building?"

I hesitated. "No one inside, but as I told the officer who took my statement, when I ran out for help, I spotted a man headed away from the facility. I think it was Saul Mandel."

"Your brother was near the building too, wasn't he?"

"Not in the beginning. But later on, yes. That's not unusual. He's curator of herpetology. It's his building."

"Yeah, it's his building." Steve Wolfe flipped his notebook shut, then pointed his thumb and finger at me like a gun. "And it's his cobra."

Matt and I argued most of the evening.

We had returned from dinner at our favorite Japanese restaurant. The food had been great, but Mei's death was on both our minds. With Matt trying his best to convince me to stay away from the murder investigations, the ride home had been especially tense.

"That place has the best sushi in town," I said, hoping to change the topic as I twisted the key in the side door lock and stepped into our kitchen. "Don't you agree, Matt?"

I spun around. "Matt, where are you?" I had assumed he'd followed me inside, but he was nowhere in sight.

"Kristy, get out of the house." Matt appeared in the doorway. He spoke in a low voice, almost a whisper. "The light is on in the den. I shut it off before we left."

"The dogs. Why aren't they here?" I suddenly realized Archie and Brandy hadn't greeted me at the door.

"I don't know, but we're getting back in the car and calling the police." He grabbed my arm, but before we moved further, Archie and Brandy bounded into the room, followed by my disheveled-looking brother.

"Sorry, I didn't hear your car pull up. I fell asleep in the den with the door closed." Tim patted Archie with his left hand. "These guys alerted me to your arrival."

"Tim, what are you doing here?" My brother held a glass of amber liquid in his right hand. From the smell, I recognized it as scotch.

"I had a fight with Barbara. Remember when you and I exchanged keys for emergencies?" He raised his glass to his mouth and swallowed. "Well, this is my emergency."

"How many of those have you had?"

"This is the first."

"Okay, go into the living room," I ordered. "I'm pouring a glass of wine for myself and then we'll talk. Do you want anything, Matt?"

"This calls for a scotch."

I carried our drinks into the living room, then settled on the sofa next to my husband. Tim stood staring out the bay window, his back to Matt and me.

"Sit down, Tim, and tell us what happened," I said.

"Barbara threw me out of the house."

"Why? Start at the beginning."

"Because of this." He fumbled through his pockets and handed me a news clipping. "It's about Mei's murder. I'll save you time. Skip down to the last paragraph." Tim swallowed his scotch in four big gulps.

My eyes focused on the end of the news article. It read: "Several board members have expressed concern about security procedures at the Rocky Cove Zoo. 'A cobra is as dangerous as a loaded gun,' stated Dr. Roland Van Sickle, noted herpetology expert and author of more than a dozen books on snakes. According to Rocky Cove spokesperson Ginger Hart, the zoo trustees are convening tomorrow morning to determine if security had been breached and to formulate a tighter procedure regarding accessibility to all zoo animals. The meeting, which will be held in the conference room of the Education building, is open to the public."

"My name's not mentioned, but the comments are about me. I'm responsible for all reptiles. Barbara wants to know how I could be so careless. She says even if the police don't arrest me for murder, I'll be fired for incompetence."

"I'm sure she'll calm down," I assured my brother. But I wondered if Tim had been careless. Was he responsible for Mei's death?

"Barbara said she made a mistake marrying me. That she put up with a curator's low salary for years, but at least I never embarrassed her. Now, she's a laughingstock."

Matt shook his head. I bristled.

"I blew up, too." Tim scratched his elbow. "She threw me out. I didn't know where else to go. Can I stay here tonight?"

"Of course," I said. Matt nodded.

"I love her, Kristy. I know she's a snob, but I can't change my feelings. I don't want our marriage to fall apart." He wandered across the room, once again facing the bay window.

I jumped off the sofa and approached my brother, touching his arm. "Don't worry. You both made statements in the heat of anger. I'm sure once you've calmed down, you can resolve your differences. Does Barbara know you're here?"

He shook his head.

"Do you want me to call and tell her?"

He nodded.

"Okay, I will. Meanwhile, you must be exhausted. Why don't you go to bed? You can sleep in the guest room."

Matt helped Tim settle in while I phoned Barbara. She didn't pick up, so I left messages on both her cell and home phone.

"She's probably screening her calls," I told Matt. "I'm guessing she doesn't want to speak to me."

"Sometimes I think he'd be better off without her," I said later that evening as I emerged from the shower, wrapped in a large towel. I'd never been that fond of Barbara, but when she and Tim had married, I welcomed her into the family and tried to be supportive and friendly. Lately, this was becoming increasingly difficult.

"I'm not defending Barbara, but she's stressed out too," said Matt.

"Only because she's embarrassed." I pulled an oversized jersey over my head and hopped into bed.

"You really think that's all she cares about? Her image?"

"I really do. Barbara loved it when Tim received honors and awards. Now, if he's not a murderer, he's a bumbling incompetent."

Matt climbed in bed next to me. "They are an unusual couple. He's really not Barbara's type."

"You're right. She was on the rebound when she married him. He's the exact opposite of her ex-fiancé who was handsome, sophisticated, and rich. But Tim was kind and caring at a time when she was vulnerable. I'm glad Barbara didn't answer the phone tonight. I would have given her a piece of my mind."

"Kristy, they have to work it out for themselves."

"I agree. For Tim's sake, I hope they get back together." I fluffed up my pillow. "He really loves her."

Matt leaned over Archie, who had wiggled his way in between us, and kissed me. After switching off the light on his side, he said, "I believe two reasonable people can negotiate almost anything."

"The key word is *reasonable*. Good night." I turned off my lamp, wondering what Tim would promise Barbara to win her back.

Chapter Thirty-Three

I knew something was wrong the moment I wandered into the kitchen and saw Matt's face.

He sat by the table with a mug of steaming coffee between his hands. I could hear the dogs in the back yard.

"How long have you been up?" I asked.

"About thirty minutes."

"Why so early? You don't open till ten today." I poured coffee into my mug.

"Don't you remember? I've another appointment at the bank about a loan to update the veterinary hospital."

Of course. With my brother's latest crisis, I'd forgotten all about Matt's appointment. "I'm sorry, honey. I've been so—"

"It's okay." Matt rose from his chair and hugged me. "Tim's problems are worse than mine. At least I'm not a murder suspect."

Still, Matt had toiled for years building up his veterinary practice and to see it destroyed by a national chain . . . This loan was important to both of us.

"The bank won't deny you the money, will they?"

"I hope not."

"By the way, where is my brother? Still sleeping?"

Matt shook his head. "He left for the zoo. There's a note for you on the table."

Owl was stretched across the yellow lined paper. She meowed loudly as I pulled the note away.

I read the handwritten message. "I left early to prepare for today's meeting on security procedures. I know the trustees will grill me about access to the snake tanks, and I don't know what the outcome will be. But before the meeting, I'm calling Barbara to see if we can work out our problems. Hope to spend the night in my own home and bed."

"He'll probably have better luck with the trustees than with Barbara," Matt said.

I imagined both would give him a hard time.

I was working at the computer when my phone rang.

"Barbara is taking me back," Tim said. "We both agree we lost our tempers."

"That's great. I mean it's great that's you're back together, not that you lost your tempers."

"Well, it's not all wonderful. She wants to see how things play out before making a final decision on whether we should stay together."

I guessed Barbara wanted to see if he kept his job, but I decided not to mention that.

"How is your prep coming for today's meeting?"

"I guess okay. I don't like speaking in public and . . . well . . ."

"What else?"

"There's no way around it, Kristy. The bottom line is the cobra was released during my watch."

Since the meeting on zoo security procedures was public, I decided to attend.

When I arrived, the conference room, which posted a capacity of up to one hundred, was more than two-thirds full. Ginger Hart was seated in the first row. Saul Mandel sat three rows behind. As I glanced to my left, I spotted Detective Steve Wolfe standing on the side, notebook in hand.

The seven members of the Board of Trustees sat facing the audience. They were positioned behind a long table in the front of the room. Name plates identified each member.

I stepped into the last row and sat down just as Tim was called to the podium.

Chairman of the Board Norm Dembrowski started questioning my brother. "How many keys are there to the room behind the snake tanks? I believe you refer to this as the snake room."

"Five. In addition to the master key that belongs to the zoo director, I have one and my three reptile keepers have the others," Tim answered. My heart ached for Tim as I heard the quake in his voice.

"These keys also open and close the individual snake terrariums, right?"

"Yes."

"Have any of these keys been reported as lost or stolen?" Dembrowski continued.

"No, sir."

"Prior to the incident, when was the last time you checked the cobra tank?"

"After the last feeding, around four-thirty in the afternoon. I personally inspected each terrarium to make sure it was locked."

"You do this every day?"

"Yes. When I'm not here, my senior reptile keeper checks. The tanks are always inspected immediately before closing. We also make sure the door to the room is locked."

"I have a question," said the gray-haired woman seated to Dembrowski's left. Her name plate identified her as Jean Jackson.

I groaned. Jackson was a state senator who had begun her political career as a prosecutor. Despite her grandmotherly appearance, she had the reputation of going for the jugular.

"According to the police report, the locks to the snake room and the cobra tank were not tampered with," she stated. "Is that true?"

"Yes."

"Is there any other access to these tanks?"

"No. If someone without a key wanted to release a snake, he would need to break into the room and then break the terrarium glass."

Jackson leaned forward in her seat. "Since that didn't happen, the only logical conclusion is that the snake was released by one of the five zoo employees with a key."

CHAPTER THIRTY-FOUR

I heard the riveting jackhammers and smelled the melting tar. I was driving by the building that was being converted into the new animal health and wellness center.

I thought about the water therapy swimming pool and other special features that would be housed here. My husband's veterinary hospital was small and outdated in comparison. Even if he got the loan for new equipment, I still wondered if he'd be able to compete.

My first stop before work this morning was Matt's veterinary hospital, in order to drop off a few old issues of *Animal Advocate* for the waiting room. As I crossed the parking lot, I noted that the dent in the car belonging to Katie, the office assistant, had been repaired.

Katie, oblivious to the noise emanating from assorted animals in the waiting area, filled out a medical chart in the reception cubicle. I handed her the magazines. "Matt has been meaning to take these but keeps forgetting."

"Thanks. Matt's in the operating room. But Abby's inoculating a cat, so she should be out soon if you want to say hello. By the way, Abby said you knew the intern who died from the cobra bite. You must feel terrible."

Before I could respond, the door separating the examining rooms from the waiting area swung open. Abby emerged, followed by a woman hugging a white Persian. As Katie prepared the woman's bill, Abby pulled me aside. "I haven't eaten anything yet this morning. Come with me to the break room. I have news."

"Good news or bad news?"

"Since nothing I say will convince you to stop investigating, I might as well help you," Abby said, grabbing a yogurt from the refrigerator and a spoon from the cabinet drawer. "I got the scoop on Linda Sancho. Jason knows an attorney who works for the same law firm as Linda's husband. You want to hear what he said?"

I smiled. Although Abby's boyfriend was up to his ears studying for the bar exam, she had him out snooping. "Why not?"

"Linda's dedication to environmental and humane causes has created problems at the zoo. Supposedly, she's fanatical. You know the type. The ends justifies the means. She won't compromise an inch."

"I've only met her briefly, but she does seem the serious sort."

"She doesn't get along with people. She's humorless. It's her way or not at all."

"I think she gets along with Saul Mandel and your Uncle Tim."

"Their concern is the animals. Her problem is with the pencil pushers, the bureaucrats who emphasize the business side of the zoo. People like Arlen McKenzie."

"But is this enough to move her to murder? And Mei certainly wasn't a pencil pusher."

"Who knows what could trigger a violent reaction?" Abby threw the empty yogurt container in the garbage and rinsed off the spoon in the sink.

I flashed back to Linda's alibi for the night of McKenzie's death. She attended Ridge River University's animal behavior conference. But I wondered if she had slipped out and returned to the zoo.

"I better go. I have patients," Abby said.

Abby returned to work and I went back to the waiting room. Before leaving, I stopped to talk to Katie. "You take classes at Ridge River University on Monday nights, don't you, Katie? Were you near the animal behavior conference? It was held three weeks ago."

"Yes. I stopped in after class. I attended the lecture on animal foraging."

"You could do that? Attend only one session?"

"Sure. Lots of people wandered in and out."

I glanced at my watch. "Time to go. By the way, I noticed in the parking lot that your car is fixed. Last time I was here, you said you had been in an accident. What happened?"

"Just a fender bender leaving Ridge River. Some lady backed out of her parking space as I was leaving."

"Was anyone hurt?"

"Nope. Only dented fenders and a taillight, but it's costing more than one thousand dollars. Can you believe that? For a dent."

"What's your deductible?"

"I didn't report it. The woman who hit me paid me in cash. She told me to get an estimate and let her know the cost. She had an accident last month and didn't want the insurance company to know about this one. She gave me the entire amount."

"That's a lot of money, but the way these insurance companies raise your rates, I guess it's worth it, especially if she had a previous accident on record. But weren't you afraid she wouldn't pay?"

"Yeah, at first. But she gave me her business card. She works at the zoo. I figured your brother could nudge her if I had a problem."

"If she works at Rocky Cove, I may have met her. What's her name?"

"Linda Sancho."

"Katie, when did the accident occur?"

"Three Mondays ago."

"The same night as the animal behavior conference?"

"That's right."

"Do you remember the time?"

"About eight-fifteen."

Grabbing my phone, I punched in my brother's number. No one picked up so I left a message. "Tim, you need to call your attorney. You're not the only one who lied about an alibi. I've proof Linda Sancho left the animal behavior conference the night of Arlen McKenzie's murder."

I was about to get ready for bed when the phone trilled. My heart pumped faster. With all that was happening, who knew what news would greet me.

I picked up. Barbara's voice was on the other end.

"Did Tim get my message about Linda Sancho?" I asked before she had a chance to do anything more than say hello.

"You mean about the hole in her alibi? Yes. He's contacting his attorney. But that's not why I'm calling. I wanted to touch base with you about Saturday," my sister-in-law said.

"Tomorrow?"

"Yes. We never set a time. How's eight? Is that too early for Matt?"

Now I remembered. Barbara and Tim's wedding anniversary was next week. Barbara had invited us for cocktails this Saturday to celebrate. The invitation had been extended several weeks ago, but with all that was happening, I couldn't believe Barbara intended to go through with it. One minute she throws my brother out of the house, the next they're celebrating an anniversary.

"Eight will be fine. I'm glad you and Tim resolved your differences," I said, not able to think of a more tactful comment.

"Well, I guess it wasn't really his fault. That bitchy Ginger Hart is causing all the trouble. I can't wait until she leaves."

"Leaves? The zoo? Isn't that premature? I know she doesn't get along with Saul Mandel, but he's only acting director. What if someone other than Saul is appointed permanently?"

"Doesn't matter. Ginger Hart's ambitions are for more than her career. Her real goal is to marry money. Big money. The type Arlen McKenzie possessed. He was unusual for a zoo director. Chances are the new director won't be filthy rich."

"Do you really think she'd seek a job with a wealthy boss in hopes of marrying him?"

"Absolutely. She tried it in her last place of employment. She was public relations director for a shopping mall and made a similar play for the mall owner. The relationship was hot for a while, but he went back to his wife. I understand Ginger was furious. She really thought he'd divorce his wife and marry her."

"How do you know this?"

"From one of my colleagues whose husband worked in the mall office. The mall owner was a big real estate developer. You may have heard his name. Jerry Rudolph."

"I have heard of him. He was a contributor to several animal causes."

"Jerry was killed in an auto accident about a month before Ginger came to Rocky Cove. I better get back to work. See you Saturday. Hopefully, a pleasant evening together will take the murders off our minds."

I scratched my head while possible scenarios flashed through my mind. Ginger fought with both Jerry Rudolph and Arlen

McKenzie right before their deaths. Car accidents could be set up. Could Ginger be a psycho bent on revenge?

"This is crazy," I mumbled. I was letting my imagination run wild. Still, it wouldn't hurt to look into the circumstances surrounding the death of Ginger's previous lover.

CHAPTER THIRTY-FIVE

The smell of burning bread permeated the room. Matt wandered into the kitchen where I was leaning over the sink, scrapping off the black top of an English muffin.

"You're up early for a Saturday," he said.

"I'm going shopping in Manhattan. I need a gift for Tim and Barbara's wedding anniversary. I want something special to cheer them up."

Matt poured coffee into a mug, pulled out a chair, and straddled it. "I don't think anything will cheer up Tim."

"You're probably right, but if it puts Barbara in a good mood, even temporarily, maybe she won't be so tough on my brother."

"But I thought they made up."

"They're back together, but I'll bet she's still giving him a hard time. And if he does get indicted, I'm afraid she'll leave him permanently." I gave up on the muffin and palmed it to Archie who never complained about my culinary abilities. "Barbara loves antiques so I thought I'd go into Manhattan and search the shops in Soho and Greenwich Village."

"Barbara would like something like that. We're not still invited to their house for drinks tonight, are we?"

"We sure are. Barbara insisted."

As Matt rolled his eyes, I held up my hands. "I've never understood my brother or his wife. But Barbara hopes a pleasant evening together will take our minds off the murder."

"I doubt it."

"My thoughts exactly." I glanced at my watch. "I better go." But before I had a chance to leave, the phone trilled and Abby's number popped up.

The phone call from Abby delayed my departure. As the train careened into the station, I skidded into the railroad parking lot, squeezed through the closing doors, and settled back for my trip into Manhattan.

After purchasing antique candlesticks in a small store in Greenwich Village, I spent the rest of the morning wandering in and out of shops and soon realized I was on the block with Booker's Amazing Pet Emporium. I stopped and stared in the window.

Twice is not an accident.

Tom Booker, the store owner, leaned against an iguana tank while deep in conversation with Linda Sancho.

I weighed my course of action. Did I risk being seen? Would Linda recognize me?

If I wanted to get to the bottom of this, I had to take risks. I slipped into the store and crept to the fish aquarium aisle, across from the iguanas. The cartons of dog food piled high in the middle row hid me from view, but I could clearly hear Linda and the store owner as they raised their voices in anger.

"What will you do?" Linda asked Tom Booker.

"Nothing. It's not my problem. Manzetti knew the rules."

"Won't he cause trouble?"

"How? Call Consumer Affairs?" Booker laughed.

A phone trilled.

"I need to answer that." He vanished into his office.

I scooted out the door, wondering about Linda's relationship with this shop. Linda had to be up to no good. But was there a connection with the murders of Arlen McKenzie and Mei Lau?

CHAPTER THIRTY-SIX

I glanced at my brother and his wife. The dark heavy bags under Tim's eyes, obvious even with his thick glasses, contrasted sharply with his pallid complexion. Although makeup hid physical signs of worry on Barbara's face, she appeared on edge. She fiddled with her napkin, almost dropped a platter of mini quiches, and jumped when the cooking timer sounded.

"Something strange is going on with Linda Sancho," I said to my brother as the evening progressed. I noticed that Barbara, who had been arranging a small platter of deviled eggs, paused to listen.

"I spotted Linda twice at a pet shop in Manhattan." While Matt left the room to return a call to his veterinary hospital, I described the two encounters at Booker's Amazing Pet Emporium, ending with, "This store has a criminal record for the illegal selling of endangered species. I'll bet this is somehow connected to the zoo murders."

Tim shrugged. "I don't know why Linda would deal with that store, but I can't imagine it relates to the deaths of Arlen McKenzie or Mei Lau. I've known Linda for five years. She's not a murderer."

"You're not either, but the police zeroed in on you because you lied about your alibi. She did too."

As Tim glanced at his feet, I had a troubling thought. "You did tell your attorney about Linda's early departure from Ridge River's animal behavior conference? You did tell him, right?"

Tim stared at his scotch.

"Tim?"

"Oh, my God!" exclaimed Barbara. "You haven't told your lawyer?"

"I've been busy. My monitor lizard developed a fungus in his claw. But I'll call Stan Margolis first thing Monday. I promise."

I shook my head. "I heard a story about Ginger Hart. Supposedly, her last lover was killed in an auto accident. Is that true, Tim?"

"I wouldn't know. I don't listen to gossip."

"Of course you don't," I said under my breath.

Matt returned, and I excused myself to use the bathroom. Since I passed Tim's study and the door was open, I peeked inside. Spread across the desk was a manila folder. Knowing I couldn't rely on Tim to keep me updated on changes at Rocky Cove, I stepped into the room and opened the folder on the chance it contained information about the zoo.

Inside was a thick report dealing with new projects proposed by Saul Mandel. Under Mandel direction, it appeared that the zoo's focus would be on research, a departure from Arlen McKenzie's emphasis on showy projects and public relations gimmicks.

I returned to the living room, where Tim and Matt were discussing reptile fungus infections. If I didn't change the topic, this could go on all night.

"Are things different with Saul Mandel as acting director?" I asked, interrupting them.

"It's a lot better." Tim's face lit up. "Saul found out about a federal grant available in herpetology. I'm applying. If I get it, I'll be able to do research on the spade foot toad."

Barbara smiled. "Only my husband would find such delight in toad research."

I ignored Barbara's remark. "What about the others on staff,

Tim? How do they feel about Saul Mandel?"

"I know Linda is thrilled with Saul. There's a possibility that the zoo will sponsor her on an Amazon field study. She's particularly interested in that geographic area." Tim sipped his scotch. "Saul's doing all the right things. He's conducting a study on our breeding program, too. The birth rate for some species at the zoo is lower than what it should be. Saul wants to find out why. Is it nutrition? Health problems? Does a habitat need a change?"

"When I interviewed Saul he mentioned how difficult it is to breed in captivity. He said every department has its problems. He gave me a few examples for my article."

"McKenzie didn't care. As long as we had a few successful births that he could publicize, he was happy." Tim swirled the ice in his glass. "The zoo is much better off with Saul as director."

"From what you're saying, I'd guess the only loser is Ginger Hart."

"Ginger will never be a loser. She's expert at manipulating people, and Saul doesn't know how to deal with that."

"Saul doesn't know how to deal with public relations either," Barbara said. "Remember, the last time we had dinner with the Mandels? Saul started ranting about how Ginger wanted him to judge entries in that contest."

"Right. The poster contest for kindergarten students, where they had to draw their favorite animals." Tim chuckled. "Saul complained, but he did serve as a judge. He always does the right thing."

Barbara shrugged, looking as if she wasn't sure she agreed. I realized my brother and sister-in-law socialized with the Mandels, and I wondered if Barbara's opinion of the curator was different than Tim's.

"Enough shop talk. Is everyone ready for dessert?" Barbara

rose from her chair. "If so, I'll set it up in the dining room. But let me first clear away the hors d'oeuvres."

"I'll help." I grabbed a cheese platter and trailed Barbara into the kitchen. Once we were alone, I asked, "Barbara, do you think Saul is capable of murder?"

"I believe everyone is capable of murder. It's like an allergy. Some people just have a higher tolerance level."

"What's Saul's tolerance level?"

"It's not that high. He has anger management issues. And he can get violent. He almost lost his job about eight years ago because of his temper."

"What happened?"

"Saul spotted three teenagers throwing bottle caps at a pregnant giraffe. He grabbed one of the kids and slammed him against the wall. It took two security guards to pull Saul away."

"That's not true," said a voice from behind.

I spun around and saw my brother standing in the doorway and glaring at Barbara.

"Saul had grabbed the boy's arm to prevent him from throwing more caps at the giraffe," Tim said. "Saul never hurt that boy. He was only protecting the giraffe."

Once we seated ourselves around the dining room table, Barbara brought in the coffee service along with individual servings of Peach Melba and a large fruit platter.

I sighed, having hoped our dessert would involve chocolate. I've always been convinced that chocolate was a universal favorite, and anyone who thought otherwise should watch the brownies disappear from a dessert buffet.

"I've a surprise to show you," Barbara said. "When I left the room, I put on my anniversary gift from Tim." She held out her right hand, displaying an oval-shaped emerald and diamond cocktail ring. "Isn't it gorgeous?"

Right now, I wanted to smack my brother on top of his head.

Matt broke the silence. "Congratulations. It's a beautiful ring."

"Yes, it is beautiful." I gritted my teeth, thinking *it's not my money and it's not my business.*

"Thank you." Barbara poured the coffee. "I want Tim to take up sailing, so my gift to him was a certificate for ten lessons at a local sailing school. Would you like to see the brochure? Let me get it." She vanished into another room.

"I didn't know sailing interested you, Tim," Matt said.

Tim smiled. "I didn't either. The most athletic activity I've ever engaged in is a game of chess. But Barbara wants to join a sailing club. She learned to sail as a teenager."

Dollar signs appeared in front of my eyes. In my mind, Tim and Barbara lived in a fantasy world. "Sailing club membership is pretty expensive. Can you afford it? I guess you can, judging by your gift to Barbara."

"Don't worry. Despite Barbara's wishes, with the murder suspicions hanging over my head, no one's proposing me for immediate membership. That's for sure."

"Where do you suppose Tim found the money for the ring?" I asked Matt as we drove home.

"I know where. Tim told me before we left."

"Are you keeping it a secret?"

"You won't like it. He got an equity loan on his house to consolidate their bills and pay Stan Margolis, who is probably the most expensive lawyer in this region. Tim took a portion of the money from the equity to buy the ring."

CHAPTER THIRTY-SEVEN

Back home, Matt fell asleep immediately, but I tossed and turned. Not only did my brother's out-of-control spending bother me, but the murders of Arlen McKenzie and Mei Lau weighed heavily on my mind. Of course, I also worried about my job at *Animal Advocate*, as well as the future of Matt's veterinary hospital. It was after three o'clock by the time I fell asleep.

I awakened to a ringing telephone.

"Abby," I muttered, glancing at the caller ID and fumbling across Archie for the phone. Matt had left the house at dawn for a golf game, and the dog now rested his head on my pillow.

"I've news," my daughter announced.

"Just what I need at six in the morning. This couldn't have waited until ten?"

"I've the day off. I wanted to call before I left for the beach. Remember when you told me about Ginger Hart's former lover, Jerry Rudolph?"

"Of course. We talked yesterday, before I left for Manhattan. I almost missed my train."

"Well, Jason came over last night after his bar review class. We did some Internet research and found a newspaper article about the car accident."

Now I was wide awake.

"The accident occurred less than two years ago in upstate New York where Jerry Rudolph was checking out property for a new mall," Abby said. "His Jaguar careened into a ravine off Route 17. The local newspaper billed it as a hit and run. Rudolph miraculously survived long enough to utter the words 'black SUV' and 'I had to swerve' to the police. The case was never solved."

I rubbed my forehead. A black SUV. Could it be the Escalade that had harassed me?

I realized any suspicions involving Ginger's role in Jerry Rudolph's accident might force the police to look more closely into Ginger as a suspect in the zoo murders. But I needed more information.

I searched the Internet and found that Jerry Rudolph's widow was still alive and living less than ten miles from my home.

I decided to pay her a visit. I considered phoning first, but thought she would be less likely to refuse to see me if I just showed up at her doorstep.

Madalyn Rudolph lived in a large colonial house in an upscale neighborhood near the water on Long Island's south shore.

"My name is Kristy Farrell," I said when she came to the door. She was a tall, athletic-looking woman of about fifty. I had read that in her youth she had been a tennis pro. "I'd like to talk to you about your husband's accident."

"My husband died two years ago. Why are you interested now?"

With what I had to say, Mrs. Rudolph would either invite me into her house or kick me off her stoop. I took a deep breath. "Your husband died after breaking off a relationship with Ginger Hart. Arlen McKenzie, director of the Rocky Cove Zoo, was Ginger's most recent lover. He was killed only a few days after he and Ginger had a major fight. I'm a person who doesn't believe in coincidences."

"You're not with the police. Who are you?"

"My brother is a suspect in the McKenzie murder. I know he didn't do it. I'm checking other possibilities."

She hesitated, then stepped aside. "Come in," she said, ushering me into a large living room overlooking the Great South Bay. "Do you think Ginger may be responsible? Do you think she might have murdered my husband, too?"

"Right now I'm just gathering information. Did the police question Ginger when your husband died?"

"No. As far as I know they didn't question anyone from down here. They chalked it up to road rage or even a drunk driver. That section of Route 17 is a pretty isolated area, so there were no witnesses. The police searched for the SUV but never found it."

Mrs. Rudolph turned and appeared to stare at a wedding photo on the mantelpiece. "I never thought Jerry's death was the result of someone setting out to kill him. I believed it was an accident. I was so distraught, I wasn't thinking straight. Jerry and I were separated for more than a year, but we had just gotten back together a few days before this all happened."

"Did you know Ginger?"

"She was the reason we separated. I never had the displeasure of meeting her, but I had friends who kept me informed. One of those friends was my husband's business partner. He said that Ginger had called in sick the day Jerry was killed. I didn't think anything of it at the time, but maybe she was upstate."

"It's possible. Did your friends tell you how Ginger reacted when your husband broke off the relationship?"

"Ginger didn't react well at all. She told everyone that she had wasted the best years of her life. I wonder . . ."

"What is it?" I said.

"Ginger had also said she'd make Jerry pay for what he did to her."

★ ★ ★ ★ ★

I phoned the police and asked for Detective Fox. Detective Wolfe picked up. I told him about my meeting with Jerry Rudolph's widow.

"You want me to investigate Ginger Hart because she knows two people who died? You think that makes her a serial killer?"

"She fought with both victims before their deaths. And neither died of natural causes. I say that's suspicious."

"I don't know about the accident upstate. It's out of my jurisdiction. But Ginger Hart had an alibi for McKenzie's murder."

"But it wouldn't hurt—"

"I don't have the time for your harebrained theories. I'm satisfied that my investigation is leading me toward the guilty party. I have a few more loose ends to tie up and then I'll go for an indictment. In the meantime, don't call unless you come up with solid evidence."

CHAPTER THIRTY-EIGHT

Tim had arranged for me to take some photographs in the reptile nursery on Monday. Once I had finished snapping photos of a baby boa who measured more than two feet long, I headed toward the exit. On my way, I ran into Linda Sancho.

"I don't know if you remember me, Linda," I said. "My brother Tim introduced us in his office. I'd like to talk if you have a minute."

"Sure." She smiled. "What is it?"

"My husband's office assistant is the woman whose car you hit at Ridge River University. You told the police you attended the animal behavior conference until ten o'clock."

Linda's smile faded. "I was gone for less than an hour. I had picked up my mother's prescription from a pharmacy earlier, but I hadn't dropped it off. The conference schedule called for a video presentation at eight, and since I wasn't particularly interested in the topic, that's when I took the medicine to my mom's place. She only lives twenty minutes from the university, so I knew I'd be back in plenty of time for the panel discussion at nine."

"But you didn't tell this to the police?"

"I have enough problems in my life right now. The last thing I need is to be considered a murder suspect." Linda nibbled the nail on her right thumb. "I should have told the police, but I took the risk that no one would find out."

"I suppose your mother will verify you were at her house."

"She was asleep. I put the medication on the kitchen counter and returned to the conference."

"I told my brother about the flaw in your alibi, and he's contacting his attorney."

"I'll inform the police that I left the university. I'll call this afternoon." Linda started to walk away, but I wasn't ready to let her go.

"Your alibi's not the only thing we need to discuss," I said. "I spotted you at Booker's Amazing Pet Emporium. That place has been cited for dealing in wildlife smuggling. Its conditions are horrid. Why would you go there?"

Linda stopped and spun around, a determination appearing in her eyes that I had not seen before. "The horrid conditions are the reason. I'm an active member of the SANAN Society."

"Sanan?" It sounded familiar but I couldn't place it.

"Yes. It stands for Stop Animal Neglect and Abuse Now. We're compiling a list of places that sell puppy mill dogs so we can mount a big publicity campaign. I checked the store out as part of our investigation."

"You were at the store more than once," I accused.

"I returned a second time to ask more questions, to get my facts straight. I had the name of a man who purchased a German shepherd puppy with serious medical problems. I wanted to find out what the store owners would do. Would they take the dog back? If so, what would happen to him?" Linda's hands tightened into fists. "As expected, they don't stand behind their dogs."

"You can prove this?"

"I'll give you the address and phone number of SANAN. You can verify my story."

"I intend to do just that."

"I would appreciate it if you didn't mention this to anyone

around here," Linda said as we parted. "I try to keep my personal life private."

My next stop was the SANAN Society headquarters, located in Brooklyn. I spent ten minutes searching for a parking space, finally securing one three blocks away.

SANAN occupied the bottom floor of a three-story building. The door was ajar so I went inside. The large room was furnished with folding chairs, a long table, old wooden file cabinets, a metal desk, and a computer that looked similar to one I'd discarded ten years ago. I spotted a small fan in the corner, but it didn't appear to be doing much good. The temperature felt hotter in here than outside.

A man with long hair beginning to gray slouched in a chair behind the desk. The nameplate on his desk read: "Alan Dysart, Executive Director." He was arguing with a woman dressed in black who was sitting across from him. The woman looked no older than thirty and wore a button that read: "Free the Animals."

"You're ridiculous," the man said. "Your plan will lose us financial support." Beads of perspiration dotted his forehead.

"You pander to everyone." The woman moved to the edge of her seat. "This is war. When will you learn that in a war not everyone will be on your side."

"Excuse me. I'm Kristy Farrell, and I'm a writer for—"

"I know who you are," the man said. "Linda Sancho called thirty minutes ago and told me you'd be checking on her."

"Is she a volunteer here?"

"She's an active member. Linda has inspected more than a dozen pet shops for our puppy mill project, including Booker's Amazing Pet Emporium. Is there anything else you want?"

"Since you've asked, I'm curious about your organization. What exactly do you do?"

The woman in black sneered. "What we should do and what we actually do are completely different."

Alan Dysart shot her a look, then turned back to me. "We promote the welfare of animals by advocating against various abuses. Right now, our major cause is the sale of puppy mill dogs."

"Linda is involved with this?" I asked.

"Of course she is," said the woman in black. "This project won't offend any of Linda's associates. This group never tackles controversial issues anymore. But what can you expect with volunteers like Linda who have careers at zoos."

"What's wrong with that?"

"Zoos are part of the problem. Animals should be free—"

"That's not our policy," Alan interrupted. "Of course, we're opposed to the roadside zoo where animals are packed into cages, but we're not against the modern zoological parks with natural habitat like Rocky Cove."

"This organization is nothing more than a bandage on an artery." The woman pointed a finger with puce nail polish in his face.

"Not true. We've always been involved with issues of animal abuse. We work through legislation, education, and public information."

"As if that's going to accomplish anything. We need to take militant action."

"It's taken us half a decade to rebuild ourselves since that militant action you're talking about."

Now it came back. Five years ago SANAN found itself in the headlines when a handful of renegade members raided pet stores, setting animals free without thought to the consequences of releasing the poor creatures on city streets. Although I didn't recall the specifics, I was sure a criminal investigation ensued.

"How long has Linda been involved with your group?" I asked.

"About six years."

What if Linda was part of the extremist faction? I wondered. What if Arlen McKenzie knew about it? He could ruin Linda's good name and career, not only at Rocky Cove but within the entire mainstream zoological community.

CHAPTER THIRTY-NINE

"Olivia wants to see you immediately," Clara said as I stepped through the office doorway.

"What about?"

"I have no idea, but she's not in a great mood. By the way, she approved your travel request to attend the animal auction."

"Well maybe that's why she wants—"

"I don't think that's why she wants to see you. She received a phone call earlier, and since then, she's been pacing around here like a caged animal. She's back in her office now."

Experiencing that sinking feeling in the pit of my stomach, I knocked on the door to Olivia Johnson's private office. I entered and faced the editor, who was standing behind her desk.

"Don't sit down," she said. "This will only take a minute."

At nearly six feet in height with broad shoulders, Olivia was an imposing figure. With skin the color of deep French roast coffee and silver hair fashioned in a short, no-nonsense style, she favored dark-colored, conservatively tailored suits, like the navy blue pinstripe she wore today. She looked to be in her late fifties, but rumor said she was seventy.

"I want to thank you for approving my travel request to attend Malur's Animal Auction," I said. "Clara told me that you gave the okay and—"

"Your articles aren't finished?"

"Not yet, but they're not due for—"

"I suggest you stick to your work and leave homicide to the

police." Olivia's eyes now focused on me like a lioness sizing up a wounded zebra.

"I received a call from Ginger Hart," Olivia continued. "A waiter at the Treasures of Zeus had overheard you talking about Ms. Hart's alibi for the night of Arlen McKenzie's murder. I've heard the rumors about your brother, and I can understand your interest in the case, but this is unprofessional."

Olivia stepped slowly around to the front of the desk. "We can't afford to alienate the public relations staff at Rocky Cove unless there's a good reason. We're an animal magazine, not a crime publication. Murder has nothing to do with us."

"What if it does?"

"What do you mean?"

"I believe the murders of Arlen McKenzie and Mei Lau are related to a scandal at the Rocky Cove Zoo."

"What type of scandal?"

"I don't know yet." I explained what I knew of Mei's worries, including her fear that the malfunctioning of the crocodile gate was caused by sabotage.

Olivia wandered to the other end of the office, standing silently for a moment. "This puts the situation in a different light. Okay. Look into it. But be careful."

"I will."

"One more thing. The zoological community networks. If you're wrong, everyone will know. Your ability to work with professionals in the animal world will be compromised. That will affect my decision as to the person I hire permanently as feature writer."

Leaving Olivia's office, I scooted down the corridor, passing Clara who was chatting with a FedEx deliveryman. I didn't feel like talking to anyone. I slumped in my chair and for several moments sat unmoving. But I realized I wouldn't accomplish anything unless I set to work.

First, I needed to find out more about the SANAN Society.

Abby knew all about animal rights and humane groups. I phoned my daughter at the veterinary hospital. In between patients, she was able to take my call.

"The SANAN Society started off about ten years ago as a protest group patterned after the student movement of the sixties and seventies," Abby said. "SANAN quickly became more radical before turning into the mainstream organization they are today. Their sit-ins had become pretty nasty. They blocked entrances to pet stores, circuses, petting zoos, any place dealing with animals. They refused to allow customers to go inside, sometimes using physical force."

"Didn't their actions become even more violent?"

"Yes. Finally, they broke into labs and stole research animals. I don't know what they did with them. But when they raided pet stores, releasing puppies and kittens on city streets, that's when the real trouble started and two factions developed."

"I remember that," I said.

"The first store they smashed was on Queens Boulevard. You know what traffic is like there. It's as bad as Manhattan. Some animals were rescued, but most were killed running out into the road."

"That's horrible. It's also a pretty stupid action for animal lovers."

"The president of the organization would agree with you. But the spokesperson for the extremists claimed the animals were martyrs for the cause."

"Whether they wanted to be or not," I said.

"A week later, they hit another pet store. This one was in Brooklyn. After releasing the animals, they set fire to the shop. Two firefighters sustained injury, one so severe he left the department on disability."

"What happened to those responsible?"

"The president of SANAN swore he'd expel any member engaging in illegal activities. He also promised to fully cooperate with the police in uncovering those responsible for the break-ins."

I twirled a strand of hair around my finger. "Did they catch who did it?"

"No. The group's board of directors threw out the more vocal of the radical element, but I hear a few still remain."

"Why? If the organization is now mainstream, why would extremist members stay?"

"According to rumors, they use the group's resources, including files and data banks."

"Have the illegal activities stopped?"

"That's hard to say. There've been a few incidents, but no one can prove members of the group are responsible. A fur salon was broken into a few months ago, the place trashed, and furs sprayed with red paint. There's talk that this involved members of SANAN, but no one was caught."

I explained my theory about Arlen McKenzie blackmailing Linda.

"I can see McKenzie tarnishing Linda's reputation with her peers," Abby said. "The man is capable of blackmail. But there's a major flaw in your thinking."

"What kind of flaw?"

"The police never discovered who was responsible for raiding the pet stores. Why do you think Arlen McKenzie did?"

"Because the police need to prioritize. They lack time and resources to devote to one case. But as the case fades in the background, tongues slip and people involved become sloppy. Besides, it doesn't matter if Linda was part of the radical faction. Some people hold you guilty by association. McKenzie would capitalize on that type of thinking."

CHAPTER FORTY

Returning home, I found a bouquet of red roses on my front step.

If Matt brought the flowers, they wouldn't be outside. But I couldn't imagine who else would drop off a bouquet.

I carried the flowers into the kitchen while examining the attached card. Addressed to Kristy Farrell, it omitted the name of the sender.

"These are flowers, not food," I said to Archie and Brandy, who stood with tails wagging on either side of me as I filled a vase with water.

I heard a car pull into the driveway.

Matt entered through the side door into the kitchen. "Nice roses. Who sent them? Do you have a secret admirer?"

"Could be. Just what I need—another mystery. Ouch!"

"Thorns?"

"That's the problem with roses."

Blood oozed from my finger. After rinsing my hand in the sink and arranging the flowers in the vase, I was still bleeding. "I'm getting a bandage. Oh, I forgot to bring in the mail. Will you get it?"

Before I located a bandage, Matt returned with an assortment of letters and a small brown box. "Here's another mystery," he said. "This package is addressed to you. I found it in the mailbox, but there's no return address and no postage."

"No postage? Maybe the same person who brought the flowers dropped it off. I'll bet there's a letter inside."

Matt placed the box along with the rest of the mail on the kitchen table, then opened the refrigerator door and pulled out a bottle of water. Owl, who had come downstairs, jumped onto the table and pawed the package. Archie cautiously approached, sniffing. Brandy trotted to the table and joined them.

Normally, the dogs and cat never stayed in the same room together. But today they ignored each other and appeared to be focused on the box.

Forgetting about the bandage, I shooed the animals away and tore open the package. Instantly, something sprung out, brushing against my arm. The creature appeared to be a frog or toad, but a most unusual one. It had golden-colored skin.

"Is this someone's idea of a joke? I don't think it's very funny."

Matt, who hadn't been paying attention, spun around. Seeing the creature on the table, he paled. "That's a poison dart frog."

I was about to grab the frog, but Matt pushed me away. "Its skin is poisonous. Don't touch it. You've got an open cut on your hand."

The three animals approached the table where the tiny frog sat motionless.

"We've got to get the dogs and cat out of here," Matt said. "If they grab the frog with their mouth, they could die."

Owl jumped onto the table and crouched down, haunches raised, ready to pounce. I scooped her up around the middle. The frog leaped to the floor.

Matt grabbed hold of Brandy and Archie. Meanwhile, Owl struggled to get out of my grasp. Anyone who has ever held a cat that didn't want to be held would realize my difficulty.

I locked Owl in the bedroom and then put the dogs in the study. When I returned to the kitchen, I saw Matt had grabbed a large pot from the cabinet and was trying, unsuccessfully, to capture the frog. Less than two inches in length, it was difficult to see despite its bright color.

"Be careful. Don't touch it with the hand that has the open cut," Matt warned as I tried to grab the frog. "Stand back. I'll get him."

When the frog leaped to a spot near the refrigerator, Matt captured him.

"We need to call the police," he said.

I nodded. "But not the local precinct. This must be tied to the zoo murders." I sighed. "As much as I dread this, I think we should call the homicide detectives assigned to the case."

"You call. I'm putting this little guy in a terrarium. Afterward, I'll find a home for him."

Matt made his way to the basement where he kept extra veterinary supplies, including a few cages and tanks. Meanwhile, I phoned police headquarters. After a bureaucratic runaround, I connected with Detective Wolfe.

"You again. I thought I told you not to bother me with your half-baked theories."

I explained the reason for my call.

"You're telling me someone is trying to kill you with a poison frog?" he said.

"Someone wants me to stop asking questions about the murders. Maybe I'm getting too close."

"Your story sounds farfetched," Wolfe said, "but I'll be over in about an hour."

Two hours later, Detective Steve Wolfe arrived and parked himself at the kitchen table.

"Would you like coffee or water?" Matt asked.

He shook his head.

"Donut?" I smiled sweetly. The detective glared at me.

"Where's Detective Fox?" I asked.

"He's out sick today." Wolfe narrowed his eyes. "What? You

don't think I can handle this alone?"

Before I could reply, Matt carried in the terrarium now housing the frog. He placed it on the table.

"This is it?" Wolfe said as he peered inside the glass at the frog. "Touching this thing could poison you? You gotta be kidding."

"The skin of this species is highly toxic," Matt explained. "At one time, Columbian tribes preparing for a hunt dipped the darts for their blowguns in the toxins from these frogs."

"And it can kill a human?"

"Poison frogs lose their toxicity in captivity. But if it just arrived from South America, and you have an open cut, it could kill you. We have no way of knowing where this frog came from or how long it's been here. It may or may not have a high level of toxins."

"Who do you think sent the frog?" Wolfe asked.

"That's what I want you to find out." I mumbled. I don't think Wolfe heard me.

"We've no idea where it came from," Matt said. "I found the package in the mailbox. No identifying marks. Just a plain brown box."

"We'll canvass the block and see if your neighbors saw anything."

"I doubt that will help. No one's home during the day."

"He's right," I agreed.

"Yeah, okay. We'll still check with the other neighbors. Who knows?" Wolfe frowned as he jotted notes on his pad. "Let's get this straight. You believe the killer suspects you're close to solving the case and sent the frog to scare you?"

"I can't imagine who else would."

"Where would a frog like this come from?"

Matt shrugged. "If you know how to use the Internet, you can buy almost anything."

"As sick as it is, it might have nothing to do with the murders," the detective said. "This could be someone's idea of a joke."

Matt ran his hand through his thinning hair. "Detective, I don't think you realize how serious this is. The frog's skin might be highly toxic. I knew because I'm a veterinarian, but my wife had no idea. If I hadn't been home, she probably would have picked it up."

"When I came home today, I found a bouquet of roses on my front stoop, sent anonymously. I pricked my finger on one of the roses."

"Whoever sent the frog, sent the flowers," Matt said.

"Yeah, sure. No one could guarantee your wife would cut herself on the roses. Chances are, she wouldn't. I can't imagine a more inefficient method of murder."

"Maybe someone wanted to scare me. Or maybe the plan was to kill off my dogs or my cat. I don't honestly know. But I'm sure someone wants me to stop asking questions. Someone is framing my brother."

"Framing your brother. Really?" The detective narrowed his eyes while shutting his notebook. "Why are you so sure your brother didn't commit the murders? Or send the flowers and the frog?"

"I'm his sister. He wouldn't send me a poison frog."

"Yeah, sure." Detective Wolfe rose from his chair and made his way toward the door. "Most premeditated homicides involve family members. Maybe he doesn't want you digging into this. Maybe he's afraid you'd uncover proof he committed the murders."

CHAPTER FORTY-ONE

I stared at my computer screen.

"It's time for a break." Matt approached me at the kitchen table. He carried two mugs of steaming coffee.

"Thanks, but how do you break from doing nothing." I grabbed a mug. "I've been trying to come up with an idea since Wolfe left."

Matt leaned over my shoulder to view the screen. "I see you've listed all the suspects, along with motives and opportunity."

"No one has an alibi for the time of Mei's death, so I can only check opportunities for McKenzie's murder. We know Linda left the animal behavior conference, and all we have is her word that she went to her mother's house. It's also possible that Ginger didn't stay at Treasures of Zeus, and that Saul slipped out of his house and returned to the zoo."

"I guess you can eliminate Amanda since she was drunk."

"I'm rethinking that. Maybe she's one of those people who act like they had more to drink than they did. She may have sobered up enough to drive back to the zoo."

"Unlikely."

"Unlikely but possible. And I've reached a dead end with Mei's journal. I'm sure there's something there, but I can't figure it out."

Matt rubbed my shoulders. "What are those numbers next to the names?"

"I'm ranking everyone on a scale of one to ten according to their ability to handle dangerous reptiles. Ginger Hart is a one. She's a public relations expert with no background in zoology."

"Why rank Saul and Amanda as fives?"

"They're scientists, but their specialties are in areas other than herpetology. They have no expertise with snakes or poison frogs."

"That you know of."

"Linda is a different story. As a wildlife nutritionist, she's involved with mammals, birds, and reptiles."

Matt wandered over to a chair and sat down. He remained silent while sipping his coffee.

"What's bothering you, Matt? I have a feeling there's more on your mind than my murder theories. Are you worrying about the new veterinary facility?"

"No. Right now I'm thinking about your safety. Two people have been killed. Now it looks like they're after you. When I saw that frog . . ." He ran his hand through his hair.

"Matt, I'm nervous myself. But I'm not backing down."

"You have this naive idea that nothing will happen to you."

"Not true. But if I did, it's certainly better than thinking something will happen to me. I'd rather be overconfident than overfearful."

"Just promise you'll be careful. Don't go off alone with anyone at the zoo and don't take risks."

"I promise. Besides, I'm leaving tomorrow, remember? I'll be in Ohio checking out Malur's Animal Auction for my article on wildlife smuggling."

"That doesn't make me feel any better. Those animal dealers aren't going to be happy if they discover what you're doing, and they play real rough."

I shut down the computer and flipped off the light. As Matt

and I headed into the bedroom, my thoughts flashed back to the two murders, the black Escalade that had almost run me off the road, and now the poison frog.

I hoped the bumpy flight to Ohio wasn't a harbinger of things to come. During the flight, I read a packet of background material Roy Maxwell had sent. Clayton Malur was a bad one. It appeared the United States Fish and Wildlife Service wasn't the only thorn in his side. The auction house owner had a history of run-ins with other federal and state agencies.

The most serious occurred three years ago when the United States Department of Agriculture had revoked Malur's license to operate an animal auction for eight months and fined him $25,000. The charges involved multiple counts of neglect under the Animal Welfare Act. Inspectors had discovered malnutrition, parasitic infections, hacking coughs, and lameness.

The report cited examples. Monkeys had torn out hunks of their fur and a few were missing limbs, caused by self-mutilation from living in cages that fell under the minimum size requirement set by law.

According to Maxwell, Malur's customers consisted primarily of hunting ranches, roadside zoos, research labs, traveling circuses, rare pet dealers, and exotic meat vendors. Drug dealers purchased lions and alligators to bolster macho images. A few buyers simply sought unusual animals as conversation pieces. No one knew where these creatures wound up when the owners became bored with their acquisitions.

At an average auction, more than a thousand animals changed hands, with Clayton Malur grossing nearly a quarter of a million dollars.

The packet also included a list of animals available at last month's auctions.

Animals for Auction

Bear cubs—Russian hogs—cougars—elk—wallabies—
Brazilian tapirs—llamas—lemurs—macaques—marmo-
sets—chimps—gibbons—camels—zebras—panthers—
kangaroos—miniature horses—ibex—reindeer—tigers—
lions—cheetahs—sugar gliders—black-footed penguins—
emus—swans—macaws—parrots—falcons—homing
pigeons—peacocks—ostriches—monitor lizards—saw-
scaled vipers—boa constrictors—pythons—Australian
kraits—black mambas—diamondback rattlesnakes—
iguanas—baby alligators—Madagascar hissing cockroaches.

The more I read about this strange place, the more anxious I
was to investigate. With its past violations for wildlife smuggling, it would add a unique twist to my story.

I rented a car at the Cleveland airport and drove more than
ninety minutes through rural communities until I reached the
Razorville Motor Lodge where I had reservations for the night.
Deciding on an early dinner, I freshened up and strolled to the
restaurant adjacent to the lodge.

Hurricane lamps illuminated each wooden table, and paintings of nineteenth-century farm scenes adorned the walls, along
with heads of dead animals. I had just picked up the menu
when a lanky, red-headed man, with legs and arms like limp lin-
guine, entered the room and slipped into an adjacent booth.

Soon a middle-aged couple joined him. The man, who was
big, bulky, and round faced with a bushy beard, reminded me
of Henry VIII. The woman had buttery blond hair, long dangling
earrings, and heavy makeup. Over a pair of tight-fitting jeans,
she wore a purple spandex top that emphasized her ample
breasts. The three started discussing exotic animals. From their

conversation, I learned they planned to attend tomorrow's animal auction.

"He can put in a special order. If anyone can get a golden lion tamarin for you, Clayton Malur can," said the red-haired man.

I strained to hear their conversation about the endangered golden lion tamarin, a small Brazilian monkey with fur around its face resembling a lion's mane.

"I heard a tamarin is difficult to obtain," Henry VIII said.

"There's no question it's gonna cost you plenty."

"And you're sure there'll be no trouble with the law?" The woman appeared to study her long scarlet nails.

"None at all. Listen, the government doesn't have the manpower to check out these things. You let us handle it. That's what you're paying for."

I sat back, processing what I'd heard. The redhead hadn't said anything incriminating. He didn't mention smuggling, but the couple didn't ask. They only wanted to cover themselves.

CHAPTER FORTY-TWO

By dawn, traffic to Malur's auction backed up on the main road for nearly a mile. Arriving at the parking lot entrance, I rolled down my window and stretched out my arm, attempting to hand my twenty-dollar admission to the fee collector, a skinhead with muscles like those found on a heavyweight wrestling contender.

He didn't grab the money. He leaned forward, apparently trying to check out the inside of my car. "No photos are allowed, including cell phones."

"I understand."

"You're not with one of those troublemaking groups, are you?" He eyed me suspiciously. "Are you a newspaper reporter?"

"No. I'm here to buy an exotic animal for my husband. It's a birthday gift." I had decided that would be my cover.

The fee collector gave me the once-over, his eyes focusing on my breasts.

I drew a deep breath wondering if he would refuse me entry. Did I come here for no reason?

He snatched the money from my hand. "Okay. Go ahead."

I hit the gas, not giving him a chance to change his mind.

The auction didn't start for another hour, but the parking lot was nearly full with trucks, trailers, and a handful of sports cars and luxury autos with license plates from more than a dozen states. As I trekked up the dirt path, carefully avoiding the occasional mounds of manure along the way, brays, roars, and

191

squeals, along with an assortment of barnyard smells, wafted through the air.

Upon entering the grounds, I surveyed my surroundings—a small, white clapboard house, three barns, and a large auction arena. I wandered through the narrow aisles of the first barn, crowded with prospective buyers and sellers.

This building's interior had been gutted, making room for row upon row of long tables. Placed atop these tables were terrariums holding hundreds of snakes and lizards. On the floor near the back sat two large crates, both marked: DANGER—VENOMOUS REPTILES.

The next barn echoed with the screeches of dozens of birds, most in cages so small their feathers stuck through the wire mesh. I jumped when a large mouse—or perhaps a rat, I wasn't sure—scurried across my shoe. I decided to leave.

Entering the third and largest barn, I gagged at the stench. Zebras and elk stood in four-by-eight box stalls with no room to turn, much less walk. Where stalls had been removed, leopards, ocelots, and cougars lay listlessly in cages, surrounded by feces and flies.

After exiting the building, I grabbed a program that someone had left on a bench and studied the list of animals for sale today. I started walking toward the arena when I spied the two people from the motel restaurant. They were talking to a man wearing cowboy boots and a cowboy hat. I lingered, hoping to hear what they said.

"I'll call you as soon as I get word," the cowboy told the other two. He shook their hands.

"Thanks, Clay. I sure hope you can get us a golden lion tamarin." The two departed.

Clay! Clayton Malur, the auction house owner. I made my way to where he stood.

"I'm interested in buying a woolly spider monkey," I said,

asking for an endangered animal that was not on today's auction flyer. "Will you have any for sale in the arena?"

"Afraid not, little lady. They're hard to come by. Very few around."

"You can't get me one?"

"I didn't say that. I just said it would be difficult. And expensive."

"Money isn't a problem."

He grinned. "We'll have to get you one that's legal, captive bred with papers and all. It may take time, but let me see what I can do."

Would the papers be forged? Proving he was still involved in illegal animal sales would be a great scoop.

I scribbled down my name and phone number and handed it to him, hoping if he called I'd be able to set up a sting with Fish and Wildlife. Then I headed to the auction arena, climbed up the bleachers, and located an empty seat as the bidding began.

The auctioneer's pitch blasted from the speaker system amid the drone of animal and human noises. In the center of the arena floor, a leopard paced in circles inside a tiny cage. It sold to a preppie-looking couple for seven thousand dollars.

Sitting further down my row was a man with a short blond beard. He appeared to be texting, but when an Indian rock python came to the floor, he looked up from his phone and focused on the auction. The bidding opened at four hundred dollars, and the first bid came from him.

"Four hundred twenty-five," called a voice from behind me.

I turned to look at the bidder seated two rows back. He wore an open-neck shirt, showcasing his hairy chest. He sported a large diamond pinky ring, and at least six gold chains hung from his neck.

The bidding escalated, and the snake was awarded to the

man with the blond beard for five hundred dollars.

The auction continued with the blond-bearded man winning the bid on a saw-scaled viper and an Australian krait. He rose to leave. I followed.

"Excuse me. I noticed you bid on several snakes," I said once we were outside the arena. "Are you a collector?"

"Why do you want to know?"

"I'm interested in buying a snake for my husband's birthday next year, and I wanted to find out about different species."

"I own a small roadside zoo." He lit a cigarette. "It's a tourist attraction in Florida."

The image of a roadside zoo flashed through my mind. These exhibits usually consisted of a few cages, cramped with animals. Not only was the admission fee high for what you saw, but the zoo served as a lure to get you to buy a cold drink, a snack, or a plastic souvenir at inflated prices.

"What type of snakes—"

"I'm here to buy snakes, not give out free advice." He puffed on his cigarette as he veered toward the white clapboard house where I assumed he would pay for his purchases.

I wanted a photo to accompany my piece but knew it would be risky. In addition to the warning from the guard in the admission booth, you couldn't move ten feet without coming across a posting of NO CAMERAS ALLOWED.

Noting that several animals occupied outdoor cages by the side of the third barn, I figured there would be less chance of getting caught if I snapped the picture there. A security guard stood nearby, talking to a teenage girl in denim shorts. While he was preoccupied, I carefully lifted my phone from my bag and photographed a caged capuchin monkey.

Then I heard Clayton Malur's voice from behind the barn. Stashing my camera away, I crept to the far end of the building and peeked around the corner.

Clayton Malur was shaking hands with a man wearing jeans and a muscle T-shirt. Even without his zookeeper uniform, I recognized him.

I watched Clayton Malur hand a wad of cash to Rocky Cove's bird keeper, Frank Taggart.

CHAPTER FORTY-THREE

"Could Frank Taggart be selling animals from the zoo?" I asked Matt during the drive home from LaGuardia airport. It was near midnight when my flight arrived back in New York, two hours late.

"No way. I told you before. Zoos keep meticulous records. You can't snatch an elephant and expect no one will notice."

"It sounds ridiculous, but what else could it be?"

"I don't know."

"First, I spotted Linda Sancho at Booker's Amazing Pet Emporium, now Frank Taggart at Malur's Auction." I shook my head. "I'm calling Tim tomorrow. Maybe he can shed some light on this."

Matt stopped short for a traffic light. "Forget the zoo. You've been working really hard. You need a break, and I can use one too. Why don't we go away for a few days? We can leave after work tomorrow." Matt put his hand on my thigh. "We can rent one of those cabins near the ocean."

"Sounds great, but I can't. Friday evening is the memorial service for Mei Lau. I'll take a rain check, okay?"

Matt removed his hand. "Sure. No problem." The frown on his face and tone of his voice said otherwise.

He remained silent for the rest of the drive home.

"Okay, what's the matter?" I asked while we undressed for bed. "Are you upset about not going away this weekend? We can go another time."

"It's not that. I think you're too involved in these murders."

"I need to help my brother. No one else is doing anything."

"Tim has an attorney."

"What's he done except increase Tim's debt by charging high fees?" I slipped an oversized football jersey over my head.

"He's kept him out of jail."

"He should be out of jail. He's not guilty."

Matt didn't respond.

"Don't tell me you think he's guilty?" I waited for an answer. "Matt?"

"I don't think you want to hear what I have to say."

"You think he's guilty?" I plopped down on the edge of the bed.

"No. I don't. But I think his trouble is of his own making. He lied about his alibi, and he's gotten himself way into debt."

I opened my mouth to speak, but Matt held up his hand. "The point is, the evidence is strictly circumstantial. Worst-case scenario, he's arrested. With a lawyer like Stan Margolis, he'll never be convicted."

"But unless the real murderer is uncovered, Tim's always going to have that stigma. People will assume he's guilty."

"I know, but right now that's the lesser of two evils."

"Not for me."

Matt snuggled next to me while grasping my hand. "I love you and I'm worried. Someone killed Mei because of what she knew. Someone tried to kill you because of what you could find out. I'm asking you to please drop it."

"I'm sorry, I can't." I jerked my hand away from Matt. "And I don't understand why you don't realize that."

Slamming the door behind me, I stormed out of the bedroom and stomped down the stairs to the kitchen. I flashed back to thoughts of my childhood. Frail and studious as a young boy, my brother excelled academically but lacked common sense and social skills.

I hated to admit it, but Detective Steve Wolfe was right. Although only a year older than Tim, I had always fought his battles.

I'd weathered other minor crises with Tim, but nothing had prepared me for this. How could Matt not see the importance of what I was doing?

Yet, the more I thought, the more I realized he couldn't act any other way. By nature, my husband was cautious and a worrier. As someone involved in medicine, he knew the thin line between life and death. If Matt put his life at risk, I'd want him to stop. Why should I be angry because he wanted me to stay out of danger?

Brandy trotted into the kitchen and rested his head on my lap.

"You always know when I'm upset, don't you?" I scratched behind his ears. As the dog moaned, I leaned down, burying my face in his fur. I sighed, realizing that I shouldn't have yelled at Matt. He was only acting that way because he loved me.

I trudged back up the stairs. Matt, propped up in bed, thumbed through a sports magazine, but he seemed to be staring at the ceiling. Archie was sprawled out next to him.

"I'm glad you're awake." I smiled.

"I'm sorry," Matt said. He tossed the magazine on the floor. "I shouldn't have criticized Tim. I know how you feel about your brother."

I nudged Archie off the bed and led the dog out of the room, shutting the door.

"What are you doing?" Matt asked.

"We'll discuss my brother some other time." I snuggled next to Matt, putting my hand on his thigh. "Right now, I've something else in mind."

★ ★ ★ ★ ★

The next morning, I phoned Roy Maxwell at the United States Fish and Wildlife Service.

"You're not going to believe what I saw at the animal auction."

"I'm sure you're going to tell me." He laughed, but I detected an edge to his voice.

"I spotted Clayton Malur passing money to one of the zookeepers from Rocky Cove."

"That's interesting."

Interesting? I'd expected more of a reaction.

"Malur's got to be up to no good," I said.

"I thought you attended the auction to get a feel for the place," he replied.

"That was my main intention."

"You'd be safer if you focused on past investigations of our agency and not on uncovering new operations. You're not a cop."

"I'm only reporting what I found to be suspicious. I'm not trying to be Eliot Ness. So, are you going to check it out?"

"Money passes hands at an animal auction for any number of reasons, most of which are not against the law. Besides, if I talk about future investigations, that could jeopardize our efforts."

"But—"

"Didn't you just hear me? I can't talk to you about current or future investigations. That means I can't tell you if we plan to check this out. Right now I'm late for a meeting, so we need to continue our conversation another time."

After hanging up, I remembered I didn't have a chance to tell him about my request for a woolly spider monkey. It was just as well. I'd wait until Malur got back to me. Then I'd ask Maxwell about setting up a sting.

Even though he didn't seem especially cooperative.

CHAPTER FORTY-FOUR

A woman screamed.

I had just arrived at the zoo. Whirling toward the right, I saw a crowd gathered by the wolf exhibit. Another spectator shrieked. Those with children hurried away.

I navigated my way around the throngs of people until the source of the horror came into view. A wolf stood near the glass partition, blood dripping from its mouth. A few feet away, another wolf, this one with a blood-stained muzzle, grasped a limp white object in its jaw.

My brother stood near the exhibit's employee entrance. I threaded my way through the crowd to reach him.

"What's going on, Tim?"

"Someone let loose three rabbits from our petting zoo. The wolves attacked and killed them. Two zookeepers heard cries from the crowd, but it was too late. The wolves reached the last rabbit seconds ago. It was Cookie, the most popular rabbit here."

Tim shook his head. "Look at the faces, especially parents and their kids. Predator and prey are nature's way, but this is not what zoo visitors are prepared to see. I can just imagine the calls and letters."

"Who could have done this?"

"Someone who wants to sabotage Saul Mandel. The trustees like things to run smoothly. The more trouble, the less likely the board is to appoint him as director permanently."

Saul was directing staff a few feet away. His normally flushed face was whitish-gray.

"I was meeting with Saul when he received the call about this," Tim said. "That's why I'm here. I figured he could use support."

By now, zoo staff had isolated the wolves into a separate section away from the public's eye. Two zookeepers swept and cleaned the exhibit, while security tried, with little success, to convince the swarms of curiosity seekers to move on.

Since there was nothing we could do, I told my brother about what I encountered in Ohio. "Tim, I saw Frank Taggart at Malur's Animal Auction."

"Frank Taggart? Why was he there?"

"I was hoping you'd know why. The auction owner handed him a wad of cash."

"That's bizarre. I can't imagine a reason."

"Rocky Cove doesn't deal with animal auctions, does it?"

"Of course not."

"What about Frank stealing zoo animals and selling them on his own? Matt said this was impossible. Is it?"

"Matt's right. All animals are accounted for. We keep detailed records. Each animal is tattooed with an International Species Inventory System number."

"What's that?"

"Zoos use it to monitor breeding. Each animal has its own number. And a necropsy is performed on any animal that dies, so you couldn't fake a death either."

"Could Frank be selling information?"

"I don't see how. He doesn't have access to data worth anything. Believe me, whatever Frank Taggart was doing, it has nothing to do with his position at Rocky Cove."

"But why would he be receiving cash at the auction?"

"My guess is, he's a private breeder on the side. That's where most auctions get their stock. I would never deal with scum like Malur, but it's not illegal."

"Is it possible Frank was at the zoo when Arlen McKenzie and Mei Lau were murdered?"

"I don't know. I guess it's possible. But as bird keeper, he only has the key to the bird exhibit and nursery. He doesn't have access to the rain forest. The same holds true for the snake room."

"Point taken." Suddenly a thought flashed through my mind. "Doesn't the zoo have any security video cameras, Tim?"

"We don't. Prior to the zoo director's death, this place was relatively crime free. About eleven months ago we experienced an incident of minor vandalism when graffiti was painted in the men's room, but McKenzie thought it wasn't enough to justify the cost of video surveillance."

"So, there's no security?"

"We have a guard at night. He's stationed in the booth by the main gate, but he does two tours of the zoo, one at midnight and the other around four in the morning. He doesn't go into any buildings, he just walks around. He checks the locks and makes sure there's no major problem with the animals."

"Wouldn't the guard be aware of who enters and exits?"

"No. We have three parking lots. His booth is located in the main one where visitors park. There are two other lots. One is for general staff, which is always locked when the zoo is closed. The other, a smaller lot, is for administration, including curators and a few other professionals, like the veterinarians and the wildlife nutritionist. We have keys to that gate so we can come and go as we please."

"Seems a little lax."

Tim shrugged then glanced at his watch. "Can you do me a favor?"

"Sure."

"I'm meeting with the zoo's head veterinarian in ten minutes." Tim handed me a chart he had been holding under his arm. "I don't want to lug this around. Could you take it to my office and put it on my desk?"

"Of course. Speaking of your office, how's Gary?"

"My reptile keeper?"

"That's the only Gary I know."

"He's back at work."

I was glad to hear he had returned to the zoo. Now I could question him about Mei.

Tim sighed. "I better go." He sounded tired and depressed.

"Isn't Barbara away at a conference until this weekend?" I asked. "Why don't you come to our place for dinner tonight?"

"A home-cooked meal from my sister? Really?"

"Let's not get carried away. Matt will throw something on the grill. I'll probably toss a salad and husk some corn."

"That counts as cooking. Seriously, I'd like company tonight. Something tells me this is going to be a rough day."

I nearly collided with Gary on my way into the herpetology building.

"How are you feeling? I heard you were sick."

"I'm better now." He grabbed the doorknob. "Thanks for asking."

"Do you have a minute? I need to talk to you." I pushed back a strand of hair that had fallen in front of my eyes.

He glanced at his watch. "I'm expected at the monitor lizard exhibit."

"Then let me get right to the point. Did Mei confide in you about her suspicions?"

"Suspicions?" He let go of the doorknob.

"Something bothering her? Maybe something illegal or unethical happening at the zoo?"

He shook his head.

"Are you sure? I thought if the two of you were close, she might have said something."

"Close? I hardly knew her. The first time we worked together was the day we removed eggs from the crocodile nest. What makes you think we were close?"

"When I saw her talking with you, she appeared agitated. It looked as if she was getting something off her chest."

"She was. But it had nothing to do with the zoo. She was complaining about a ticket she got at a speed trap about a mile from the zoo. I guess she needed to vent and I was here."

"But when Mei was bitten by the cobra, you acted strangely. Right after that, you took off from work. You've been gone a long time."

"I had the flu. I really was sick. As for my strange behavior, that's true. But not because of anything Mei told me. I've been fascinated with reptiles since I was a kid. I knew the danger, but I never witnessed a serious problem until two weeks ago."

He blushed as he stared at the ground. "First, the crocodile nearly attacked Mei, then the cobra bite. It made me gun-shy, or I guess I should say reptile-shy. When I returned to work, I discussed this with Tim. I'm better now." Gary glanced again at his watch. "I should go."

Once Gary left, I paraded up to the front desk, where Mary sat sorting the mail. "My brother asked me to put this in his office," I said, holding up the chart.

"His door is open as usual. Go right in."

There wasn't an empty space on the desk, so I placed the chart atop a stack of papers. Turning to leave, I spied three keys dangling from a large metal ring hanging from a hook near the door.

Despite Tim's insistence that he always carried the key to the snake room, knowing my brother's absentmindedness, I suspected it might be on that ring. Tim frequently spent time away from his office. What would prevent someone from stealing the key, making a copy, and returning the original?

I needed to find out if any of those keys unlocked the snake room door, and the only way to do that was to try them. I could ask Mary, but I didn't want to take the chance that she might mention it later to Tim. I shuddered. I didn't want to be in that small enclosure, surrounded by venomous reptiles, even if they were in tanks and couldn't get to me. Snakes gave me the creeps. Still, if one of the keys granted access to the area behind the terrariums, the list of murder suspects expanded.

I peeked outside at Mary, still engrossed in the mail. I grabbed the key ring, dropped it in my bag, and strolled out the door, calling good-bye.

I hurried through the public portion of the reptile exhibit until the staff entrance to the snake room came into view. Before inserting a key, I glanced over my shoulder at the crowds, looking out for zoo employees. They would know I didn't belong.

Certain no staff was in the immediate area, I attempted to unlock the door. The first key didn't fit. I twisted and jiggled the second key. Then I tried the third, but the lock still didn't open. The key for the snake room wasn't here.

"Kristy!" a voice called. "What the hell are you doing?"

Less than ten feet away stood my brother.

"I thought you were meeting with the zoo's veterinarian," I said.

"It was cancelled. Do you want to explain what you are doing?"

I explained why I'd taken the keys.

"Those three keys are for places I rarely go—the lecture hall, the uniform closet, and the old file room," Tim said. "Don't you think I'd want the police to know if another suspect had access to the snakes? That would take suspicion off me. You are so stubborn."

"I prefer to be called persistent," I said, trying to lighten the situation.

I was about to leave when Tim said, "At least some good came of your escapade."

"What do you mean?"

"Those keys reminded me that Mei was working in the file room. I completely forgot she had been transferring information from archived material onto our computers. I need to clear out her stuff so I can send someone else in there to continue her work."

"Stuff? What stuff?"

"Mei liked to spread out. Her desk in the herpetology office was overflowing, so she moved some of her personal belongings to a small desk in the file room."

I formed a crazy theory—a real long shot.

"Did the police know about this?" I asked.

"Probably not. As far as I'm aware, they only checked her work space in herpetology. Do you think it's important?"

My brother was a scholar and very intelligent, but I couldn't believe his lack of common sense. "It could be. Let's take a look."

The file room was located in the basement of the Education building. As Tim opened the door and flipped the switch, fluorescent light illuminated the area. I followed him down the steep, narrow stairs, carefully holding on to the banister. About a dozen metal file cabinets hugged the plaster walls.

"What are you looking for?" Tim asked as I headed toward an old wooden desk located in the far corner.

"I'll know if I see it." Mei referred to writing all her thoughts in her diary. I had assumed Mei's journal was that book. But now, thinking back, I realized the journal only contained information concerning work assignments—no thoughts or personal feelings. And Mei had never used the word *journal.* She specifically referred to the book as a diary.

Did another book exist?

After sneezing from the dust, I searched the first two desk drawers with no luck. Only memos, office supplies, and five candy wrappers. But when sorting through the third drawer, I found a book inscribed *My Diary.*

"Got it," I said.

"What's that?" Tim asked.

"Something that may hold clues to the murders."

"Shouldn't we contact the police?"

"Eventually."

"But, Kristy—"

"I've got to get back to the magazine office. I'll see you tonight, Tim. Don't forget. Dinner at my house at seven."

CHAPTER FORTY-FIVE

Stepping inside the *Animal Advocate* office, I heard an unfamiliar male voice as the door to the editor's room opened.

"I appreciate anything you can do. I'll talk to you next week," a man said as he exited Olivia's office.

Dressed in an open-neck blue oxford shirt and khaki slacks, his tanned skin and muscular physique led me to believe he spent lots of time outdoors. As he passed by and nodded, I guessed his age to be mid-fifties.

"Oh my God, the facial similarity is nearly identical. Is that who I think it is?" I asked Clara, although I was sure of the answer.

"Your competition's father. That's the senior Schuyler Adams."

"Was he here about his son?"

"I don't know. He was in Olivia's office for nearly an hour." Clara shook her head. "Olivia never spends that much time with one person."

Upset as I was, I realized fretting about Schuyler Adams wouldn't accomplish anything. Right now, my focus needed to be on Mei's diary. I marched to my cubicle and settled down with the book.

I flipped through the pages that appeared to contain lots of personal information, including comments about her friends and love life. There was some mention of her work at the zoo, but mostly as it related to her feelings toward other staff members. She described Saul and Tim as brilliant but absent-minded, and Amanda as serious and aloof. She thought Ginger was a jerk, and she claimed to hold a deep respect for Linda.

Then I came across an entry dated about eight weeks ago. Scribbled under the date was the following: "Need to talk to McKenzie about this. Nothing makes sense." Below that statement was a list of strange terms and numbers.

Rhynchopsitta terrisi—3—2
Amazona vittata—4—2
Anodorhynchus hyacinthinus—3—2
Poicephalus gulielmi—4—3
Nyctea scandiaca—6—2

Were these terms Latin? I wondered if Anodorhynchus hyacinthinus was a flower—a type of hyacinth? If these were botanicals, perhaps Amazona vittata referred to a plant from the Amazon region. Whatever they were, they sounded scientific.

Who would be familiar with science terminology?

A doctor.

Since Matt wasn't thrilled with my involvement, I phoned Abby.

"Hi, Mom. I'm a little busy right now."

"You also sound down. Is anything wrong?"

"Jason and I had a fight."

Damn! "Did you break up?"

"I don't want to talk. I have to go—"

"Wait. Don't hang up. I called for another reason."

I told her about the list in Mei's diary. "These words may be Latin or Greek. Maybe you know what they mean?"

"Fax me a copy. I have two patients to see, but after that I'll look it over."

After faxing Abby the information, I continued reading the diary, finally coming to an entry dated a week before Arlen

McKenzie's death. The writing dealt with Mei's thoughts concerning the late zoo director.

It read: "A zoo director's job is about leadership. And leadership is about character. I don't know Arlen McKenzie personally. I can only go by what others have said, and I'm aware of how unreliable that can be. Something is terribly wrong at Rocky Cove. I think I know what's going on, but I'm not sure. I need to make contact with McKenzie and tell him what I discovered. Then I'll know if my theory is right, and I'll know what type of man he is."

Later that afternoon, Clara barged into my cubicle. "This just came over the fax. It's for you, Kristy."

"Thanks." I read the message.

"It doesn't make sense." Clara hovered by my desk. "Do you understand it? Is this important?"

"I understand it, and it is important."

Clara lingered.

"Thanks for bringing this to me." I smiled.

Clara left.

I stared down at the fax. Abby had sent back the list. Next to each term she had written:

Maroon-fronted parrot—Rhynchopsitta terrisi—3—2
Puerto Rican parrot—Amazona vittata—4—2
Hyacinth macaw—Anodorhynchus hyacinthinus—3—2
Jardine's parrot—Poicephalus gulielmi—4—3
Snowy owl—Nyctea scandiaca—6—2

At the bottom of the paper, she had scribbled: "These birds are all endangered species. But I have absolutely no idea what the numbers represent. Do you?"

I hadn't a clue.

Chapter Forty-Six

It was one of those quick summer storms. The driving rain pelted the cedar shingles on the house. Gazing out the big bay window, I knew the local roads would soon flood as the rain came down faster than the storm drains could handle.

When Abby arrived, I breathed a sigh of relief.

"It's like a monsoon out there," Abby shook off the water. "Is Uncle Tim here yet?"

"I expect him any moment." I glanced out the window again but didn't express my concerns. Tim was a horrible driver, always preoccupied with his work instead of paying attention to the road.

"Thanks for inviting me to dinner, Mom. Can I help?"

"Obviously, the barbecue has been moved indoors. Let's go chop some vegetables for the salad."

"I apologize for my abruptness this morning," Abby said. "I didn't want to discuss Jason."

"I shouldn't have pushed."

"Jason and I are talking again. We're having dinner the night after the bar exam to see if we can work out our problems. He wants to move to Santa Fe. That's where his family is from. His uncle is president of the local bank and offered him a job in their legal department. If he takes it, he wants me to go with him." Abby sighed. "I want to stay here."

"I hope it works out," I said, afraid my face showed my feelings. I liked having my only child nearby. But what I wanted most was her happiness. She'd need to make her decision without input from me.

I began chopping onions with a vengeance.

Tim had been expected at seven. After seven-thirty, I gazed out the bay window. The rain had let up a little, but the slick on the roads could still be dangerous.

Matt wandered into the living room and rested his arm on my shoulder. "I'm sure everything is okay. You know your brother. He probably got busy at work and lost track of time."

By eight, still no Tim. I nervously nibbled a potato chip. "He should have called. Something is wrong."

"Have you called him?" Abby plopped down on the sofa.

"No one picks up the phones at the zoo after hours. I left a voice mail message on the odd chance he'd listen before he leaves. I wish he had a cell phone."

"He doesn't have one?" Abby asked. "Everyone under ninety has a cell phone."

"He had one but lost it last week and hasn't replaced it yet. He's lost three so far this year. If it doesn't look like a reptile, he can't keep track."

Matt smiled. "Knowing Tim, I'd guess an emergency popped up."

I phoned Tim at home, hoping he'd stopped off on the way, but I got sent to voice mail.

"Barbara's away on a business trip, right?" Matt asked.

I nodded, then set to work on a crossword puzzle but couldn't concentrate. I rose frequently to look out the window.

The phone rang. Matt grabbed it.

"Not interested." My husband hung up and turned to me. "That was a home remodeling telemarketer."

"I think we should contact the police," I said.

"About the telemarketer?"

"No. About my brother. They'll know if there have been any accidents."

"Why don't I drive to the zoo?" Matt pulled the car keys out of his pocket. "They have twenty-four-hour security. I'll ask the guard at the front gate to check if Tim is still there."

"Zoo security didn't help the night of McKenzie's murder," I said.

Before Matt could respond, the dogs, barking loudly, rushed out of the living room and into the kitchen.

I dashed into the kitchen and peeked out the window. "It's Tim."

"What happened?" I swung open the side door.

"Sorry. We had another crisis at the zoo and I completely forgot about dinner." Tim dripped water on the floor as he made his way to the table. He yanked out a chair and dropped down. "Someone sent an anonymous letter to the Board of Trustees. He or she accused Saul Mandel of plagiarism on his doctoral thesis."

Matt wiped up the water. "That's a damn serious charge."

"I know, but it's not true. Saul absolutely denies it."

"Did the letter include proof?" I asked.

"None at all. The writer claims proof will be sent within the next few weeks, but several of the trustees are overreacting."

"But if it can't be proven—"

"Doesn't matter. At the next meeting, the board planned to appoint Saul as director permanently."

"You think now they won't?"

"Not only will the appointment be postponed, but one of the trustees is so upset about the possibility of bad publicity that he's contacted other board members. He wants Saul out as acting director."

"Before he gets a chance to prove himself?"

"You may be innocent until proven guilty in a court of law,

but that doesn't necessarily hold true in the job market."

"So what will happen?" Matt switched on the burner under a large pot of water for the corn.

"I think he'll stay as acting director. Luckily, the majority of trustees want evidence of plagiarism before taking action. They're afraid of a lawsuit. As for the permanent position, it doesn't look good. The board doesn't like controversy."

"I guess you're right," I reluctantly agreed.

"Anyway, that's why I'm late. When Saul addresses the Board of Trustees next week, he'll be questioned on this issue. We both stayed tonight to determine the best way to handle the situation. I hope you weren't worried."

"Let's take our coffee into the den, Mom," Abby said. The clock read almost midnight. Tim had departed ten minutes ago. Matt, who had an early-morning appointment, was on his way up to bed.

"Good idea. I could use a second cup. It helps me think." I poured a refill, then accompanied my daughter into the other room. Before settling down on one of the comfy recliners, I opened the three windows. There was a delightful breeze and I loved the smell of the night air after a rain storm.

"So?" Abby said.

"So what?"

"You said coffee helps you think. What are you thinking? I noticed at dinner you were unusually quiet."

"What if Saul Mandel did plagiarize his doctoral thesis?" I said. "Wouldn't that give Saul another motive for murder?"

"Yeah, it would."

"And what about Mei's suspicions about wrongdoings at the zoo? Could that be related to the plagiarism charges?"

"Uncle Tim seemed to think the accusation is ridiculous."

"Tim understands reptiles. When it comes to people, he's always been naive."

CHAPTER FORTY-SEVEN

Friday night was the memorial service for Mei Lau. Held at a turn of the nineteenth century gray stone Methodist Church, Abby and I slipped into the last pew as the service began.

Abby leaned over and whispered in my ear, "Tell me again. Why am I attending a funeral for a woman I don't know?"

"This is not a funeral. It's a memorial service. You're here to observe. I'm hoping we gain insight into a reason for Mei's murder."

"I'll be sure to pay attention for hidden clues in the eulogy."

I shot my daughter a withering look while handing her a hymnal. Still, I knew her sarcasm masked how upset she was. Abby was only a few years older than Mei. The young woman's death only emphasized her own vulnerability.

When everyone rose to sing "Amazing Grace," I noticed my brother seven rows in front, sitting next to Amanda Devereux. Also in the pew were Linda Sancho, Saul Mandel, and Ginger Hart.

I wondered about Tim and Amanda sitting together. The police considered my brother to be the prime suspect in Arlen McKenzie's murder. Did Amanda think the same thing? If so, how could she stay so calm and civil? Not to mention the fact that on her right side sat Ginger Hart, her husband's lover.

After the service, Mei's aunt received visitors in the fellowship hall. Dressed in a simple black suit with black stockings and flats, she wore her gray hair in a small bun atop her head. I guessed her height to be about four-eleven and her weight under one hundred pounds.

"I'm so sorry," I said. "I don't know if you remember me. I was your niece's English teacher."

"Of course. She talked about you all the time. You were a godsend after her parents died. It's so thoughtful of you to come here tonight." Mei's aunt cried softly. "Why would anyone do this to that poor child?"

A woman who looked to be Mei's age wrapped her arms around the aunt. "I'm sure the police will catch the person who did this." She spoke with a slight Jamaican accent.

Mei's aunt regained her composure. An elderly couple approached to pay respects. Abby and I offered condolences again and moved on.

The church's women's guild provided refreshments.

"I want something cold," Abby said. "I wish they had bottled water, but I think I'll have to settle for punch."

As Abby took off in the direction of the punch bowl, I wandered toward the other side of the room where there was a short line for coffee. Much to my relief, my brother and his colleagues had left at the end of the service. I didn't want to meet up with Ginger tonight. My inquiries at Treasures of Zeus had angered the public relations coordinator, and although I had no intention of backing down, a memorial service was no place for a confrontation.

I had finished pouring coffee into a cup when a hand lightly touched my arm. "Hi. I'm Sondra Champion. Mei's roommate."

I turned and faced the young woman who had embraced Mei's aunt a few minutes ago. Tall and willowy, with skin the color of café au lait, she was smiling, but her dark eyes radiated sadness.

"I'm Kristy Farrell. I taught Mei—"

"I know. When you introduced yourself to Mei's aunt, I recognized the name. Mei was so happy running into you at the zoo."

"I felt the same way about seeing her." Wondering if Mei had confided in Sondra, I zoomed right to the point. "Did Mei ever talk to you about trouble at the zoo?"

"Trouble? What type of trouble?"

"I don't know, but something bothered her. Did she ever mention her work?"

"Once in a while she'd talk about her research projects, but to tell the truth I never listened that carefully. Mei could get technical. I'm a graduate student in American history. Talk to me about the United States Constitution, not the DNA of zebras."

"Did she ever speak about the people she worked with?"

"Only the public relations coordinator. I believe her name was Ginger. Mei didn't like her, although I think they got along okay. Oh, once she mentioned Arlen McKenzie."

"Really? What did she say about him?"

"That she'd soon discover if he had any substance or whether he was all show like everyone claimed."

"After McKenzie's murder, did you notice a change in Mei's behavior? Was she nervous? Afraid of anything?"

"Now that you mention it, she did seem jittery, especially the night before she was killed. I was headed to Boston the next day to do research for my thesis. I was a bit preoccupied and didn't think anything of it at the time, but, yes, her mind was elsewhere. She seemed on edge. Do you think that's related to her death?"

"I do, but I don't know how."

"Is there anything I can do to help?"

"Maybe. Are Mei's belongings still at your place?"

Sondra nodded. "The police searched but they didn't find

anything of interest. I told Mei's aunt she could collect the things any time she wanted, but I don't know when she'll feel up to it."

"Could I take a peek sometime?"

"Sure. How about now? I only live a few minutes from here. You could follow me home."

"Great. My daughter is with me tonight. Okay if she comes?"

"Comes where?" Abby said. "They ran out of punch and I didn't want to wait until they made more. Oh, I see iced tea."

"No time. We're leaving now." I grabbed my daughter's arm, introduced her to Sondra, and explained that we were going to search Mei's old room. "Maybe we'll find something that will help."

We exited the building and were in the parking lot when Sondra said, "I don't know if this is important, but the Saturday before the murder, a woman stopped by the apartment asking for Mei. When I told her Mei wouldn't return until late that evening, she seemed upset. I asked if she wanted to leave a message, but she said no."

"Did the woman give her name?" Abby asked.

Sondra nodded. "Linda Sancho."

"Mei's room is to the left," Sondra said as we entered the living room in the small apartment. "It's the way she left it when she went to work that last morning. I'm afraid it's a little messy."

I smiled, thinking of Mei's desk at school. "I can imagine."

"To make matters worse, I'm a neat freak."

"Were there problems living together?"

"I'd pick up after Mei in the beginning, especially since we shared the bathroom. We argued occasionally, but finally I mellowed." Sondra's eyes filled with tears. "I don't have to worry about that anymore, do I? Shows you how petty most problems are."

My eyes moistened as I impulsively hugged Sondra.

She led us into Mei's bedroom. Papers, books, and assorted trinkets littered the top of her desk and dresser, and clothes were strewn across her unmade bed.

"Now that the police are finished, I'll clean up in here. I want the room presentable when her aunt comes."

"Where's her computer?"

"The police have it. But I don't think they found anything on it. I gave the receipt to her aunt." Sondra paused. "I'll leave you two alone to search. If you need anything, I'll be in the kitchen."

Sondra wandered out, leaving the door ajar. I searched the corner desk while Abby rummaged through the dresser. I wasn't sure what we were looking for, but hoped something would pop up.

"No luck yet?" Sondra strolled into the room about forty minutes later with a mug in her hand. Steam rose from the top.

"Nothing. We've looked everywhere. I guess we'll go."

"Would you like something to drink first?"

"Is that coffee I smell?"

"I just made a pot. Do you want some?"

"I never refuse coffee. I'll have a quick cup. Black. No milk or sugar."

"You drink too much coffee, Mom."

Once in the kitchen, I spotted more than a dozen cookbooks on the shelf near the refrigerator.

"Who likes to cook?" I asked.

"Both of us. But most of the books are mine." She handed me a mug. "Mei got most of her recipes off the Internet. She kept them in that folder at the end, the one with all the papers sticking out. She never organized them, but she could always find what she wanted."

Sondra grabbed the folder, opened it, and began straightening out the papers, one by one. "Two nights before her murder, she made a delicious penne ala vodka with peas and artichokes, using this recipe."

Abby, who stood next to Sondra, stared down at the folder. "Mom, you need to see this."

I looked. Scribbled on the bottom of the sauce-stained recipe was the following:

Rhynchopsitta terrisi—3—2
Amazona vittata—4—2
Anodorhynchus hyacinthinus—3—2
Poicephalus gulielmi—4—3
Nyctea scandiaca—6—2

555-3287

"Do you know why this list is here?" I asked, instantly recognizing it from Mei's diary.

Sondra examined the paper. "No idea."

"Do you recognize the phone number?"

Sondra shook her head.

I pulled the phone out of my bag and punched in the number on the paper. After four rings, I reached voice mail, where I listened to the following message:

"You have reached Linda Sancho."

CHAPTER FORTY-EIGHT

My cell phone trilled as I drove Abby home from Sondra's apartment. I glanced down at the number. "It's Tim. Why would he be calling me at this hour?"

"It's not even ten. Why don't you answer and find out?"

"This is not good," I said to Abby after I finished talking with my brother. "Tim heard a rumor from a friend who works in the courts. The district attorney is convening a grand jury on the zoo murders on Monday. Tim's the target."

"Do you think they'll indict him?"

"Yes. The way the system is set up, a prosecutor could convince a grand jury to indict a ham sandwich. And the circumstantial evidence is damning."

"But I thought the district attorney was super cautious."

"Obviously Detective Wolfe convinced him to go for it. I know Tim is innocent, but how do you prove it? I've reached a dead end and time is running out."

"Sometimes the best thing you can do is give your mind a rest," Abby advised.

"Easier said than done."

"Stop thinking about it. Spend the weekend doing something completely different, and on Monday you'll be refreshed and ready to tackle the problem again."

Later that night, while Matt snored contentedly, I stared into darkness as dozens of thoughts squirreled through my mind. The more I investigated, the more frustrated I became. All five suspects had strong motives. Nobody's alibi was ironclad. I couldn't make heads or tails out of Mei's diary. Linda's name constantly popped up. Was Ginger a psycho serial killer? How drunk was Amanda? Were Saul and Tim the only ones who had access to both the snake room and the rain forest?

I turned over, pushing up my pillows. Abby was right. I needed to clear my mind. Maybe then, I'd come up with an idea.

The next day, determined to give my mind a rest from wildlife smuggling, endangered species, and murder, I drove to a nearby shopping mall. At the last minute I wanted to find a dress to wear to a theater production and cocktail reception that evening.

After trying on a horizontal black and white striped dress that made me look like a zebra, I spotted the perfect blue sheath. I spent the remainder of the day browsing in the mall, finally wandering into a bookstore where I spotted a book about poisons. While thumbing through the table of contents, I discovered a section on snake venom.

According to the author, the venom of each species is unique. Russell's vipers are primarily hemotoxic, attacking the victim's circulatory system, destroying capillary walls, causing internal bleeding, and breaking down tissue, often resulting in kidney failure. Victims may bleed from the eyes and mouth. The cobra, on the other hand, is filled with neurotoxins that block nerve impulses to muscles, resulting in paralysis of the heart and lungs. A few snakes, such as the Mohave rattlesnake, contain a combination of both.

Whether or not death occurred after a bite depended on a number of variables including the victim's age, size, and health, as well as the species of the snake and the amount of venom injected. That last element, the amount of toxins released, depended on specific factors, one being when the snake ate its last meal. A snake injects more venom on an empty stomach than on a full one.

I shut the book and rubbed my forehead. To maximize the chances of Mei receiving a lethal dose, the murderer needed to ensure the cobra hadn't eaten. Who controlled the reptile feeding schedule? The answer was the curator of herpetology, my brother Tim.

CHAPTER FORTY-NINE

"What a day!" Matt strolled through the side door and dropped down on a chair next to the kitchen table.

"Problems at work?" I asked.

"No. Just the usual busy Saturday." He glanced at his watch. "I guess we better dress soon for that thing tonight."

"That thing? Don't you mean the play and fundraising reception?"

"Yeah. That thing. I suppose it's too late to get out of it."

"Of course we have to go. Barbara is co-chair of the committee, and we promised her. She's been nagging us to attend her functions, and we've always had an excuse."

"You couldn't think of one this time? At least we have time for dinner. Come on." He started up the stairs. "Let's get this over with."

"It's a play, Matt, not a dental appointment."

"I know, but—"

"But nothing." I folded my arms in front of my chest. "Tim wants to stay home tonight, but Barbara convinced him they need to keep up appearances. Tim needs us for moral support."

"Wow! You look great." Matt straightened his tie as I descended the stairs in my new blue dress.

I smiled, knowing I looked good but that I'd look better minus twenty pounds.

"What a shame we can't ditch this affair and go out for a

romantic dinner." Matt winked. "Followed by an even more romantic night at home."

"We can accomplish half your wish. We have time for the romantic dinner."

We dined at our favorite Italian restaurant then drove to the theater, located on the old Cranston estate, which dated back to the Revolutionary War. The league had converted the stable into a small theater with the purpose of providing an outlet for Long Island's playwrights and performers. To raise funds, the group frequently held cocktail receptions in conjunction with new plays.

After the third act ended, Matt and I strolled with the rest of the theater patrons through the sculptured garden to the manor house. The reception was taking place in the great hall, a stately room with mahogany walls adorned with oil paintings of fox hunts and English gardens. The crowd attending tonight's affair included many of Long Island's movers and shakers.

"How long do we have to stay?" Matt asked.

"We just arrived. We'll have a drink, mingle, make small talk . . . Oh, I never expected to see her here."

Linda Sancho stood only a few feet away. This was the first time I'd seen her wearing makeup. Although she wasn't beautiful, she looked elegant in a tea-length cream-colored lace dress, her black hair piled atop her head. Next to her was a man, slight of build, with black wavy hair and large dark eyes.

"Come on, Matt. I want to introduce you." We approached the couple. "Hello, Linda. Did you enjoy the play?"

Linda's eyes widened, first appearing startled, and for a fleeting moment, frightened.

"Oh, yes," she said, finally acknowledging me.

Before Linda could introduce the man to her right, he stuck out his arm for a handshake. "I'm Linda's husband, Manuel Sancho. Do you work at Rocky Cove, too?"

"No, but I'm spending time there writing an article for *Animal Advocate* magazine."

Linda crumbled a napkin in her hand. "There's Evan," she said to her husband. "Didn't you want to see him?"

"Yes. I need to speak to him." Manuel Sancho smiled. "Please excuse us. I'm sure we'll meet again."

"I don't understand." I shook my head as Matt and I maneuvered through the crowd to the bar. No pomegranate martinis were available, so I ordered a red wine and a scotch for Matt. "Linda obviously didn't want us to talk to her husband. But why?"

"What are you whispering about so seriously?" someone behind me said.

Recognizing Barbara's voice, I turned and faced my brother and sister-in-law.

"We ran into Linda Sancho and her husband," I said. "I didn't expect to see them here."

"It's business," Barbara explained. "Manuel Sancho's law firm is a major contributor to the performing arts."

"Is that who I think it is?" Tim motioned toward the middle of the room, then turned toward the bar and ordered a scotch.

Barbara nodded. "It certainly is."

About a half dozen men gathered around a woman in a slinky black dress and silver stiletto sandals.

"Ginger Hart. What's she doing here?" I asked.

"She's dating the assistant producer of the theater group."

"Really? I can't imagine her dating an assistant anything."

"This assistant is heir to a fortune. His family owns real estate, manufacturing plants, restaurants, a major retail chain . . . He could buy and sell a dozen production companies."

Matt chuckled.

As I glanced in Ginger's direction, I noticed the public relations coordinator appeared to be the center of attention amid her little group. Ginger was a woman who never underestimated her own appeal and her effect on men.

"By the way, did you see Amanda? She's here tonight," Tim said, grabbing his drink from the bartender.

"Amanda Devereux?" I scanned the room.

Barbara discreetly nodded toward the right side of the hall. "There she is. Doesn't she look fabulous?"

Amanda wore a peach cocktail suit and moved effortlessly from group to group, stopping only for the briefest conversation. She worked the room like a seasoned politician.

"Amanda always attended these functions with Arlen. I think he used it as a way to network, but she really seems to enjoy the arts. It's my guess she plans to continue her involvement with the group." Barbara waved to a couple near the cheese and fruit display. "I need to say hello to the Weinbergs. I'll see you later."

"Since I'm not on call tonight, I'm getting another scotch," Matt said. While he tried to grab the bartender's attention, Tim pulled me aside.

"I hinted to Amanda about Frank Taggart attending the animal auction," he said.

"Hinted? You're the most unsubtle person I know. How did you hint?"

"I told her you saw Frank at Malur's Animal Auction."

"Why would you come right out and tell her, Tim? What if they're in cahoots? Did you think of that?"

Tim's face flushed. "Amanda is rich and highly regarded in her field. I doubt she'd be involved in some petty scam."

"But even so, why would you come right out and tell her?"

"Because she's probably the only one at the zoo he talks to. If he's an animal breeder on the side and sells to Malur, I thought he might have mentioned it to her. Unfortunately, he didn't. She knows nothing about his life beyond the zoo."

"Is she going to question him?"

"Absolutely not. Whatever he does, Amanda is adamant it has nothing to do with Rocky Cove. She agrees with me that he probably has a side business as a breeder. She doesn't understand how anyone can deal with the likes of Malur, but she feels Frank's activities on his own time are his own business. And as his boss, she has no legal right to interfere."

"She sounds more like a lawyer than a curator."

"I can see her point," said Matt, who had returned to the conversation with his second scotch of the evening, third if you counted the one at dinner. "I'm sure Amanda just wants to be careful. People sue so easily."

"She also asked if you're sure you saw Frank at the animal auction," Tim said. "Could it have been someone who looked like him?"

"No. It was Frank. I'm sure."

A waitress approached with a tray of hors d'oeuvres. While Tim and Matt chose from an assortment of lobster rolls and shrimp puffs, I headed to the ladies' room. I began rummaging through my bag for a comb when the door swung open and Linda Sancho barged in.

"Kristy, I apologize if I seemed rude earlier. My husband doesn't know about my involvement with the SANAN Society. I was afraid you might say something. If we run into each other again, please don't mention it."

Before I could respond, Linda exited.

"Linda Sancho followed me into the restroom." I'd joined up with Matt on the far side of the room. Tim had gone off in search of Barbara. "Linda wants to keep her membership in the animal rights organization a secret from her husband. My theory keeps growing stronger."

"What theory?"

"That she murdered McKenzie because he's blackmailing her," I said, slightly exasperated that Matt couldn't remember what I'd said. "I always thought her vulnerability was within the zoological community. Now I think McKenzie threatened to tell Linda's husband about her involvement with the animal rights group. Manuel Sancho is up for a partnership in his law firm, Webster, Mayer, and Hammond. It may have to do with that."

Matt let out a low whistle. "If Linda's past activities involved a radical group of any sorts, her husband could kiss that partnership good-bye. Webster, Mayer, and Hammond represent old money. I went to college with the son of one of the senior partners so I know a little about the law firm. It's super conservative. The last thing Manuel Sancho needs is to be embroiled in a controversy."

As Matt headed to the end of the bar to grab some peanuts, Tim returned without Barbara.

"I'm glad I have you alone for a minute," he said.

"What's the matter?"

"Barbara doesn't know about the grand jury. She has no idea that the District Attorney wants to indict me. Please don't mention it."

"But you can't keep that from her. What if it was leaked to the newspapers?"

"My attorney would know before that happens. If so, I'll tell her. Here she comes. Matt's with her. Please, Kristy, don't say anything."

"Kristy, I wanted to let you know that Professor Layne is here." Barbara pointed toward the north side of the room.

"Good. You mentioned she might come tonight." I turned to face my husband. "You remember Professor Layne, don't you, Matt? Back when I was teaching, I brought her into the high school as a guest lecturer on the theater. I want to say hello."

I also wanted to get away from Tim and Barbara. I had no desire to be part of my brother's deception.

Matt said, "I'll stay here."

"Me too," Tim said. "Professor Layne works with Barbara on the league's fundraising. She's too much of a character for me. Nice lady, but weird. Definitely weird."

CHAPTER FIFTY

Professor Alicia Layne tended to stand out in a crowd. A large woman, tonight she wore a caftan-style cocktail dress of deep purple, making her look like a giant plum. Her short silver-streaked black hair was adorned with a purple orchid.

Aside from teaching drama at a local college, the professor performed in summer stock theater. She most recently appeared in Noel Coward's *Blithe Spirit* as the medium, Madame Arcadi, a role suiting her perfectly.

I threaded my way through the throngs of people. To my surprise, I found the professor engaged in conversation with Amanda Devereux.

I said hello to both, then added, "I haven't seen you in ages, Professor Layne."

"Kristy Farrell. It's so good to see you." Professor Layne extended her arms for a hug, engulfing me in waves of purple. "I heard you left teaching? What have you been doing?"

"I write for *Animal Advocate* magazine. That's how I met Dr. Devereux. I interviewed her for an article."

Professor Layne motioned toward Amanda with her hand. There was a ring on each finger. "Did you know that Amanda is a former student of mine? I still believe my theater arts class provided her with the confidence she has today. Do you remember, Amanda? You were such a mousy thing."

Amanda smiled, remaining perfectly poised. I winced. Tact had never been Alicia Layne's strong suit.

A waiter with a tray of champagne offered drinks.

"I shouldn't, but I will." Professor Layne reached for a glass. "I have high blood pressure, but I adore champagne."

Since I was tonight's designated driver, my one red wine would be enough. I refused the champagne. Amanda hesitantly grabbed a glass.

Professor Layne gulped down half of her drink. "Dee-licious. Do you remember when you acted in some of the productions on campus, Amanda? You were quite good."

Amanda smiled. "I'll never forget it."

Professor Layne swallowed another two gulps, emptying her glass and placing it on the tray of an unsuspecting waitress passing by. I noticed Amanda hadn't touched her drink. Had her alcohol problem ceased since she no longer had the stress of a philandering husband?

"You had talent and interest in so many areas, but ornithology was always your first love, wasn't it?" Professor Layne said to Amanda.

"Yes." Amanda's gaze veered away. "Oh, I see someone I must speak with. Please excuse me."

Once the zoo curator left, Professor Layne shook her head. "Poor Amanda. I keep telling her to get in touch with her feelings. She holds everything inside. Always poised and proper."

I questioned this image of Amanda. She had lost her cool the night of McKenzie's murder, when she drank so much that staff drove her home. And a few evenings before the murder, Amanda had aggressively confronted her husband about his relationship with Ginger—right in front of Mei Lau. But even Mei claimed that it was out of character. I had to admit, when I saw Amanda sitting at Mei's memorial service between Ginger Hart, her husband's lover, and my brother, the number one murder suspect, I was surprised at her self-control. Amanda Devereux was an enigma.

Professor Layne reached out, snatching another glass of champagne from the tray of a nearby waitress. "It's not good. At our last fundraiser I told her to stop acting like the Queen of England and react like any normal wife would in the same situation."

"What situation?"

"Oh, that's right. You weren't here. Didn't your sister-in-law tell you?"

"Tell me what?"

"Arlen McKenzie was hitting on her?"

"Hitting her? Do you mean physically abusing her?"

"No. Not hitting her. Hitting *on* her. He was making a play for her." Professor Layne winked. "He was flirting shamelessly."

"He was flirting with his wife?"

"No, no. He was flirting with your sister-in-law." Professor Layne made a sweeping gesture with her arms.

"Let me get this straight. Arlen McKenzie was flirting with Barbara?"

"That's right. And Amanda acted as if nothing was going on."

"What did Barbara do?"

"I really hate to say."

I didn't believe that for a minute. The Alicia Layne I knew loved to gossip. "Please tell me what Barbara did."

"Well, I suppose it's okay to talk. In the beginning she flirted back. She went along for a little while, but as Arlen became more . . . shall we say amorous? . . . Barbara tried to avoid him."

"Did Tim notice?"

"My dear, everyone noticed." The professor waved a jeweled hand in another sweeping gesture. "You couldn't help it."

"Did Tim say or do anything?"

"He mostly looked embarrassed."

"That's it?"

"Well, at one point, when Arlen admired Barbara's necklace
. . . a little too closely, if you get my drift . . . your brother's face
turned redder than a Bloody Mary, but he never said a word."

"I can't believe this."

"At least your brother showed emotion. Amanda stood there
looking like a new addition to Mount Rushmore."

"What's bothering you?" Matt asked during the drive home. I'd
been silent for most of the ride.

"I'm getting discouraged. The more I delve into the two
murders, the more I discover information to implicate my
brother."

"What do you mean?"

I told Matt about Arlen McKenzie and Barbara. "That just
adds to Tim's motive to want McKenzie gone," I said.

"True. But all the suspects had good motives. It seems everyone who knew McKenzie hated him."

"There's more. I read in a book today that a snake produces
less venom on an empty stomach than after a meal. Tim would
know that."

"That's common knowledge for anyone involved in zoology. I
could have told you the same thing. I'm pretty sure all the
suspects would be aware of that, not just Tim."

"Yes, but Tim could manipulate the cobra's feeding schedule."

"He's not the only one. There's someone else who'd be aware
of the snake's mealtime and would also have a say in the matter."

"Of course." I banged my hand on the steering wheel. "Matt,
you're right. I was so focused on Tim, I forgot about the person
involved with the diets of all the zoo animals. The wildlife
nutritionist."

Linda Sancho.

CHAPTER FIFTY-ONE

"When the phone rings, I expect to hear my brother calling from jail."

While Matt was upstairs, still asleep, Abby and I sat in the kitchen, savoring early Sunday morning cups of coffee and warm breakfast buns. The aroma of cinnamon filled the air.

"I wouldn't worry. I talked with Jason last night." Abby bit into her cinnamon bun and finished chewing. "He said the evidence against Uncle Tim is good but not great. Enough to win an indictment but not the trial that follows."

"And Jason has so much legal experience," I said dryly.

"He has graduated from law school, Mom."

I refilled my cup. "By the way, how are things between you and Jason?"

Abby shrugged. "I told you. We're waiting until he takes the bar exam to sit down and discuss our problems. I'm glad I have some time before making my decision. I'm sure I can get a veterinarian job in New Mexico. If competition from the health and wellness center is as tough as anticipated, Dad may need to cut staff. If I leave here, it might make things easier."

"Don't base your decision on that."

"I don't really want to leave. All my friends and family are here. I love Dad's veterinary hospital and—"

"Do you love Jason?"

"Yes." Abby smiled. "As I said, there's lots to consider. But not this morning."

"Okay. Then let's get back to the murders. The most damning evidence is that Tim has keys to both the snake room and the rain forest."

"So does what's his name . . . Saul Mandel. His motive is strong too."

"I know. Linda also has strong motivation, and her name pops up in the strangest places. But Tim swears she doesn't have access to the snake room. Neither does Amanda or Ginger." I sighed. "If Tim didn't commit the murders, by process of elimination, Saul must be guilty. Tim doesn't believe it, but I can't think of any other possibility."

"Unless someone else had gotten hold of the keys."

"That's what I'd like to believe, but Tim insists he keeps the keys to the snake room on him at all times. So do his reptile keepers. He claims Saul keeps the master keys locked up too, and no one else has access."

"Does Uncle Tim keep the keys with him when he sleeps?"

"I don't know for sure, but I would guess not." I smiled at the thought.

"That widens your suspect list."

"What do you mean?"

"Ask yourself who wouldn't want Uncle Tim to lose his job? Who would also have access to the keys at night? Who could easily sneak out and have a copy made? Your answer is Aunt Barbara."

"No way. Stretching my imagination as far as it will go, and this *is* a stretch, I can envision Barbara injecting poison in Arlen McKenzie's arm. But there's no way she'd handle a live cobra."

"Listen to my theory," Abby pressed. "You're not going to like it. Uncle Tim wouldn't kill Arlen McKenzie just to keep his job, right?"

"Of course not."

"But I think he'd kill for one reason. To protect Aunt Barbara. Suppose Mei discovered that Barbara murdered Mc-Kenzie. Tim would kill Mei to keep her from talking. It has the makings of a Greek tragedy. She kills for him. He kills to protect her."

"You have a flair for the dramatic."

"Aunt Barbara reminds me of Lady Macbeth. Although Aunt Barbara is not as earthy. She'd never use a dagger. Too messy. Poison is her method."

"Stop it. This is ridiculous. Tim would never kill anyone no matter what the motive. And Lady Macbeth never committed murder. She convinced her husband to do it." The English teacher in me couldn't help correcting Abby.

"I know that, Mom." Abby sounded exasperated. "I only meant Aunt Barbara is stronger and more ruthless than Uncle Tim."

"That's not a joke?"

"No, I'm serious. As Uncle Tim's wife, Aunt Barbara is no stranger to Arlen McKenzie. I'm sure he'd agree to meet with her."

My daughter had a point. I flashed back to the theater benefit and Alicia Layne's gossip concerning McKenzie and Barbara. I conjured up images of my sister-in-law arranging a clandestine meeting with the zoo director.

"I know it seems farfetched, but the more you think about it, the more logical it becomes," Abby continued. "Look where Aunt Barbara works. A pharmaceutical firm that manufactures medicines, some of which contain venom."

"But she works in the office. The labs are in a different community."

"I bet she still has access to snake venom."

Suddenly, I remembered. "Your scenario won't work. Barbara has an alibi for the McKenzie murder. She attended a retirement dinner that night."

"An alibi that hasn't been checked. If Aunt Barbara wasn't a suspect at the time, I'm guessing the police wouldn't have bothered to verify her whereabouts."

"I don't believe this theory of yours, but I'll find out what time Barbara left the retirement dinner."

"How will you do that?" Abby drained her coffee cup.

"I'll call her office midday tomorrow. She always goes to lunch with the pharmaceutical representatives on Monday. Amy, her assistant, answers the phone. Hopefully, Amy attended the retirement dinner too. I'll talk to her and see what she knows."

"What if you discover Aunt Barbara lied?"

"I haven't gotten that far. One step at a time."

Once Abby left, I sat back and chewed my cinnamon bun while thinking this case was full of improbable theories. But Barbara a murderer?

CHAPTER FIFTY-TWO

Early Monday morning, the phone rang.

"Is this Mrs. Farrell?" the voice said.

"Yes."

"Clayton Malur, from Malur's Animal Auction. I've good news. I can get you a woolly spider monkey."

Then he told me the cost.

"I didn't realize it would be quite so high. It may take a little time to raise the money." I needed to stall until I contacted Roy Maxwell at United States Fish and Wildlife about setting up a sting.

"You said money wasn't a problem. How long do you need?"

"I'm not sure. Probably—"

"I'll give you three days before I find another buyer." He ended the call.

I punched in Roy Maxwell's number and explained the situation. "Wouldn't it be great to prove that Clayton Malur is still involved in illegal sales?"

"We can't authorize a sting just because you feel he's smuggling. There needs to be some evidence."

"It's more than just me." I told him about the couple in the Razorville restaurant who were seeking a golden lion tamarin from Malur.

"None of this is evidence. The tamarin might be perfectly legal. In any case, a sting can't be arranged that easily. Malur will have papers verifying the woolly spider monkey you're buying was bred in captivity and not stolen from the wild. Same as with the golden lion tamarin. We'd have to find out if the documents are forged."

"That's exactly what I want you to do."

"Proving documents are forged is difficult. Often the paper trail is impossible to follow. That's why he contacted you so quickly. If it were easy to prove, he wouldn't have called until he checked you out."

"But—"

"I wish you'd let me know you were doing this," Maxwell said. "In fact, you shouldn't be doing this at all."

Later that day, I sped off to the Rocky Cove Zoo. I needed to verify statistics for my story on breeding endangered species. After that, both my articles would be done.

I quickly gathered the information I needed in the zoo library and was headed toward the exit when I ran into Ginger Hart.

"How's your murder investigation coming?" she asked. "Asking any more questions at Treasures of Zeus? Still playing Sherlock Holmes?"

"I'm sorry if my checking your alibi at Treasures of Zeus upset you. I'm verifying the whereabouts of everyone with keys to the rain forest, not just you."

"I have an ironclad alibi."

"No. Not an ironclad one. You could have scooted out of Treasures of Zeus, driven to the zoo, murdered Arlen, and returned to the restaurant without anyone realizing you were gone."

Ginger planted her hands on her hips. "If you checked your facts, like a competent reporter, you'd have discovered I didn't have my car that night. I hitched a ride with friends. Without transportation, it would be impossible to get to the zoo and back in the time involved. Or did you think I would take a taxi to commit murder?"

"I'm trying to help my brother."

"Maybe you should face the fact that your brother could be the murderer."

"You can't believe that. The evidence is purely circumstantial."

"True, but the evidence leans the most toward him. Anyway, I'm clear. And I don't have hard feelings."

"Glad to hear that." I turned to leave.

"By the way, I'm aware there's another applicant for the feature writer position at *Animal Advocate,*" Ginger said as I began my trek down the path.

I slowed down.

"One with impressive credentials, I might add," she continued. "Your editor assigned him an article on the Siberian tiger. I've been working closely with him to ensure he obtains all the material he needs." Ginger smiled maliciously. "I guess you didn't know about him, did you?"

Schuyler Adams!

During my drive back to the office, all I could think about was Schuyler Adams's feature story on the Siberian tiger. I couldn't believe no one at work, including Clara, had told me.

There were no spaces on the street so I pulled into the municipal lot behind the *Animal Advocate* building just as a red sports car zoomed out of the parking area, nearly crashing into me.

I recognized the driver.

"Schuyler Adams just sped away, Clara," I said, stepping into the office. "Was he here to see Olivia?"

Clara didn't look up from her work. "I think so."

"What do you mean, you think so? Olivia can't sneeze without you knowing it."

Clara raised her head. "Okay. He had an appointment."

"Do you know about the article he's writing on the Siberian tiger?"

Clara nodded.

"And you didn't tell me?"

"The last time we discussed him, you looked so upset. Besides, I hoped he'd mess up the story."

"I doubt he'd do that." I couldn't help but smile at Clara's loyalty.

Clara lowered her head, staring at a blank paper on her desk.

My smile quickly faded. Her demeanor indicated she knew more about this situation than she let on.

"What aren't you telling me, Clara?"

"Olivia took Schuyler to lunch Friday. At La Scala."

My heart sank. At La Scala, offers were extended and deals finalized.

As if reading my mind, Clara added, "I don't know for sure if he's locked up the job, but he was talking with Olivia for more than an hour today. When he left he said he'd see me soon. And he was smiling."

"I need a caffeine fix." I poured coffee into a mug and wandered down the hall. I desperately wanted the permanent position as feature writer. I couldn't remember when I had enjoyed my work as much as I had this last month.

But there was more. Looming on my mind was the opening of the new animal health and wellness center. Matt thought the impact of the new facility on his veterinary practice could be disastrous. I needed this promotion and the accompanying salary raise, no matter how meager it might be.

Back in my cubicle, I sloughed behind my desk, staring at the blank computer screen. But worrying wouldn't accomplish a thing. Until I heard officially from Olivia, anything could happen. Meanwhile, I'd focus on proving my brother's innocence.

Although I felt I was grasping at straws, my next step was to check out Abby's theory concerning my sister-in-law's alibi. Glancing at my watch, I noted it was ten minutes past one. Since this was lunch time for many corporate executives, I phoned Barbara's office. With any luck, she would be out of the building and I could ferret the information I needed from a member of her staff.

Barbara's assistant answered the phone. I had never met Amy, but we'd spoken many times on the phone.

"Barbara's at lunch with the pharmaceutical reps," Amy said. "You can reach her on her cell if it's important. Or do you want me to have her call you back when she returns to the office?"

"No thanks. I'm heading into a conference in a few minutes, so I'll reach her at home tonight." I zoomed right to the point of my call before Amy picked up another phone line. "Barbara said she had a great time at that retirement dinner a few weeks ago. Did you enjoy it, too?" I tried sounding as casual as I could.

"I sure did, but I paid for it the next day. Most of the group left after dessert, but a few of us hung out at the bar. I had to take the train back to Long Island, so I didn't get home until after midnight and I'm up at six."

"That's the problem with city functions when you commute from the suburbs. Barbara usually rises before six, too. I'll bet she scooted out of the dinner early."

"I don't know. Come to think of it, the last time I saw her was during the cocktail hour."

CHAPTER FIFTY-THREE

My phone trilled as I was driving. I let it go to voice mail and played it back when I arrived home.

"This is Barbara. I need to talk to you, Kristy. Please call me as soon as you hear this message."

Had Barbara found out about my call to her assistant and figured out what I was doing? Or was there more trouble with my brother? Had the indictment been handed down? I called back and Barbara answered on the first ring.

"What's wrong?" I asked, my heart pounding. "Your message sounded urgent."

"There's something I need to discuss with you."

"Sure. What is it?"

"Not on the phone. Can we meet tomorrow?"

"Of course. Is it Tim?" I wondered if my brother told her about the grand jury.

"I really can't talk now. I've a one o'clock appointment at the nail salon across from my office. Can you meet me there? You could get a manicure too and we could chat. I'll make the appointment for you."

"That's fine, but can you at least tell me if Tim is in more trouble."

"I'd rather talk in person. It's complicated. I'll tell you everything tomorrow."

It's complicated? I hung up, wondering why the secrecy.

★ ★ ★ ★ ★

The nail salon was crowded with women trying to squeeze manicures, pedicures, and other assorted beauty treatments into their lunch break. When I arrived, Barbara was in the waiting area, sitting on a high-back wicker chair next to a potted palm and sipping from a bottle of sparkling water. This place was big on ambiance, and I had no doubt this would be reflected in their prices.

I slid into a chair across from my sister-in-law.

"Okay. What's this about?" I asked.

"I need your help. But let's wait until we're called for our manicures. That way we can have some privacy."

"In here? The nail stations are less than two feet apart."

"I arranged for Lu and Jenna to do our nails. They work out of the little alcove in the back. No one will hear what we're saying."

"Lu and Jenna will."

Barbara waved her hand dismissively. "That doesn't matter. The point is several of my coworkers come here for treatments. I don't want them to overhear our conversation. We should be called in about five minutes."

I realized that once we settled down at our manicure stations, my sister-in-law would immediately start explaining what was bothering her. If I wanted to verify Barbara's whereabouts for the night the zoo director was killed, I'd need to question her right now.

"You couldn't alibi Tim because you were in the city for a retirement dinner and didn't return home until midnight, right?" I asked.

Barbara nodded.

"How did you get in? Did you drive?"

"Long Island Railroad."

"Did you travel with coworkers?"

"No. I returned home alone. No one else takes the same line. Why are you asking me this?"

"Oh, no particular reason. Matt likes to drive to Manhattan, and I like the train. I'm always interested in how others feel about this."

"I prefer the train."

I sighed. As far as finding witnesses to the time Barbara left the retirement dinner, I had reached a dead-end. But that didn't mean she'd lied. Still, could Abby's theory be right?

A few minutes later, we were shown into the main salon. I sneezed. Probably a reaction to the allergens in the room. The four vases of lilies displayed throughout the salon couldn't mask the strong odor of nail lacquer and polish remover.

I settled in my chair. "Now, what's so important, Barbara, that you needed to talk to me privately?"

"Tim told me Saul may not be appointed permanently as director. With the trouble at the zoo, there's a growing sentiment among the trustees to bring in an outsider."

"That's too bad, but why are you so upset about it?"

"Because there's also a growing sentiment to do a sweep of all top staff and that would include Tim. If they do hire someone other than Saul as director, the new person may decide to bring in a new team."

"You mean Tim would lose his job?"

"The Board of Trustees has decided that any pending employment contracts or new hires should wait until a permanent director is appointed. So yes, it's possible a new director may choose not to keep Tim, especially since he's the leading suspect. Not that I think he'll be arrested."

I realized that Tim still hadn't told her about the grand jury.

"But you can't stop rumors, and the zoo runs on good public relations," Barbara continued. "Of course, no one would admit that's the reason. Tim and I need your help, Kristy."

"Me? What can I do?"

"Tim needs positive publicity. In your article on the Rocky Cove Zoo, could you emphasize the work Tim's done with breeding reptiles? He could be the main focus of your story."

"My article on captive breeding is completed."

"Can't you change it?"

"No. It's an overview of the zoo's breeding program for all endangered species, not just reptiles."

"Well, you could include the others but concentrate on Tim's work."

"If my editor thinks I slanted the article to fit my personal agenda, she'd fire me on the spot, and I wouldn't blame her. The purpose of the story is not to boost Tim's career."

"I didn't realize you were such a moralist."

"Come on. I'm doing my job. It's my first assignment."

"Your story is more important than your brother?"

"Finding out who killed Arlen McKenzie and Mei Lau would help more than some puffed-up article." I lowered my voice. "Until the real murderer is discovered, Tim will always have that shadow over him. If he's arrested for murder, it wouldn't matter if he single-handedly saved all reptiles from extinction."

"So you're not changing the article?"

"What part of 'doing my job' don't you understand? No, I'm not changing it. But I can tell you that Rocky Cove's breeding program is excellent. All three curators come across in my story as innovative and dedicated because it's the truth. If the trustees read my story, maybe they won't change staff."

Barbara narrowed her eyes while we walked to the drying machines. "Well, I guess we'll find out, won't we?"

Chapter Fifty-Four

Something was up. I spotted Matt's car in the driveway when I returned home. My watch read five, and Matt rarely came home before six. As I entered through the front door, I found him slouched in his armchair with the *New York Times* on his lap. But he wasn't reading it.

"Is something wrong?" I asked.

"It was one of those days."

"What happened?"

"One of my hydraulic examining tables broke. It will cost a fortune to replace. And Lucy Garone's cat almost escaped out the front door."

I rubbed the back of his neck and shoulders. "Didn't anything good happen today?"

"I guess so. Lady Snow gave birth to her puppies."

"That's great news." Lady Snow was an Alaskan malamute show dog owned by Matt's best friend, Jake. "How many puppies?"

"Only four. Three males, one female."

"Four is small for a malamute litter, isn't it?"

"Litter sizes vary."

I rubbed Matt's shoulders as he sat silently, his muscles in knots. Meanwhile, his statement about litter sizes kept flashing through my mind. But I didn't know why.

He finally spoke up. "Your brother called today."

"Oh? What did he want?" I felt my muscles tense as I

wondered if there was more news about the impending indictment.

"On top of his legal problems, which seem to be mounting, he's afraid of losing his job," Matt said.

"I know." I told Matt about my meeting with Barbara at the nail salon. "She's desperate. She always puts on a showy front. It's not like her to ask for help."

"Mike Murphy, one of the zoo trustees, had been one of my clients before he moved to Manhattan. Tim asked me to talk to Mike on his behalf."

"Are you going to?"

"I don't know. It's awkward. I haven't spoken to Mike in more than four years. I don't even know if I can find his phone number." He sighed. "Besides, I honestly don't believe it will do any good."

"Do you really think the trustees won't renew Tim's contract?"

"It's possible. If that happens, Tim and Barbara won't be able to keep up the payments on their home equity loan. They could lose their house. And they won't be able to pay their attorney fees."

"And it's pretty likely Tim will be indicted next week."

Archie padded into the room, plopping down next to me. I spotted a large scratch under his right eye by his nose.

"What happened to Archie?" I knelt down beside the dog.

"I wanted to talk to you about that, too. The situation between Owl and Archie has escalated. Archie cornered Owl by the refrigerator. She scratched his face. It will be fine, but that's not the problem. Owl's not working out. We can't keep her." He grabbed my hand and squeezed it. "I promise, we'll find her a good home."

"I know. But if she's adopted, I won't see her again."

I fought back tears, thinking how ridiculous this was. My

dream job was down the tubes, my husband's business in danger of failing, my daughter might move away, my brother faced the possibility of jail, and I was about to cry because of a cat.

CHAPTER FIFTY-FIVE

I woke at sunrise.

"Matt, are you awake, yet? Why don't we go out for breakfast?"

He rolled on his side, pulling his pillow over his head.

I couldn't get back to sleep. It was too early to go to the zoo, but an idea popped into my mind. A brisk walk on the ocean boardwalk would clear my head and refresh me for the day. I showered, dressed, made a thermos of coffee, and headed out to my car. It was only a fifteen-minute drive from my home to the local beach.

Soon the beach would be crowded, but at this hour I shared the boardwalk with a handful of joggers and early-morning walkers. Sea air always invigorated me. Later on, it would be mixed with the smell of sunblock, but not yet.

By the time I finished my walk, more beachgoers had arrived. Settling down at a table near the concession stand, I poured my coffee and sat back, momentarily inhaling the salt air and listening to the waves crashing on the shore. Gazing at the horizon, I was hypnotized by the rolling water—until my concentration was interrupted by a nearby conversation.

A boy of about four, a girl who appeared to be a preteen, and a young woman I guessed to be their mother occupied the next table. The girl's grumpy expression indicated she'd rather be home in bed than participating in this early family outing.

The woman had apparently brought breakfast from home for

the children. She sat patiently while the boy played with the bowl in front of him. "Travis, eat your cereal. You too, Ashley."

"No, I hate it," the girl said.

The woman sighed. "You're the one who insisted I buy this brand because it has strawberry chips."

The girl looked up from staring at her blue nails. She leaned over and grabbed the box. "This cereal is a rip-off. The picture on the label is full of strawberry chips, but only two chips are in my bowl. It says right on the box you get one hundred chips. I bet you don't get ten in the whole box."

The mother snatched back the carton and appeared to examine the label. "You're wrong. It doesn't say that. It says you get *up* to one hundred strawberry chips. That's a common advertising gimmick."

"It's not fair."

"Advertisers often like to emphasize the maximum but they only give you the minimum."

The girl returned to staring at her nails while her mother cleared off the table.

Something about that conversation bothered me, but I didn't know what. I sat there, savoring my coffee and gazing out at the whitecaps and rolling waves.

Then it came to me.

Hurrying to my car, I began putting it together. The lone baby eagle I saw on my first visit to the Rocky Cove Zoo's bird nursery. Tim's statement about the zoo's low birth rate with certain species. Matt's comment on how litter sizes varied. And now a mother's casual remark about maximum and minimum.

As I pulled onto the parkway, I realized that was what the numbers in Mei's diary meant. Back home, I raced up the stairs into the study and dragged one of Matt's veterinary books from the shelf to the desk. I thumbed through the index but couldn't find what I needed. As for trying the Internet, I wasn't sure where to start the search.

I headed to the bedroom to wake up Matt, but stopped short. Matt disapproved of my involvement and wouldn't go along with my scheme.

Instead, I grabbed my phone and punched in Abby's number.

"Is it daytime yet?" she grumbled.

"Yes, it is. I think I know why Arlen McKenzie and Mei Lau were killed, but I need your help. I have a theory, but I won't know if it's correct unless I verify certain facts." I told Abby what she needed to find out.

"I'll check and get right back," she said.

Ten minutes later, Abby called. We talked for a few minutes, and I outlined my plan.

CHAPTER FIFTY-SIX

I grabbed the phone and punched in another number.

"My plan will work," I said, "and it's the only chance we have." I argued for nearly ten minutes. "Good. I'm on my way."

I ripped a sheet of paper off a pad, jotted down a number from the phone book, and stashed it in the zippered compartment of my bag. Before leaving the house, I stuck my head in the bedroom doorway. "Matt, I'm headed to the zoo. See you later."

"Yeah, later." Matt hugged the pillow, covering most of his head. He mumbled something I couldn't decipher.

Despite everything on my mind, I chuckled. Matt slept soundly. When he awakened, he wouldn't remember a thing I'd said.

On my way out, I grabbed another reference book from the study. But this one, a paperback, had nothing to do with zoology.

When I pulled up to the entrance booth at the zoo, the security guard leaned out. "We don't open for another forty-five minutes."

"There should be a pass for me signed by Tim Vanikos. I'm his sister, Kristy Farrell."

"Right. I didn't recognize you. He dropped the pass off earlier." The guard motioned me into the parking lot.

Before exiting my car, I pulled out my cell phone, along with the paper stored in my bag's zippered compartment, and punched in the number written on it.

"Stone Mount Pharmacy," a man said.

"I'm calling for Amanda Devereux," I said. "She'd like a refill on her prescription."

"What's it for?"

"I don't know. I can't read her handwriting. I work for her and she left me your number, along with a note to call for a refill. She wants it by six tonight. It's the same one you delivered to her house a few weeks ago. Does she have more than one prescription on file?"

"Let me look." He put me on hold.

While drumming my fingers on the steering wheel, I impatiently glanced at my watch. Moments later, the pharmacist returned to the line. "The only prescription I have is for Flagyl, but it calls for no refills. This is a real powerful drug. She'd better talk to her doctor if she feels the infection hasn't gone away."

After ending my call, I grabbed the paperback from my bag. It was a guide on the side effects of prescription drugs. I read the section on Flagyl.

"I was right," I murmured, hopping out of the car and hurrying down the path to the ornithology office.

The zoo buzzed with activity. Chattering monkeys scurried toward a fat-faced zookeeper as he slipped into the exhibit toting two buckets of what was probably their breakfast. Along the path, two sanitation workers swept the pavement, while a security officer whizzed by me in a yellow jitney.

I tried convincing myself that nothing could happen with all those people here. But I jumped at the sudden roar of a lion. Although the cool morning breeze had yet to be replaced by the humidity and scorching heat of midday, I perspired under my blouse. Nerves.

I veered down a side path, and upon reaching ornithology, I discovered the door was locked. I noted with apprehension that there were no zoo employees working in this immediate area. Finally, I spied Amanda Devereux heading my way.

"Good morning." With a smile, Amanda strolled up the walkway to the building. "How did you get in here before opening hours?"

"I was given an early-admittance pass because I've another interview," I lied. "But I need to talk to you first."

"My schedule is particularly busy today." Amanda reached for the door and pushed her key in the lock. "Perhaps you could make an appointment for another time. If you call public relations—"

"I know who murdered your husband."

Her face showed no emotion, but her body tensed and she curled her fingers into fists.

"My evidence points to Frank Taggart," I said.

"I find that hard to believe." Amanda's voice stayed calm. "Do you have proof?"

I nodded.

She hesitated only a moment. "Even though what you say sounds farfetched, come into my office and we'll talk."

Amanda unlocked the door. I trailed her through the main room until she ushered me into her private office.

"Sit down," she said. "I need to use the restroom, but I'll be right back."

I sunk into one of the soft, black leather chairs, then shifted impatiently in the seat.

Amanda returned to the room, sat down, and folded her hands on the desk. "Suppose you tell me what this is all about."

"I found a list of birds in Mei's diary. All are endangered species and next to each bird are two different numbers. I believe the first number represents the eggs produced at the zoo. The second number refers to the eggs that Frank Taggart reported as produced."

Amanda frowned. "Why would Frank report fewer eggs than there actually were?"

Bingo. I smiled. "I think he stole eggs of endangered species and sold them on the black market. You never know how many eggs a bird will lay. Most species lay within a range of one to three or two to four, right? My theory is that when birds at Rocky Cove produced the maximum, or close to it, Frank reported the minimum and sold off the difference."

I pulled the list out of my bag and handed it to the curator.

Maroon-fronted parrot—Rhynchopsitta terrisi—3—2
Puerto Rican parrot—Amazona vittata—4—2
Hyacinth macaw—Anodorhynchus hyacinthinus—3—2
Jardine's parrot—Poicephalus gulielmi—4—3
Snowy owl—Nyctea scandiaca—6—2

"So, for example, the maroon-fronted parrot laid three eggs but Frank only reported two and sold off the other," I said, pointing to the list. "These are rare birds. Some of their eggs sell for thousands of dollars."

"This's incredible." Amanda looked down at the list, then shook her head in apparent disbelief.

"Don't act surprised. You were in on it."

She jerked her head up, her face showing no emotion.

"Before I showed you the list, you said it didn't make sense for Frank to report fewer eggs than were laid," I said. "But at that point I had only said the numbers were different. I hadn't used the word 'fewer' or suggested anything like that. How would you know unless you were part of the scam?"

"It was a logical conclusion. And I don't see what this has to do with my husband's murder."

"Mei discovered this scam while interning in ornithology. The day before McKenzie's murder, she had been pulled off her regular duties to help work on photo sessions with the zoo director. I think that's when she told your husband of her suspicions. Then he confronted either you or Frank with the information, and one of you killed him."

"Ridiculous!"

"I wasn't sure until this morning which one of you did it. You could have given your rain forest key to Frank. But that bothered me. Sticking a needle in someone's arm from behind . . . I couldn't imagine Arlen McKenzie letting Frank get that close. It had to be you."

"I have witnesses who will swear I was home."

"No. Your witnesses can verify they *drove* you home. Claiming you were too drunk to drive back is a lie. And a superior acting job. Professor Layne said you were good, and the role of a drunk isn't that difficult to play."

"You can't prove any of this."

"Actually, I can. Mei mentioned stopping by your home a few days before the murder. You received a delivery from your pharmacy while she was there. I know you can't drink alcohol with a good number of prescription drugs, so I played the odds, hoping a long shot would come in. I figured you used the Stone Mount Pharmacy since there's really no other place close by. I called them this morning and found out your prescription was for Flagyl."

I reached into my bag and pulled out the reference paperback on prescription drugs. "You can't mix Flagyl with alcohol. It will make you violently ill. Would you like me to read the warning?"

I flipped to the page. "Combining with alcohol can cause nausea, vomiting, dizziness, diarrhea, and abdominal cramping. In rare cases, it can cause seizures."

I slammed the book shut. "You wouldn't drink alcohol if you took this. I also noticed at the theater reception that you took champagne, but you never drank any."

Amanda folded her arms across her chest. "This makes you think I killed Arlen McKenzie and Mei Lau?"

"No. Not Mei. I think Frank murdered Mei. Reptile keepers have keys to the snake room, and Frank originally worked in herpetology. All he needed to do was make a copy before he transferred to your department. I know the key says 'Do Not Duplicate' but there's always someone willing to break the law for a price, especially with Frank's contacts."

"She figured it all out. Pretty smart, isn't she?" said a voice from behind.

I turned around. Frank Taggart blocked the doorway. In his gloved right hand he clutched a hypodermic needle.

"When I went to the restroom, I called him on my cell phone," Amanda said.

As I returned my gaze to Amanda, a smile, cold as a Minnesota winter, spread across her face.

"I told you it was a big mistake to show her the bird nursery." Frank approached me, brandishing the hypodermic needle in the air.

"That had nothing to do with it. She discovered the information in Mei's diary. You never should have let Mei see what you were doing. You were thinking with your pants, not your head."

"How was I to know that the little bitch would read the records and notice the difference in the number of eggs?"

My body felt cold. Still, I needed more information. And, most importantly, I needed to stall. "Why did you use snake venom to kill your husband? That's an unusual method?"

"Frank keeps several snakes at his home, including a Russell's viper, so we extracted the venom. Arlen didn't realize I'd injected him until it was too late. Of course, we also took the zoo's cobra," Amanda said. "We thought by using the snake, we would cast suspicion on Tim, and we were right."

"But why blame Tim?"

Amanda shrugged. "Nothing personal, but he was vulnerable. Tim had motive. That motive, combined with the use of venom as the method of murder, would make him a leading suspect, and no one would think of us. Frank and I had decided to wait until we were sure your brother wouldn't have an alibi. When I discovered that my husband and Tim planned to meet earlier in the evening, we knew that would be the time to do it."

"Enough talking. We have to get rid of her." Frank Taggart's eyes had a wild man's look.

"But how do we dispose of the body in daylight?" Amanda leaned forward, placing her hands on the desk.

"We'll stash her in one of the crates in the back room and get rid of her later. I've plenty of room in the car. I drove the Escalade today."

Escalade. Of course. He was the one with the black car. Tim might remember what the other curators or administrators drove because they all have reserved parking spaces near each other. But he wouldn't know what kind of car a bird keeper drove because they parked in the general employee lot. And it sounded like Frank didn't bring the Escalade to the zoo that often.

"So you're the one who followed me and tried to run me off the road," I said.

"I happened to be dropping off papers in your brother's outer office when he gave you the McKenzie address. I overheard everything, and I knew you were about to stick your nose where it didn't belong. I figured I could scare you off."

"Another idea of yours that didn't work," Amanda said, glancing at her watch. "We've got a problem. The zoo will open shortly. What if someone barges in here while we're hiding the body?"

"That won't happen. Your clerical staff is at computer training this morning. Besides, to make sure we wouldn't be interrupted, I locked the front door when I came in. This is a perfect time for murder, Amanda. We only need a few minutes."

I stared at the needle. "What type of venom are you using this time?"

"I didn't have time to obtain venom. This is filled with an animal tranquilizer. Enough to kill a tiger."

"What if she told someone about coming here?" Amanda rose from her chair. "What if they look for her here?"

"Zoo employees saw me enter the building," I added quickly, "and my daughter knows I'm here. And why I'm here."

Momentarily, I watched fear flash through Frank's eyes. He glared at Amanda. "When you arrived, was anyone here?"

"No, but she had to come through the front gate. That means the security guard saw her."

"He probably thinks she came to see her brother. I'll administer the overdose in the storage room. There are several large crates, so that way we won't have far to carry the body. After everyone leaves for the day, I'll put the crate in the Escalade, drive off, and dump her in the pine barrens. Someone will find her eventually." Frank laughed. "Tim will be the leading suspect. Murdering your own sister. Juries hate that."

I winced as Frank gripped my shoulder with his left hand. In his right hand, he clutched the hypodermic needle upright. "Let's go."

It felt like tiny spiders crawling around my intestines. This wasn't going as planned. I needed to stall.

"You won't get away with this," I argued. "My brother is aware of everything. I spoke with him before I came here. He told Saul Mandel, too."

Frank tightened his grip on my shoulder, pushing me toward the back room. "I don't believe you."

"You should believe her," called out a booming voice. Saul Mandel barged into the room, followed by Tim.

"It's about time," I yelled at my brother. "What took so long?"

"I wasn't sure this crazy plan would work, but it did," he said.

"Tim, what are you and Saul doing here?" Amanda asked. All color had drained from her face.

"When Kristy laid out her plan for me on the phone this morning, I called Saul right away. We rushed here and hid in the adjacent storage room before you arrived. Leaning against those thin walls, we heard everything."

Amanda collapsed into her chair. She quickly regained her composure, but her face remained ashen. "How did you get in this building? It was locked."

Saul jangled a set of keys. "The back door. I'm acting director, remember? I have the master set to every lock in the zoo."

Frank pushed my brother against the wall and darted out of the room. I heard the front door slam.

"Stop him!" I yelled.

"He won't get away," Tim said. "The police should be here any minute, Kristy. We called once we were sure of your theory."

I heard sirens in the distance. Moments later, I peered out the window at the flashing lights—and Frank Taggart in handcuffs.

CHAPTER FIFTY-SEVEN

"Olivia wants to see you. Right now," Clara announced, the moment I entered the *Animal Advocate* office. It was the day after the arrest of Amanda Devereux and Frank Taggart.

"I'll bet she made a decision about the job."

"I don't know."

I stepped into the private office of the editor-in-chief. Olivia Johnson rose from her chair and moved to the front of her desk. She wasn't smiling or frowning. For the first time since I had begun working for the magazine, I couldn't read her face.

"Well, you certainly were right about a major scandal at the Rocky Cove Zoo," she said. "The stealing of eggs from endangered species is definitely something our readers want to know about. I'd like to do a special feature on it and include the two murders. We'll bump the story on the Siberian tiger."

I felt my jaw drop. "Wasn't the Siberian tiger article written by Schuyler Adams?"

"Yes, a freelance assignment. We can save it for a future issue." Olivia coughed. "That young man is an excellent writer."

I fell silent.

Olivia smiled, something she didn't do often. "But you're an excellent writer, too. Congratulations. I'm giving you the feature writer position."

"But I thought . . ." I decided not to complete the sentence.

"You were about to say you thought I had chosen Schuyler, weren't you?"

"Yes."

"I thought seriously about Schuyler, but he made a statement that caused me to hold back."

"What did he say?"

"During lunch at La Scala the other day, Schuyler said one trait possessed by all great journalists is persistence. He's right. And no one is more persistent than you. That's when I decided the job was yours."

I grinned. "That's terrific. Thanks so much. You won't regret it."

"Don't thank me too much. There's talk that *Animal Advocate* may be bought out by a major publishing conglomerate. If that happens, no one knows what staff will be kept on or what direction the magazine will take. There's also the possibility that *Animal Advocate* will go under. I honestly don't know how long any of us will be working here."

Olivia appeared to stare at the photo on the wall of a falcon in flight. "But this is all in the future." She turned back, facing me. "Right now you have a job. Our next issue will focus on marine life. Be here nine sharp next Monday and you'll get your current assignments, although I can tell you now that one will be on ocean predators."

"I can't wait."

"By the way, you'll be working with Schuyler."

"Schuyler?" Olivia always liked dropping bombs.

"Schuyler has been accepted in a graduate program. When I told him I was giving you the job, he decided to enroll." Olivia grinned. "His father wanted him to continue his education and is happy the way things have worked out. Anyway, as part of the curriculum he'll be interning with us for credit."

CHAPTER FIFTY-EIGHT

Two nights later with a mug of coffee in each hand, I joined Matt in our den. Earlier in the day I'd been on the phone with Roy Maxwell from Fish and Wildlife, then with my brother.

"I still can't believe what you did." Matt dropped his newspaper on the endtable and grabbed one of the mugs. "I can't believe Abby encouraged you. And your brother went along with your crazy scheme."

"We needed proof. And it worked."

"I don't care. It was still dangerous."

"I was never in any real danger. Tim and Saul were in the adjacent room."

"I've never met Saul, but your brother doesn't inspire confidence in a life-threatening situation. This whole egg scam doesn't make sense. Amanda had everything going for her, including marriage to a multimillionaire. Why would she take the chance?"

"It makes sense once you know the whole story. Frank Taggart spilled all the details to the district attorney in exchange for a lighter sentence."

I sat down in an armchair across from Matt. "Amanda's marriage was in trouble from the start, and she knew it wouldn't last. She made a decent salary at the zoo, but she has expensive tastes, way beyond the salary of a curator. Living with McKenzie, she had the estate in Stone Mount, a condo in Manhattan, expensive cars, jewelry, but with the prenuptials, if they divorced, she could never afford to live like that."

"Okay, but—"

"When Frank started working in ornithology, he hinted to Amanda how much eggs of endangered species would fetch on the black market. Amanda read between the lines, so they went into business together."

"It's that lucrative?"

"You bet. Remember, Mei's list only included the six cases where she physically saw the eggs in the nest and then noticed the difference in the reports. The operation was much larger. I understand they had an egg from a Lear's macaw that sold for five figures."

Matt let out a low whistle. "And it's all cash, of course. Tax free."

"That's another charge they'll be facing. Tax evasion."

"But how did they pull off the scam?"

"Frank was in charge of the bird nursery. The other bird keepers rarely went in. When they did, he made sure none of them had any knowledge concerning the number of eggs."

"How did Mei find out?"

"She was in the nursery only once. But that was enough. Frank had a computer glitch, and he didn't want to call in technical services. Mei's college minor was computer science, so she figured she could help. He expected her to focus on the computer, not nose around the facility. He wrongly assumed that, as an intern, she wouldn't be at the zoo long enough to catch on."

"When Mei told Arlen McKenzie what she had discovered, did he try to stop it?"

"More than that. McKenzie was getting ready to file for divorce. When he found out about the egg scam, he insisted Amanda resign as curator. Then she'd have nothing. No job. No rich husband. And he made another fatal mistake. He told

Amanda he hadn't decided if he would notify law enforcement or let her go quietly."

"So she murdered him because she couldn't be sure he wouldn't report her to the authorities," Matt said.

"Right. The next day, she arranged to meet with him in the rain forest at nine-thirty that night. She said she could show why the exhibit was producing big cost overruns and how the problem could be fixed."

"But why nine-thirty? Wouldn't he be suspicious?"

"Amanda made up a story about having a meeting and not being available until then. The rest is history."

"Then she inherited his fortune."

"He hadn't changed his will yet. It's ironic. She killed because of the scam, and once McKenzie was dead, she didn't need to sell the eggs anymore. I understand she told the police she wanted to stop after McKenzie's murder, but Frank wouldn't let her."

"Who killed Mei?"

"Frank. At first, he tampered with the crocodile barrier, causing it to malfunction. When that didn't work, he didn't have much time left. He knew Mei would be working on inventory Friday morning. Frank grabbed the cobra from its tank, threw it in the storage closet, then barricaded Mei in there."

"Did Frank send the poison frog?" Matt asked.

"Yes. He wanted to scare me off the case." I didn't mention the incident with the black Escalade, having decided some things were better left unsaid.

As Matt strolled into the kitchen to fetch dessert, I thought about the black car involved in the hit and run of Ginger Hart's former lover, Jerry Rudolph. It had nothing to do with the murders at the Rocky Cove Zoo. I wondered if that crime would ever be solved.

"It looks like Clayton Malur will be doing heavy jail time

too," I said as Matt handed me a plate of crumb cake. "First he's charged with receiving and selling stolen property from the Rocky Cove Zoo. But that's not all. Malur got caught selling a golden lion tamarin that had been smuggled into the country. It turns out the couple who bought the animal are special agents for the United States Fish and Wildlife Service, working undercover."

"You're saying the illegal sale of a golden lion tamarin computes to heavy jail time? Endangered species laws aren't that tough."

"There's more to the story. It seems Malur committed another crime. This one comes with stiff penalties. Drug smuggling."

"You're kidding?"

"A while back, Roy Maxwell sent me a press release about a federal interception of boa constrictors filled with cocaine-stuffed condoms. They were enroute to an animal import business. But I didn't know the whole story. It turns out the owner of the business chatted like a mynah bird to the feds. In exchange for a favorable plea bargain, he provided the DEA with information as to the origin of the drugs."

I bit into a piece of crumb cake. "He also confirmed rumors about a second shipment of cocaine-filled snakes due near the end of the month. Can you guess their final destination?"

"Malur."

"You got it. So this time, instead of confiscating the cargo, Fish and Wildlife, along with the Drug Enforcement Agency, allowed the shipment to continue as planned. In the meantime, the undercover couple who bought the golden lion tamarin introduced Malur to a friend who collected rare parrots. They let it be known that this friend sold drugs on the side and needed a new connection."

"This friend was DEA, right?"

"Exactly. Malur sold the 'friend' cocaine yesterday, and the Drug Enforcement agents made an immediate arrest. Now Malur's hotshot lawyer can't claim his client didn't know the snakes contained coke."

I paused to sip my coffee. "I couldn't understand why Roy Maxwell was so annoyed at my plan to set up a sting. Now I know. He feared my interference would blow the DEA sting."

"Well, I'm glad Malur is finally getting what he deserves. What about that pet store in Manhattan?"

"Booker's Amazing Pet Emporium? They don't appear to be involved in the illegal pet trade anymore. At least, there's no evidence. However, the authorities issued violations for unsanitary conditions. I understand the animals were seized and the owners charged with neglect. The store is currently closed down."

"Someone must have reported the conditions," Matt said.

I smiled. "Yes, someone did."

"Let's hope the owners don't get off with a small fine and open a new pet business a few months from now."

"I agree."

The front door slammed shut. Abby paraded into the room. She kissed both Matt and me before saying to her father, "I picked up a litter box and cat food."

"Did you get a cat?" I asked, wondering if this meant she wasn't moving to New Mexico. Or she was planning to take a cat along.

Abby grinned. "Not just any cat. I know how tense it's been here with Owl and the two dogs. Owl really needs a home without other animals. If it's okay with you, I'd like to take her."

"That's a perfect solution. I'll miss her a lot, but at least we'll get to see her when we visit you. But I thought one of your roommates was allergic?"

"Our lease is up and my roommates want to get apartments of their own." Abby grinned. "But that works out well. Jason and I have decided to get a place together. He's not taking the job in Santa Fe. He accepted an offer at a Manhattan law firm."

"I knew about the cat, but I didn't know about Jason moving in," said Matt.

I knew he wasn't pleased with our daughter's new living arrangements, but he'd get over it. He liked Jason, too.

Abby plopped down on the sofa. "I want to hear the latest news about the zoo and Uncle Tim's job. What's happening to everyone?"

"I got the whole scoop," I said. "The Board of Trustees convened yesterday and appointed Saul Mandel as director permanently."

"What about the plagiarism charge?"

"Totally untrue. It was Amanda Devereux who had sent the anonymous letter accusing him of cheating on his doctoral thesis."

"But why would she want to ruin him? He didn't know about her scam. Or did he?"

"When Saul, as acting director, decided to look into some of the zoo's low birth rates, Amanda knew it was only a matter of time before he discovered discrepancies in ornithology. She had to make sure he didn't stay at Rocky Cove, and she figured a plagiarism charge would get him fired."

"Do you think Saul will be a good director?" Matt asked.

"I know the staff is pleased at the appointment. Whether he'll be able to handle the business side of running the zoo remains to be seen. But Tim feels confident that Saul will step up to the job."

"What about Uncle Tim?" Abby leaned down and scooped up Owl, who had come into the room and was rubbing against her leg.

"Good news." I beamed. "Not only will Tim remain as curator of herpetology, but he'll also be promoted to assistant director."

"Aunt Barbara must be happy. That should help their marriage."

"Well, she's definitely happy. Since Tim wasn't arrested, she wasn't embarrassed, and now she can brag about his new position to her friends. As for the marriage, that will still be as one-sided as always. Tim will continue adoring her."

"What about Ginger Hart? How do you think she'll get along with Saul Mandel?"

"Ginger took a new job. She's now director of public relations for the Long Island Performing Arts Center."

Matt laughed.

"According to Tim, the zoo is hiring a new coordinator for public relations," I said. "One who has a genuine interest in wildlife. She has a graduate degree in marketing, but her undergraduate major was zoology. I think she'll work well with Saul."

"What about the zoo's wildlife nutritionist?" my daughter asked.

"Linda will remain at Rocky Cove. The position was put back in the budget. I also formulated a theory as to why Mei jotted Linda's phone number on the bottom of the penne recipe. I wasn't the only one Mei wanted to tell about her findings. We'll never know for sure, but I believe she also wanted to confide in Linda."

"Why Linda?" Abby asked.

"Mei didn't know the exact reason for the discrepancy in the number of eggs reported, but I'm sure she had suspicions. She planned to talk to me, but I don't know that much about birds. Linda is familiar with all types of animals. She could confirm Mei's suspicions or come up with an idea of her own. And I think Linda was the only one in the zoo whom Mei totally trusted."

"Did Mei ever get a chance to talk to Linda?"

"I don't think so. Linda told Tim that she and Mei never got together."

"Well, I'm glad this is over." Matt leaned back, looking more relaxed than he'd looked in weeks. "I got the bank loan, too. Let's hope that helps me stave off the competition from the animal health and wellness center. Their facility is scheduled to open in two months."

The doorbell rang. Matt returned to the den with a bouquet of red roses. "These were just delivered for you."

"I'll watch for thorns. There's a card this time." I read the note: "Thanks for all your help. I might be sitting in jail if not for you"

The note was signed by Tim.

"Wow. That's so unlike Uncle Tim to think of sending flowers. But he's right," Abby said. "Even if the police didn't have enough evidence to arrest him, that shadow would have hung over his head. Now he's cleared, thanks to you."

"You helped, Abby. I couldn't have done it, if you hadn't translated the list of endangered birds from Mei's diary."

"No, Mom. *You* realized the importance of the list and then figured out the meaning of the two numbers next to each bird. You put it all together."

"I am persistent," I said and then grinned.

Matt grinned back. "I'd say stubborn, but it's a great quality in you."

ABOUT THE AUTHOR

Lois Schmitt has worked as a freelance contract writer for Remedia Educational Publishers. Her most current assignments included a series of nonfiction pieces featuring national parks, as well as several nonfiction pieces on New York City landmarks. She is also the author of *Smart Spending* (Scribner Children's Books).

Ms. Schmitt currently teaches economics at Nassau Community College. She served as media spokesperson and education coordinator for the Nassau County Office of Consumer Affairs.

Her interest in animals, the focus of her mystery, is evident by her membership in the New York Zoological Society, Best Friends Animal Society, the Marine Mammal Center, and the ASPCA.

She is a member of the Mystery Writers of America.